Hunted by Fate

NEW YORK TIMES BESTSELLING AUTHOR
SHANNON MAYER

This one's for you.
Yes you. Chin up, Starshine,
the world is waiting for you to
burn bright and change the impossible.

SHANNON
MAYER

Hunted by Fate

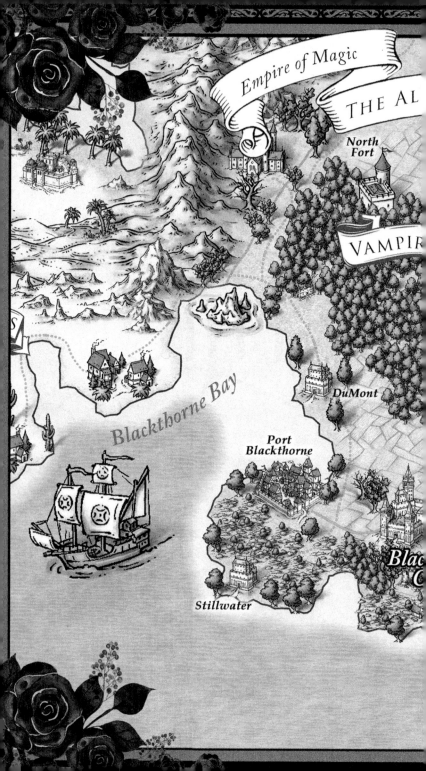

Prologue

Long Ago...

T he fire crackled, dancing and flickering, throwing shadows across one side of the combatants' faces as they studied the game board.

"Evangeline, you have barely touched your drink, do you still think I would poison you? You must admit, that was a long time ago."

Her eyes didn't leave the board as she reached for her goblet of blood-spiced wine. She slid her fingers around the thick pottery stem and clutched it lightly, bringing it to her perfectly painted lips.

The board was scattered, and there was only one way she could see beating the wise king of the Werewolf Territory.

Distraction.

Lifting the goblet to her mouth, she took a sip of the overly-bold, crimson liquid. "It is hard to tell, old friend, if it is poison or just terrible wine." Her lips quirked as she lifted her eyes swiftly to his and then away again. In that single glance, she still saw the same interest as always.

Lycan barked a low laugh. "Our wine is not that bad, Evangeline. Better should you choose to drink it more often."

He growled her name, and she kept the shiver from showing by leaning forward and moving a piece on the board. He spoke of wine, but she knew what he was asking for, and it was much more than sharing drinks with him. "I would think that you have learned by now, I cannot."

"Your husband dishonored you and even if he had not, he's long dead. You owe him nothing," he said softly, placing his hand at the edge of the table, their fingers a breath away from touching.

She slowly lifted her eyes to his. "And as I have said, time and again, this is not a thing that can be. Not for either of us."

Forcing herself to pull her hand back, she did not drop her gaze from his, and the tension grew, the air heating between them until she could barely breathe with the images that tumbled through her.

One kiss had bound her soul to his in a way she would never understand. She should have set him aside and never glanced his way again.

His lips twitched and he dipped his head in her direction. "I cannot lower my eyes, Evangeline, but I will acquiesce to this contest of stares, for if I do not, I cannot be certain your clothing will remain intact."

The gasp was involuntary and her heart tripped over what he was suggesting.

"I am—"

"I know what you are, Evangeline. I have never forgotten it, or that stolen kiss in the midst of a thunderstorm that left me craving a woman I could never have. There can be no other for me. Not truly. I know this. I have long since accepted this. Just as you need to accept that you feel the same, deep down in your heart. Why else would you be here?"

His words were bold, and they made her forget the reason that she had asked for the secret audience with him. Certainly, it hadn't been to have a scandalous affair that would leave them both stripped of their titles, ravaged by their kin, and left for dead. No, that was not why she was here, though watching his mouth tip into a half smile, feeling the pull of his body as it leaned toward hers...she should have known this would not be so simple.

"My nephew Edmund has become a real danger," she said softly. "I am at a loss."

Lycan leaned back in his chair, dropping his eyes to the board as they both acted as though they hadn't been mere seconds from something that was forbidden to both of their kinds. "What kind of danger?"

Evangeline stood, her silken skirts rustling the only sound as she made her way to stand by the fire. Staring into the flames was far safer than staring into Lycan's deep brown eyes. She would lose herself in them if she was not careful.

"He is young, only twelve yet, and I would hope that perhaps his actions are a product of his youth, and not something more. Something...terrible." She clasped her hands in front of her, clutching an edge of the silk.

Lycan joined her at the fire, side by side. Not touching, but so very close.

"Tell me."

If her brother, King Stirling, found out she'd spoken of his son Edmund's deeds outside the royal house, she would be condemned to death. But she had to protect the ones who needed her.

"It started young when he was barely able to walk, he would torment the small animals he was able to catch—"

"Our pups do the same," Lycan said with a wave of his hand, "it is the way of a predator to learn to hunt young and toy with its food."

She nodded slowly and then turned to meet his gaze. "But do your pups drag out the pain of their victims? Do they laugh and delight as those that they feast on cry for hours? I've seen your pups, they kill quickly when that time comes. And if they do not, they are stopped. Corrected by their elders."

He was silent, his expression grave as she hurried on, for fear she would stall and not be able to tell the worst of what she had buried inside.

"He...looks for those who would trust him now. He has learned to manipulate at a rate that is terrifying, and his father turns a blind eye because he is heir to the throne." She lowered her voice to a whisper. "I have found three human maids with limbs removed, tongues cut out, horrendous acts upon them...and when I found them, Lycan, they were not dead. Edmund is...I fear he is becoming a monster."

The wolf king had gone quiet beside her, the stillness of a hunter on edge, ready to attack.

"You wish me to kill him, then?"

She grabbed his hand before she could stop herself.

"Gods, no! I would not have you put yourself in danger like that, Lycan. We need good men. Men who fight with honor, and for the love of their people." Her throat tightened as she stared up at him. "I may never have you in my life, but I cannot imagine The Empires of Magic without you in it. That is not a world in which I wish to live."

That truth should not have escaped her, and yet it slipped out.

She pressed on before she could dwell on her admission. "And Edmund is still just a boy. A troubled one, but death? No." She shook her head furiously. "He is still my nephew, and I cannot forsake him so easily."

He stared down at her, voice hoarse. "Evangeline...why would you share this with me if I cannot help?"

She released her hold on him and stepped back, but he followed until she was pressed against the rock wall. The heat of the fireplace at her back, the heat of the wolf king in front of her, and all she could do was stare up at him.

"There is another child, Lycan. A secret child. Just three days ago, he nearly did the unthinkable and attempted to murder his own sibling. It was sheer luck that I found them in time and stopped him."

Lycan continued to close the distance between the two of them until his chest brushed up against the curve of her body. Nostrils flared as he closed his eyes and dipped his head so that his mouth was against her neck as he spoke.

"Speak plainly, Evangeline, for I find myself unable to think clearly at this moment as the blood rushes to places other than my mind. What are you asking of me? What is it that you...*need*?"

His voice had dipped back to a growl and she found herself unable to look away, to put her own thoughts into an order that would allow her to speak.

But for the child she'd sworn to protect and loved as her own, she had to do this.

She pressed her hands flat on the rock wall behind her and gripped the stone tight. The urge to lean into him, to curl her body around his was a deep-seated craving that left her praying she could be strong enough.

"I need you to protect the child that Edmund would kill," she whispered.

Lycan's eyes dipped to her mouth. "And in return?"

Her lips trembled as she spoke a dangerous truth once more. Of all those she knew in her life, he would smell out the lies. "You have my heart. My soul. For the rest of eternity, there will never be another man for me. You own me, even though we can never be. Is that not enough? To know that you and you alone carry my heart in your hands? If I could give you more, I would, but I would not endanger you, or any of those that I love and protect by...giving you the last of me."

His eyes softened and his throat worked as he seemed to struggle to find words.

"There is no woman like you in this whole grand world, Evangeline. I would secret you away, run to the human's realm and leave this all behind if you would come with me."

Her lashes fluttered across her cheeks as he lifted a hand to brush away a tear. "I cannot. I have my responsibilities, as do you. You have your own family to care for—people you love. They would be in danger if you left."

His body slowly eased against hers until she was pressed tightly between the wall and his hard-muscled frame. "I know all this; it does not mean I cannot wish for more. To wish for a life free of those responsibilities to be with the one soul that sings to my own." His mouth rested once more against the sensitive lines of her throat, breathing her in.

Unable to still her hands any longer, she brought them up slowly and cupped his face, allowing her fingers to run across the stubbled line of his jaw, to feel the heat of his blood just under his midnight dark skin.

They stood there, breathing each other in, holding to the moment as much as they held to one another. A stolen time, a memory that would be tucked away and kept safe, for the precious warmth it would offer when the nights of winter rose and grew cold around them.

"Lycan."

"My love," he whispered.

Her breath caught in her chest and she struggled to get the words out. "Do you promise me? I must know that Edmund will have someone to stop him if and when the time comes. The child is illegitimate, but the Oracle has already spoken of the strength and power that will reside within—a strength that will rival Edmund's one day."

A sigh slid from his chest and he seemed to struggle to move, to step back.

The loss of heat was immediate, her hands sliding from his face, her eyes welling uncontrollably at the thought of what she'd lost. Of what she must give up in order to save those she loved.

"Your tears tell me there is more to this than what you are saying." He brushed a thumb across her cheek and captured a tear.

"We cannot meet again, Lycan," she choked on the words. "My brother has always suspected it wasn't the fearful villagers on the mainland who killed my husband in the battle at the ravine all those years ago. I know you killed him for what he did to me, but the rage in you...it was not lost on Stirling. In spite of my vow to never marry again and play the part of the properly grieving widow, he is no fool. He knows there is something between us, and he would cut us both down. A truce is one thing, but accepting a love match between a vampire and a werewolf? Never. I do not care for myself, but for those who need me. And for you. I would not have you hurt for me, not for anything."

The wolf king bowed his head, then slowly, so slowly went to his knees. "To live a life without you, Evangeline, my heart? My kind are not meant to be kept from their heartmates. They are not meant to live without the one that makes their wolf howl to the sky for joy."

She bit her lower lip hard enough to draw blood, but even that was not enough to keep her from moving. From dropping to her knees before him. "My wolf king, there will never be a day when I do not think of you. When I do not wish you with me at my side." She struggled through the tears that now streamed down her cheeks, staining the silk top of her dress. "I will see you in my dreams every night, and I will hold onto you there. For it is the place where we can be together. Only there that I can be myself, and tell you how my heart sings only for you. That my blood burns only for you."

She pulled his forehead to hers and held him there. The minutes slid by too fast, and she knew that she had to leave. The sun would be rising soon, and here in the wolf territory, there was no protection for her against it.

A knock on the door shattered the moment.

"My king. There is an hour before dawn," a gruff voice called from the other side of the door.

Lycan smoothed his hands over her face, trying to stop the tears from flowing but he could not.

"I would move the stars and moon for you if I could," he said softly, "But if the only thing you ask of me is to protect a child, then I will do that with all I have in me. We will find a way to keep him safe from the sun."

Evangeline took his hands and stood, rising in a single graceful movement, fighting to pull herself together. This was the moment. This was the time to be the duchess she'd been trained to be her whole life. To squash her emotions, to pull herself together. To protect those who could not protect themselves.

Still, she clung to his rough hands, a lifeline she was not yet ready to cast away. "She needs no protection from the sun. The child is born of a human mother."

Lycan's eyes went wide. "A rarity indeed."

She raised her voice, calling to her maid, "Anna, come out now and bring our little one with you."

A side door was pushed open, and a young woman stepped into the room with a bundled-up toddler in her arms.

Evangeline slowly released the king's hands and stepped toward the maid. "Come to me, my dear one." She held out her arms, and the child reached for her, a wide grin spreading across a cherub-blessed face.

She allowed herself one last squeeze and one last kiss, then turned to the king. "Your Majesty."

As if on cue, the child waved at Lycan, giggling. "Hallo."

His eyes softened as he shook his head. "Such a terrible task you have set me, Evangeline."

"I am aware." She took in a shaky breath. "I will write if I can. To stay connected. To help."

His eyes shot to hers, understanding flowing between them unspoken. She would write to the child, and to him.

A dangerous correspondence.

Stepping close to the king, she lifted the child into his waiting arms, more tears spilling down her cheeks.

"Mama?"

Lycan froze and stared at her in question.

Evangeline dipped her head and stepped back as she clutched Anna's hands. "I have raised this child as my own. I am giving you the other half of my heart, Lycan. You are the only one I trust."

You are the only one I love.

Did her eyes tell him what she should have said earlier?

He dipped his head in her direction as Anna tugged her back. "Duchess, the sun will be rising, we must go. We must go now."

But every step backward was a step away from the two she loved the best in this world.

Two that she could never see again...

CHAPTER 1

Sienna

Gods be damned, we were running out of time.

The rain lashed against my face as we rode hard through what remained of the night, Bethany to my right, and William, now first in line for the vampire throne to my left. Assuming he lived through this. His head bobbed, chin touching his chest, a steady trickle of blood dribbling from his nose.

"Will?" I called his name out over the pounding of the hooves and the wind whipping around us.

He wobbled and tipped to one side, his body listing like a ship in a storm.

Bethany cried out, but she was nowhere near enough to stop him from falling.

I pressed my right leg against Havoc's side and the horse shifted closer to Will and his mount. Reaching out, I grabbed his arm as he nearly toppled over, and, gritting my teeth, held him in his saddle.

Barely, just barely. He was not a small man, and I wasn't sure how long I could keep him upright.

We needed shelter, and we needed it quickly before Will ended up sprawled on the hard-packed earth in worse shape than before.

"Bee!" I called over the whipping winds, "we need to find a place to stop for the night!" I prayed she had some sense of where we were, which was ridiculous.

Bethany hadn't been allowed out of the castle much more than myself and the other girls that were brought in for the Harvest Games, but hope springs eternal.

She shook her head helplessly as we pressed on. "I've been looking. I haven't seen proper cover anywhere."

Hanging onto Will with all my strength, riding through the wild weather, I had nothing to distract myself with other than my own thoughts.

This mess that I was in was mostly of my own making. I'd willingly let myself be captured by the Collectors on the mainland, thinking I'd go to the werewolves and thus rescue my friend, Jordan. Instead, I'd been purchased from the auction pens by the vampire contingent, stuffed into a corset, and made to take part in a dangerous game of ballgowns and death threats. All while searching for a way to get to Jordan before it was too late.

Flash forward a few weeks and the situation I'd thought was already *pretty* bad had gotten far, far worse. The King was dead, and suddenly I was on the run with the young vampire prince headed toward the Werewolf Territory, while his maniacal elder brother hunted us down. I had no illusions about that particular bit. I could almost feel it under my skin, Edmund's eyes searching for us.

Of course, there was the middle brother I could have been thinking about instead.

Dominic.

The General. I blinked and I could see him in the tub, feel his hot, smooth skin below my fingertips. Feel his even harder cock—

"Here," Will rumbled and I jerked in my seat, flushing even under the slap of the rain and wind.

"What?"

He lifted a shaking hand and pointed off the path we were following. I didn't see anything, but I turned Havoc toward the section of the forest he'd indicated. Thick with brush, the jackpines leaned in tight to one another, but I could just see the slightest break in the treeline showing...something man made.

The sound of the rain began to fade, and a thick snowflake floated from the sky, clinging to my lashes.

As heavy as the rain was, the white blanket that began to fall around us was thicker even than that. Soon, we wouldn't be able to see three feet in front of us.

"Hurry," I hollered to Bee. "The snow will cover our tracks."

And buy us time to deal with whatever injuries the young prince had suffered.

Gripping Will's arm as tight as I could, I half led, half pushed us toward the barely-there path between the trees.

The branches were saturated and if we hadn't been soaked before, shouldering our way through the brush would have done the trick.

Ten minutes and we broke through the thick bush, sticks and evergreen needles in our hair, and into what I would, in normal circumstances, call a shitty little shack. But in our current state of need, it looked like the bloody Taj Mahal to me.

It was no bigger than a large horse stall, maybe twelve by twelve, with a metal pipe sticking out of the tin roof, so it was set for a fire inside. To the right was a simple, covered shelter for the horses with a tie rail on the inner edge, and only one wall to block the very worst of the wind.

I felt bad for the animals, but there was nothing to be done about it. It was better than nothing at all.

Without words, Bee followed me in dismounting. Between the two of us, we heaved Will through the now flurrying snow and into the small shed.

"Here, there's a light," Bee said through chattering teeth. The click of a turning striker, and then a lantern bloomed to life, pushing back the darkness.

There was no mattress, but a stack of coarse blankets sat piled in the corner.

"Lay one out," I grunted, nearly buckling under the weight of holding Will up myself.

Bee grabbed the blankets, laying two down, and keeping one aside.

"Here," she said, rushing back to Will's side. His legs took that moment to buckle completely and he crashed to the ground, collapsing against Bethany.

"Will, you have to help us!" I pleaded as I pulled on his arm to roll him off her.

He didn't respond, didn't so much as twitch.

"Grab his hand. We have to drag him." I gritted my teeth as I wrapped my fingers around his forearm. His skin was icy cold, and even in the dim light, I could see that it was beyond pale and dipping into tones of blue.

My stomach bottomed out at the sight. The temperature had just dropped, but it was not *that* cold outside. We needed to do something and we needed to do it fast.

After five full minutes of swearing and sweating, the two of us finally managed to wrestle him onto the makeshift bed.

"Check him for wounds while I deal with the horses." I turned away, and was out the door before Bee could argue. Though I doubted she would... Not when it came to Will.

The three horses had made their way into the small shelter on their own, huddled up together as they took solace from the snowstorm swirling around us. I tied each of them to the rail and set about looking for feed for them.

Which also gave me a moment to think about what our next step would be. Obviously, first things first, we had to get Will back on his feet. There was no way he could stay upright in the saddle as he was, and there was no way we'd make it all the way to the Werewolf Territory without him. Or even be assured we wouldn't be ripped to shreds if we did manage to get there.

Hell, even with Will in tow, that seemed like it was still a distinct possibility. Maybe even more than a possibility. It wasn't like the vampires and wolves got along.

Around the back of the small shelter, there was a wooden storage box full of feed for the horses.

Fresh feed.

I paused and looked it over, nerves humming to life. Was it normal to have a place in the middle of nowhere fresh stocked with fodder for horses? Unlikely, but I wasn't in a position to question it, so I shoved my discomfort aside, grabbed the feed, and stuffed it in front of Havoc and the other two.

Water was next. Ignoring my aching back, I found a bucket and slogged my way to a creek that was nearby, taking it back three times for the horses.

All the while, wondering just whose hut this was, and would they be showing up soon to reclaim it?

More and more, I knew we would have to move quickly. Even if it weren't for Edmund, we couldn't afford to get captured by some overzealous vampire lordling thinking to get in good with the new King.

Breathing hard, sweating, and shivering at the same time, I stepped back into the little cabin and leaned on the door.

Bethany was laying next to Will, the lantern casting a dim glow over them both. She turned her pale face toward me. "His heart is so slow, Sienna. I think...I think he's dying."

I bowed my head, my hopes slipping away in a rush. Immediately I pushed that defeatism away.

"Then we have to help him *not* die then, don't we?" I looked at her and then tapped my finger to my neck.

Her eyes widened. "You mean...feed him?"

"The horses are barely hanging on as it is, and we already know animal blood isn't as potent. We're all he's got, Bee. If we don't help him now, then we might as well just ride away and leave him behind. Because you're right. I think he's dying, too."

I shuddered and, under the cold and weight of my sopping wet clothes, it was all I could do to keep standing.

"We need a fire," she said, straightening. "No one will be looking for us out in this weather so the smoke won't give us away."

As if to punctuate her words, the wind picked up, rattling the one window, throwing snow against it, blocking the world from view.

The small stove was already prepped for being lit, including a good stack of wood next to it.

I put my hand to my face. "Bloody hell. I know we do. But it's a risk."

"A risk we have to take." Bethany was already making her way toward the fire, and I gently pushed her back to Will.

"No, I'll start it. You...do you know how to...feed him? Do we cut ourselves or do you just hope he's still with it enough to bite?"

"I'll try the latter for starters. Vampires are born, not made, so I'm in no danger of being turned."

I dropped to my knees in front of the small potbelly stove, thinking about being bitten by a vampire.

Being bitten by Dominic to be precise.

Not that he ever had, but the idea of his fangs sliding into me as he held me against his naked body had a whole other kind of shiver running through me.

Something was seriously wrong with me.

I laid the wood in the small stove and used the small striker to light the kindling. In a matter of minutes, I had the fire going with the tinder-dry wood. Someone had for sure been here ahead of us. And that someone had set this small place up for themselves. We needed to be gone before they got back and found us Goldilocks-ing their cabin.

"Sienna, I need help," Bethany said softly, taking my attention away from the fire. "I can't get him to bite me."

I turned to see her pressed against him, his head turned so that his mouth was against her neck. But there was no reaction from him, no mouth movement at all.

"Try your wrist?" I shuffled over to her, my body chilled through, but I would survive.

I was not certain that Will would.

Taking Bethany's hand, I lifted her wrist to Will's mouth and together we pushed her skin against his fangs.

She gasped as they punctured through.

"Come on, Will. Please don't die." Her words were choked with tears that had nothing to do with the pain of his fangs breaking her skin open.

I moved to her other side and held Will's head as Bethany's blood dripped into his mouth, rubbing his throat to force the first few drops of it down.

"He should start waking up," she murmured, shooting me a panicked look. "Why isn't it working?"

The minutes ticked by as she massaged her wrist and flexed her hand to keep the blood flowing, and I massaged his neck to keep it going down his throat. Her tiny wounds weren't coagulating so that much was in our favor.

I shimmied out of the outer layers of my dress and laid it on the floor next to the wood stove, then helped Bethany do the same so that we were both down to our thin slips.

Drier, but still freezing.

"Here." I picked up the final blanket and laid it across her shoulders.

"What about you?"

I knelt beside Will's torso.

"There has to be a wound, something that is making him not respond." I was hoping for a cut that we could just patch up, but I had a horror-filled, sinking sensation that perhaps the young prince was not going to make it after all.

The duchess's words rang in the back of my head.

"Take care of him, save him."

But it was the thought of Dominic's face that firmed my resolve once again. I had to try.

Sliding my fingers across his chest, I fanned the shirt he was wearing. Nothing was visible on his upper body.

I opened up his shirt further and didn't see any wounds on his belly. I worked my hand under his back, but there was nothing. Not even a scratch. The few bruises he'd had when we'd first started out were gone.

I lifted my head to look at Bethany, a slow horror dawning on me. "The king was killed with poison. The same person wants Will dead. There are no wounds on him—it must be the same poison."

Bethany's eyes closed and a tear slipped out. "Can we save him?"

I sucked my lower lip into my mouth and held it a moment before nodding. "We are going to do everything we can. We need to get him awake enough to ride, to get out of here. Then we are going to find the werewolf king and beg for help. Okay?"

The plan sounded so very simple, yet both of us knew it was anything but.

Bethany looked across at me. "You're a good person, Sienna."

"No, I'm not, because we need him too. Our chances of survival are better if Will is alive." I took a breath and motioned for her to move. "Wrap your wrist. See if there is anything tucked in a floorboard or a hidden cupboard for food and I will feed him for a bit."

"I could stay with him, I don't feel bad. I'm not even lightheaded." Bethany's one hand was splayed across his chest, the other holding the side of his face as her wrist dripped into his mouth.

I knew she had feelings for him, she'd all but told me when we'd still been at the castle that she secretly loved him.

"I would never step between you, Bee," I put a gentle hand on her arm. "This doesn't mean anything at all."

She looked away, guilt written on her face. "And you love Dominic. You're right, I'm being stupid."

I wasn't going to argue with her about my supposed love for Dominic.

Lust?

You bet your bottom dollar that I wanted that man more than I knew was good for me and my future health.

But love?

Love was...not something I could say was even real, not in this world of intrigue and politics, of life and death.

"I love Jordan," I said softly. "He is why I'm here, *he's* family."

Bethany nodded dubiously, but said nothing, making room for me. I knelt beside Will, already knowing that what we were doing was so that we could say we tried. If blood had been the answer to the King's poisoning, he would have survived and Edmund would not be on the throne and us in this mess.

I knew with all my heart that our efforts were for Bethany. Her last goodbye to a love that could never be—a maid and a prince of vampires was never going to be anything, any more than a human slave and vampire general could be...

I held my wrist close to Will, but at the last moment paused, pulling the butterfly pin from my hair. Somehow, it felt like a betrayal to allow him to use his fangs on me. I refused to acknowledge whom I would be betraying as I stabbed at my skin in one, quick motion. The sharp point of the pin instantly punctured through my flesh. Crimson blood welled and flowed, and I let it run down my hand to drip off my pinky finger into Will's mouth.

Three drops, and I could have sworn that his labored breath grew more even.

Four drops and his eyelids fluttered.

A groan slid out of him and then he moved like lightning. His mouth latched onto my wrist and he was clinging to me with a strength that defied his near death a moment before.

"Bethany!" I shouted her name as I struggled to free myself, panic gripping my chest. But Will was not letting me go. I might as well have been cemented to him.

She grabbed him and we fought to free my wrist from his mouth as the wind battered around us.

Bending her mouth to his ear, she whispered something to him and as fast as it had happened, he let go, flopping onto his back with a deep breath.

His eyes flickered open and he stared at the ceiling.

His voice was hoarse. "I should be dead. I saw my mother beckoning me to the grave."

I grimaced and held my arm to my chest, feeling the bruising spread already.

"Well, oddest thank you I've ever heard, but you're welcome."

CHAPTER 2

Dominic

The smell of damp peat moss filled my nostrils as I approached the little village an hour's ride from the castle, but it was the eerie silence that had me reining in Ares.

A sense of unrest snaked its way up my spine as I took in the scene before me.

Dozens of huts and cottages lined the cobbled street, their chimneys belching smoke, but there was not a soul in sight. I *snick*ed my tongue and urged Ares forward, one hand on the hilt of my sword.

It didn't require supernatural powers to sense that something was very wrong here.

"Go away!" a hoarse voice called in the distance.

I turned to see an old woman waving a gnarled hand at me from her open window.

"Don't you know there's an outbreak, stupid boy? No strangers allowed here in Belladonna until the bloodworms are kilt!"

"I've no plans to stop, woman. I'm just passing through to get to the forest."

"No strangers passing through, either," she hollered. "For all we know, you could have a bellyful of the vile creatures even now! Go on, turn 'round and go back the way you came!"

I knew that there was no true outbreak on the horizon—that my brother Edmund, the new King, had infected his own people with the deadly worms in order to cover up his murder of our father using one—but these poor fools had no way of knowing that. They would spend the next months–maybe even years–living in fear, cowering in their homes, while Edmund continued his reign of terror, unchecked.

But as much as I wished I could stop and soothe their fears, there were more important matters at hand that I needed to deal with.

In the two days that had passed since my father had died, the palace had been in utter chaos. Edmund's advisors had talked him down from his initial plans to murder our brother Will in cold blood in order to ensure he didn't incite an uprising, but that hadn't stopped him from imprisoning Will and wounding him grievously from what I'd been able to find out. The new king had also threatened to murder all the women participating in the Harvest Games and brashly declared an imminent return to the old ways.

Ah, yes. The good old days, when vampires could brutalize humans and every other species without consequence. When there were no rules except those made at the whim of the King himself. When we were every bit as monstrous as those tales told by the humans 'round a campfire in the dark of night. We were everything they feared and more.

Despite my own attempts, it had been Edmund's trusted counsel who had convinced him that giving our father a proper funeral—not just a perfunctory burial, but a true royal send-off with all the respect, pomp, and circumstance he was due—was the first order of business. Without that, Edmund stood little chance of gaining the genuine loyalty of those who had loved and admired King Stirling. Edmund was powerful, but not powerful enough to dismantle centuries' old traditions that required at least the illusion of civility and diplomacy *before* the bloodletting and murder started.

The event would commence the following morning and last all day and night.

Forty-eight hours of a head start for my younger brother, my woman, and her maid.

Forty-eight hours until I was meant to hunt them down like dogs, with Edmund at my side.

Forty-eight hours for Will to feed from Sienna's smooth, sweet neck and—

I let out a snarl and shoved that thought away. I couldn't afford to get distracted by feelings of jealousy and rage. There was precious little time and much to do.

I snatched the shield from my saddlebag and held it high, flashing the royal family crest to the old woman who still glared at me through her window.

"Close your shutters and mind your business, on orders of the King."

Without waiting to see if she obeyed, I dug my heels into Ares' flanks and rode on. Less than a mile further, I reached the tree line leading into the forest. Ten minutes later, a quaint little house came into sight.

With a silent prayer, I dismounted my horse and led him to a trough filled with clean water.

Please let him have forgotten all about her...

"I wondered if you'd come to see your old mother in a time like this." Her voice was the same as ever, a little sharp, and a lot wary.

I turned to see my mother standing in the doorway, a sad smile spread across her still-beautiful face. Her raven locks were long and lustrous, and her figure was that of a woman in her prime, but her troubled blue eyes revealed her age. They showed the wounds of her past as clearly as any scar across the skin.

A sigh of relief rolled through me as I made my way up the stone path to her door. "Mother. I'm glad to see you're well."

She let out a delighted peal of laughter as she waved me in. "I have to admit, I'm rather surprised myself. When I heard of Stirling's demise, I was fairly certain I'd reached the end of my time on this earth. I imagine that sadistic prick has got a lot on his plate right now, but he'll come for me soon enough."

Sadistic prick being Edmund. She never called him by name.

"That's why I'm here," I said, stepping inside and swiping my muddy feet on the mat. "Before he does, we need to get you someplace safe."

"Safe?" she said with a wry smile. "In the Territories?" She leaned in to pat my cheek. "Sweet boy, safety no longer exists here. Surely, you realize that?"

She led me into the great room and drew me down to sit beside her on the sofa.

"I do," I acknowledged with a grim nod.

"Even you are only safe until he has his house in order. Once the dust has settled, he'll have your head. You are far too strong. You command far too much respect and loyalty for him to keep you around. It was only Stirling's edict that shielded you from his wrath."

"I'm aware." And if things went my way, Edmund would be long dead before the dust had time to settle.

"So how do you plan to ensure your survival? I couldn't bear to lose you, my son," she whispered, lacing her fingers with mine.

"First, by getting you out of here."

"I already told you, there is nowhere in the Territories that—"

"Exactly. That's why you will need to go beyond the Veil...or what used to be the Veil. I've secured you safe passage to Verona, in Italy. That is still a city where many of our kind live in peace and comfort. You leave tonight." She opened her mouth to argue, but I cut her short. "Hear me out, stubborn woman. You want me safe?"

She clenched her jaw, but then nodded. "Of course."

"Then help me." I squeezed her hand, imploring. "Mother, I love you dearly, but your presence is a weakness. All Edmund has to do to get me back in line is threaten to harm you. With you safe in Italy for a time, I can focus on usurping the bastard and hastening his journey to hell where he belongs. Then, if you wish, you can come home."

She let my words marinate for a long moment. "And what of Will?"

"I'll go and rescue him once I have a plan in place to take down Edmund."

"Do you have something in mind?"

Her mind was no doubt already flashing through the potential scenarios. King Stirling had commented more than once that I'd taken after her, and in this he was not wrong.

"I've worked out nearly half a dozen prominent families who I believe would help plan his assassination if called upon," I said, watching her for a reaction. I was not disappointed.

My mother let out a snort. "Aristocrats, especially of the vampire variety, are loyal to the hand that feeds them. Sure, there might be a few with principles, but the only way to suss them out is by posing the question. And if you've picked incorrectly?"

she shrugged one deceptively delicate shoulder. "You've sealed your fate, along with that of the kingdom."

And there was the rub.

"Then I'll do it the old-fashioned way. Alone. I'll be armed at the funeral, playing the part of loyal General to the king. Then, when we raise our swords in salute, I'll remove his head from his neck."

She studied me carefully. "Yes, there's a chance that there are enough of his detractors present that you get away with it. But it's just as likely that you are murdered by one of Edmund's loyalists on the spot." She held up a staying hand. "I know you don't care if you die, but remember, that leaves Will out there, unprotected."

Along with Sienna.

I raked a hand through my hair with a growl.

"So, what do you suggest, then? I just retrieve Will and run, like a coward? Leave my people...*my soldiers* at the mercy of a sadistic tyrant?" I shook my head furiously. "I won't do it."

"And I would never ask you to," she assured me gently. "Edmund must die. And his loyalists need to be buried beside him. But why does it have to be at your hands? Why can't you do what's been done since the beginning of time and hire someone to do it for you?"

I stared at her, nonplussed. Who in their right mind would risk the wrath of the Vampire King for coin?

Understanding dawned on me suddenly, and we spoke at the same time.

"The Vanators."

An elite cadre of vampire hunters who had spent the past fifteen years trying to wipe our kind off the face of the earth. Our mortal enemies, if we had any, it was them.

"To invite them into our home would be tantamount to suicide," I said.

She raised one brow and cocked her head. "Yes, but for whom? Not you."

I let that thought roll around in my brain for a long moment. Could it be done?

They were money-hungry, there was no doubt of that. And they would leap at the chance to take down the keystone to our empire. Edmund's cruelty was legendary even beyond our borders. If anything, the Vanators overstated it when they spread their recruiting propaganda. Could they be trusted to make a deal?

Would they trust me enough to come onto our lands?

The possibility was there—and that gave me pause. "If you agree to leave quietly on the ship tonight, I will consider it."

She didn't have to know that I was already considering it, leaning into the idea. If it helped assure her obedience, more the better.

"Fine. I'll pack a trunk now and be ready by nightfall."

I let out a sigh of relief and rose. "The boat will be waiting for you at Southwind Estates at midnight. Tell Teresa you've come for a visit. Once you're in Verona, stay put until you hear from me. Swear it?"

She rolled her eyes and criss-crossed her heart with a finger. "I swear."

"If all goes to plan, I'll see you within the month." Two weeks for her to get to Verona, and an additional two weeks to make sure Edmund was dead.

Her gaze went soft, tears glazing her blue eyes. "And if it doesn't?"

I pulled her in for a tight squeeze, pressing a kiss to the top of her head.

"Then I'll see you on the other side, Mother. Safe travels."

I headed for the door and didn't look back. One responsibility down, and what felt like several thousand more to go.

When I stepped back outside, a sugary dusting of snow had covered the ground. Well out of season, but still a boon.

That meant there would be even more toward the colder eastern border. Hopefully, with that cover and the extra time, Sienna and the others would make it out of Edmund's reach before our hunt got underway.

Slightly mollified that my most immediate concerns were taken care of, I mounted Ares and raced back toward the castle. Now came the much more difficult task of figuring out how to not only stall Edmund, but to stop him completely. And there was only one person left in Blackthorne Castle that I trusted enough to help me do it.

The snow had ceased again by the time I reached the palace training grounds, and my soldiers were busy sparring. I spotted Scarlett's flaming hair in the distance as she shouted at a pair of fresh recruits swinging their blunted cutlasses wildly at one another.

"My *mother* could swing a sword more smoothly than that! Unless our enemy is a blind chicken, you're both bloody well fucked if you don't get it together! Come on, now, boys!"

For the first time since I'd heard the news of the king's death, my lips twitched into a smile.

I had to hand it to her. My Captain of the Guard was an excellent substitute in my absence.

"Captain."

Scarlett turned her head toward me at the sound of my voice.

"Let's give the lads a break, shall we? I need to speak to you in private."

She tipped her head in a curt nod. "You heard the General. Go take a piss, get something to eat, and meet back here." She turned to the group of two dozen others. "All of you, take thirty."

With that, she tugged her black cloak more tightly around herself and fell into step beside me.

"Where have you been all day?" she murmured for my ears only. "I was getting worried. You know he'd as soon kill you as send you on a mission."

"I had some business to take care of."

She didn't press and I didn't offer to elaborate.

"We'll talk at the tavern," I said, jerking my chin toward the squat building twenty yards away. "I don't trust that the soldiers' quarters aren't being monitored."

When we stepped inside, by tacit agreement, we both headed toward the crackling fire.

"Two ales, please," I called to the barkeep as I took a seat in front of the hearth.

"Every time I see your ugly mug, I feel a sense of relief," Scarlett admitted in an unusual display of affection. She shrugged off her cloak and then folded her muscular frame into the seat across from me. "If you try to go after Will and the two women without him, he'll hunt you down like a rabid dog, you know. Although, I'm pretty sure he's going to do that anyway," she admitted with a wince.

"Everyone keeps telling me that," I grumbled in reply. "I'm starting to get a complex."

The barkeep set two sloshing steins of ale on the table between us but when I held out some coins, he waved me off.

"On the house. May His Highness rest in peace, General."

He left us without another word.

"Lots of people are still loyal to the dead king," she observed lightly. "Maybe a coup wouldn't be as difficult as we think."

I glanced around and then leaned closer. "It would be far easier if Edmund were dead. And I have a plan to make that happen."

Once I told her about the Vanators and the beginnings of a strategy I'd devised on the ride from my mother's house on how best to utilize them, she was quiet for a long time. So long that I almost wondered if she'd drifted off.

"Scarlett?"

"Sorry," she said, jerking her gaze from the fire and snapping back to reality. "I was just thinking of how fucked things have been since the Veil fell. Or maybe it was always like this?" She shrugged and then let out a mirthless chuckle. "In any case, as you know, I'm in. Whatever you need me to do, I'm at your command."

I *did* know, but in a time when very little was certain, it was nice to hear.

We'd agreed about the Vanators. If the opportunity to pick Edmund and his men off during the hunt did not arise, she would make contact and extend my offer. It was dangerous, but I was hoping that she would not have to even reach out to the

Vanators. If all went as planned, Edmund would be dead before the hunt was complete.

For the next hour, the two of us pressed our heads together and began the long, laborious task of turning my germ of an idea into a military offensive. But all the while, one corner of my mind couldn't stop from wondering if Sienna was still out there in the bitter cold. If she was alright.

And if my brother was at her neck, drinking from her.

Taking what was mine.

It was all I could do not to flip the table before me and begin the hunt in earnest.

Monstrous, indeed.

CHAPTER 3

Sienna

"We can't stop for long," Will said, his voice barely audible over the whipping winds.

We'd only been back on the road for an hour, and I was no more thrilled than he was to be off the horses in broad daylight.

"We have no choice," I replied, shooting the young prince a probing glance.

There was no denying that he looked slightly better than he had the night before. Our blood along with a night's rest had clearly helped. His cheeks had a bit more color, and he was steadier in the saddle. He had a long way to go to get back to his normal strength, though. If we were ambushed right now by even two healthy vampires, despite his fighting acumen, we'd be dead meat. But Bee's mare had started limping a mile back, and we needed her if we had any chance to get to the werewolf border before Edmund's men hunted us down.

I turned and made my way toward Bee, whose face was pinched with worry as she rifled through our saddlebags for some of the apples and dried beef we'd brought.

"We should've gone the direct route, over the bridge," Bee murmured, shooting Will another concerned look. "I don't know if he's going to make it..."

"He's going to make it. I think we've only got a couple more hours ahead of us." Assuming the mare had just picked up a stone, and it wasn't working itself into a full-blown abscess or infection... "Besides, if we'd gone to the bridge, we'd have been picked off by guards."

I didn't let her see my doubt. It was tough being in charge, knowing every decision I made could cost us all our very lives. But it was too late to change course now. We needed to forge ahead and make the best of our current lot.

"Hey girl," I cooed softly as I approached the bay mare. "What's going on? Will you let me take a look?"

She tossed her head, eyes rolling as I got closer.

"Shh, you're alright. You're okay, sweet girl."

Whether it was the tone of my voice or my strange new—I wouldn't call it power, that was way too terrifying—ability to connect on some deeper level with animals, she calmed almost instantly as I laid a hand on her heaving side. I wish I could say the same for myself. The horse's pain rolled off her in waves, coursing through my fingertips.

It was bad news; it wasn't even as simple as a stone bruise. I ran my hand down the back of her leg, the heat pulsing off the thick tendon. She'd injured her main flexor tendon pretty severely–a pull or a tear, I couldn't be sure. But either way, she was in a lot of pain. The mare had muscled through the last leg of our journey because she was a good girl, but she wouldn't be able to go much farther. Not with the weight of a person on her back. And as hard as we'd been pushing them, there was no way either of the others could bear two of us. I wished I had some sense of how close we were, unless...

Come on. You can do this.

I closed my fingers around the mare's leg and then let my eyes drift shut.

Don't think about the cold. Don't think about the fear. Just feel.

Desperately, I dug deep, searching to call the same power to my fingertips that I'd used to heal Havoc just a couple of days before. Only I didn't know how I did it then, and I didn't know how to do it now.

"Come on, come on..."

There, deep down, in the pit of my very soul, a tiny spark–

"Godsdamnit!"

I stepped back, mind reeling. It was like I was running on empty. I'd used up all my stores of energy on my own horse, and left myself near dead doing it. I felt alright now, considering, but this was all new. I had no idea how long it would take to get back to full strength, especially on little food and even less sleep. And I still didn't have a handle on how any of it worked.

"We can't stay here in the open any longer," Bee's low voice sounded just inches from my ear. "You and Will saddle up and go. I'll stay here with her."

Fury shot through me as I whipped around and slapped her right across the cheek.

If I wasn't so mad, I might have laughed at her stunned expression.

"The fuck you will," I snapped. "That's a death sentence and you know it. Now stop acting foolish and help me think of an actual solution to this problem."

There was a long silence as she stared at me, wide-eyed. "I-I can't believe you just slapped me," she said finally, rubbing at her cheek with a frown.

"You deserved it. And besides, I learned it from you," I reasoned. "I think it was my second day, and we were going to be late for some meeting with the Duchess. I was yammering on and on about something and then *crack*. I hate to admit it, but it helped." I paused and eyed her intently. "Did it help?"

She let out an indignant sniff and shrugged. "It helped me get a headache, if that's what you mean."

"What's the verdict?" Will called from where he sat ten yards away, propped against a nearby tree, his voice weak.

"We'll take her as far as she can go, and then go the rest of the way on foot," I replied, eyeing the landscape ahead.

"Excellent." He waved a hand. "Carry on then."

Bethany smiled at him and I rolled my eyes. He might be heir to the throne but he could barely stay on his horse. As if he had some say in where we went right then.

A thick, dense fog had rolled in, making it hard to judge how far we had to go, but I refused to lose hope. We had to get to the border.

It was the only way to save Will and Bee... The only way to see Jordan again.

But again, it was the thought of Dominic that spurred me into action.

"Bee, you and Will eat some of that food while I try to wrap her leg for some support."

"Look alive!" Will shouted suddenly as he struggled to rise and reached for his sword. "We've got company!"

My pulse kicked up a notch as adrenaline coursed through me.

I yanked the dagger from its sheath at my hip and wheeled around.

"Get behind the horses!" I hollered to Bee, desperately searching for a sign of movement in the dense fog surrounding us.

A massive wolf came loping into view just a moment later. I'd thought I was mentally prepared for what a werewolf might look like, but I'd been gravely mistaken. This thing was the size of a Subaru, with coarse, reddish fur and teeth like Ginsu knives. It padded toward me, ears pinned back against its massive head.

We'd planned to throw ourselves at the mercy of the wolves, but at the border, in a strategic way. This animal had come onto vampire territory for a reason, and by the looks of it, that reason was to hunt. I'd heard tales of some werewolves slowly slipping into madness since the fall of the Veil. Whispers amongst the maids and even Bethany had mentioned it.

Could this wolf be one of those slipping?

Again, I tried to access that tiny ember inside me to even make a connection with the creature, but in my panicked state, it was nowhere to be found.

Blood roared in my ears as I dropped into a fighting stance. I was under no delusions that I could win this battle, but I wasn't going down easy.

"Come on, you ugly bastard," I said, beckoning him with one hand, "let's dance."

The wolf came to a sudden stop and cocked its head at me. Then, a moment later, it began to shake. I watched in awe as the beast's limbs crackled and stretched, writing...changing.

A moment later, a giant wall of a man stood before me. The long, unkempt ginger hair, the thick beard...the Glasgow smile.

"Lochlin!"

Dominic had all but admitted his ally and friend Loch was a werewolf, but seeing him shift right in front of me was a shock to my already overtaxed system.

"Aye, lass. 'Tis I," he said with a grin. "I'd hug you but..."

I followed his gaze and realized I was still holding the dagger in front of me, ready to gut him. "Sorry." I resheathed my knife and then closed the distance between us. "What are you doing here?"

"What are *you* doing here, is the real question. Are you trying to get yourself killed, then? You're only a few miles from the border. I was out hunting and could smell your horses. It's so rare that the bloodsuckers come close to the border this far east, especially in weather like this, I had to come take a look. See who was fool enough to get close."

He turned, surveying the space around us. "Prince William," he said, nodding at Will in greeting.

"Loch," Will managed, slumping against the tree and sliding back down to his bottom again.

"Sienna?" It was only then that I remembered about Bee. She was cowering next to her mare, face as white as a sheet.

"It's okay, Bee. This is Loch, a friend of Dominic's."

He's going to help us, I hoped.

"Speaking of the devil, where is the General?"

About that...

"He, um, he and Duchess Evangeline sent us away. Edmund was planning to execute Will—hell, he almost managed it already—so we took him and a few horses and headed your way. The Duchess said we should ask your people for sanctuary." I realized I was babbling but couldn't seem to stop. "If we explain that we want to stop Edmund from breaking a longstanding truce and bringing chaos to the Territories, I'm sure they'll listen. Won't they?"

Loch's dark, soulful eyes were locked on mine and I tried not to squirm. "So you're telling me that *Dominic* sent you away? Dominic told you to do this?"

"Yepper. He did," I said, nodding confidently. "He knew Edmund was going to have us all killed, so he told us to run to the border and request an audience with the wolf king."

"Strange. Because there is no king. Not any longer. There is only a wolf queen. And I'm fairly certain I told that to Dominic the last time we spoke, dinna I?"

The wolf-man closed the last of the distance between us and stared down at me, making the most of his size. His voice was so low, I had to strain to hear him.

"But what's even stranger, lassie, is that our forces just received intel that the General and the new king are putting together a hunting party for the three of you as we speak. So tell me...who's lying?"

I stared at him, unblinking, as I processed his words.

We'd known Edmund was going to be on our tail, but Dominic? What the hell was going on here? Was he so furious that I'd disobeyed his orders to stay put that he would turn on me?

"It's a ploy. He has no choice but to lead the party if he wants to protect us," Will called. "He would never hunt me down."

But me, on the other hand? Hard to say. He was going to be pretty pissed off that I'd completely ignored his directive to stay put, that much was for certain.

"Okay, so I lied," I said with a shrug. "Sue me. It's been a rough few days, to say the least. But everything except the Dominic part was true. If we stayed, Will would be dead and I would be as good as. The Duchess did tell us to speak to the wolf king. Maybe she didn't know about the shift in power?"

Lochlin seemed slightly less suspicious as he nodded slowly. "That's likely. It was a recent change and even though she knows the former king, I don't believe they're in regular communication. I'm not so sure this is a wise plan though, lass." He turned and made his way toward Will, popping a squat beside him. "'Tis a risk, William. Even if the powers that be are open to an alliance, the full pack will not be easily swayed. Many centuries of bad blood will muddy the waters."

"If your leader is strong and has their respect, they'll listen, won't they?" Bee piped in, eyeing Lochlin warily.

"She is. They do. But there is a mental sickness touching some of our kind since the fall of the Veil. Most are fine, but those afflicted become paranoid and increasingly violent. I'm not sure..."

"Please, Loch. We have nowhere else to go. Our mare is injured, Will is hanging on by a thread...if we turn back, we die for certain. Your queen is our only hope."

Bethany piped up, her voice soft, "This weather is brutal as well. We don't even know what to make of it at this point, or when it will break."

Lochlin closed his eyes and tipped his head back to face the sky. "For fuck's sake, alright then. I'll take you to meet the queen. But I'll no be making any promises. This could go badly. For all three of you. And for me."

The relief that coursed through me made my knees weak. All the caveats in the world didn't matter at this point.

He was taking us to the Werewolf Territory. At least we'd have a chance, and if luck was on my side, I'd even get to reunite with Jordan.

I shot Loch a grateful smile and went to help Will stand.

"Let's get this show on the road then, shall we?"

CHAPTER 4

Dominic

T he morning of King Stirling's funeral dawned sharp, crisp and cold. Each breath I took iced the back of my throat, down into my lungs. But that was not what had my attention. No, Edmund's first decree as a new monarch had my skin itching.

Instead of a burial in the manner of our people, a simple wooden box, arms crossed and a chunk of oak clutched in the hands, Edmund had decided to do something less traditional.

"Is he seriously going to burn his father's body? Does he not realize how that looks?"

I didn't turn to Raven as the vampire lord stopped to stand next to me. He'd arrived the night before, late as usual, but still in time for the funeral.

"It does appear so," I said. "And I believe that he is sending a message to any who would cross him."

Step out of line and you'd find yourself burning on a pyre of your own.

Raven shot a look at me. "Why? What is he hiding?"

I arched a brow at him. "What do you think?"

Because there was the rub. A body burned to ash could not be picked apart. There would be no autopsy to see just what had killed the old king. No one would ever find the worm or any evidence that would help turn the tide against Edmund.

It wasn't good, but I had to pick and choose my battles with him, and I'd already pressed for an elaborate sendoff fit for our father in order to buy Sienna and Will a further head start. Pressing for more and more concessions would only raise his suspicions.

Raven gave a slow nod. "Well, I could take a few guesses. But perhaps I should wait for the gambling hall to make my bet? What do you think we could find there?"

His suggestion to visit the gambling hall had already crossed my mind in hopes that I might get some idea of which way the wind was blowing gossip-wise. Now, with Raven along for the ride, I could act as though I was escorting a visiting dignitary.

"After you, Lord of Seattle." I tipped my head in his direction.

He laughed and clapped a hand on my shoulder. "Good man."

Turning quickly, he strode through the slowly gathering crowd. The fire would not be lit until noon, mimicking the midnight hour. Then it would burn for a full two days.

I kept my eyes traveling over the people we passed. Looking for...something. An indication of subterfuge, of hope, of anything that could be of use. As of yet, all I had for certain was Scarlett and a few of my closest men at arms on my side.

I was not even fully sure I could trust Raven, despite his nature to avoid conflicts. That in itself was not going to work in my favor if this coup came down to a true battle.

"Whatever happened to that scrappy little street urchin you won at the auction?" Raven asked as we made our way through the streets and toward the Boar and Blade Inn. The best gambling den in the city, as well as home to some of the best drink.

His words sunk into me. "She took part in the Harvest Games."

"Really? Did she do well? So hard to see under all that dirt. She had a great figure though, not the usual type for your lot." He laughed. "Me on the other hand, I may have lain awake more than once wondering what she looked like clean and naked—"

I didn't recall moving. I was next to him and then the next second I had him by the throat and pinned to the wall of the closest building. As soon as I realized what I'd done, saw his eyes wide and felt his pulse under my hand, I let him go.

"My apologies, Lord Raven." I gave him a stiff bow. "Perhaps you'd best go on without me."

The bastard though, he could not help himself. Crowing with laughter, he grabbed my arm, obviously unconcerned with what I'd just done.

"Tell me it isn't so! Tell me that...she did not get under your skin, did she? Or just under your body? No, gods of the night no. Wait, wait! You...care for her?"

His laughter turned more than a few heads our way—seeing as we should have been grieving the king and not having a lark. Catching himself, he settled for a hearty chuckle. "Oh, this is too sweet. Tell me everything."

I closed my eyes and struggled to breathe. "This is not the time, Raven."

His smile was wide, and I could see that he was truly barely contained. "Oh, I beg to differ, it is exactly the time. Where is she? I should like to meet the one who finally caught your eye and not just your cock."

My jaw clenched and unclenched, fangs aching at the root. "She ran away, with Will." There, let him chew on that.

Raven's mouth hung open as he stared at me. "Say that again, my ears must be plugged with cotton—"

"You heard me clearly." We'd reached the pub, and I waved at the door, urging him to enter. "We will discuss her later. Not here."

"Well, if we must wait, then I will do so on pins and needles." He laughed again as he went ahead of me, seeing as he was a titled Lord and I most certainly was not.

Making his way to the upper floor where the gambling took place, I let him get more than a few feet ahead of me as I scanned the room. Round tables were set up along the edge of the walls, and the gaming pits that were sunk slightly into the floor dominated the center of the room for the dicers. At the far end were a couple of men set up with tables, a sign on each. One read, "Death by murder," the other, "Death by chance."

Subtle.

Several of my own soldiers were there, and they tipped their heads in my direction. I returned the gesture but left them to their own devices as I made my way over to where Raven had slid into a card game. I took a chair just behind him so that I had my back more to the wall, and I was able to watch over Raven as if I were his bodyguard.

More than that, I was able to watch the men who made their way toward the two tables.

Those that bet on the death by chance were of no concern.

Those that bet on the death by murder...well, they were far more interesting.

A lordling from Teresa's Southwind Estates by the crest on his left shoulder. Young. Nervous. His eyes darting left and right as he stepped up to the "death by murder" table and laid down a substantial amount of coin. Even from where I sat, the glitter was excessive for one so young.

"Name," the bookie barked.

The young one cleared his throat a few times. "Nicholas of Southwind."

Teresa's son. Interesting. He was a handsome lad, and I could see that, once he'd filled out some, he'd have the ladies flocking to him. But he couldn't have been more than sixteen, and still had a long way to go for growing up.

"Here's your marker." The bookie slid a stamped round wooden token. It would have all the details of the bet on it.

I watched him go, hurrying back down the stairs. Raven threw some money on the table, his concentration solidly on his game.

So I thought.

"Tell me, General, have you at least seen her naked yet?" Raven asked so casually that I didn't quite absorb the question at first.

"What?"

"The girl, the one you like, have you seen her naked yet?"

Gods, he was baiting me, and I couldn't allow myself to bite. I needed to focus on the task at hand, not on remembering the lush curves of Sienna's body under my hands, or the soft touch of her mouth on my cock.

I stood and left him to his gaming as a second figure approached the betting tables.

Once more, this figure went straight to the 'murdered' side of things.

Duke of Layton, cousin to Anthony, plunked down a significant amount of coin on the table. "Take my bet."

The same sniveling voice, the same cringing attitude.

I stood right behind him so that when he turned, he was forced to look up, craning his neck. "Duke, I'm surprised to see you here. Were you not removed from court by my father?"

His smile stretched across his face, like a snake's mouth. I half expected a forked tongue to flick out. "Ah, but he's dead, isn't he? I don't suppose you know anything about that?"

Around the room, the other men went still, turning and watching our interaction.

I didn't smile back at him. "You seem rather certain the king was murdered."

"Well it's obvious, isn't it? Who else would want him murdered but one of his sons? And since one of those sons has run away, we can all guess at the culprit, can't we?" He slid sideways and made his way around me.

It took all I had not to throttle him.

There were other ways to dismantle his body and reputation. "Did they ever find the child that you fathered, Layton? Or are we still pretending you didn't dismember her and eat her alive?"

An intake of air around the room, the duke paused. "Good day, gentlemen."

And then he was gone.

If I were to put my money on any of the vampires in that room being tied to Edmund, it would be that one. Easy enough seeing as his cousin was deep in Edmund's pocket.

"General." The bookie stood. "You be scaring off business, do you mind?"

Jaw ticking, I strode across the room. Raven was completely capable of taking care, and I knew that if he heard anything of interest, he'd let me know. Of the vampires around me, he was one of two that I was certain of. And in his case, it was mostly due to the fact that he had remained in Seattle for most of his life, avoiding the politics of the court.

I made my way back toward the castle, my mind working through the possibilities.

I still had multiple snakes to weed out before I made my move. The suggestion of my mother weighed on me, using the Vanators to strike at Edmund.

If things went south, and we had to use the Vanators, the danger only increased.

I lifted my head, coming back to the present as I stepped inside the castle courtyard. Scarlett had the men practicing for the procession. I watched for a moment as the humming of the staves filled the air with an eerie dissonance that I felt all the way to the marrow of my bones.

They would do Stirling proud.

Turning away, I picked up my pace, climbing a set of stairs and hurrying toward Edmund's chambers.

In front of his door there waited three servants in an unsteady line. All three women, all three human.

Crying.

"What are you doing here?" I asked, my voice sharp.

The maid at the head of the line struggled to speak. "The King asked for each of us to come to his chambers in turn."

I looked at them and then at the door just as a scream erupted from within the room. The three women stifled cries of their own, the one in the middle sinking to the floor.

"Leave, all three of you. Go," I commanded. "I will deal with any fallout."

Curtsying to me, the two on their feet grabbed their companion and dragged her down the hall, away from Edmund's chamber.

I put my fist to the door and rapped sharply with my knuckles. "Your Majesty, a word."

Another muffled scream.

"I am otherwise engaged," Edmund said, his voice as silky as ever.

I was not sure that I could save the woman in the chamber, but I would try.

I did not want to think on why it was so important at that moment to save a human maid, but I suspected it had a great deal to do with an auburn-haired, golden-eyed vixen. She would have wanted me to help.

"Your Majesty, it is important. I would not disturb you otherwise."

Silence, then footsteps, the clunk of something heavy, the crack of wood.

"Fine. Enter."

Steeling myself, I opened the door and stepped across the threshold. The smell of blood and viscera hit me like a punch in the face. If it had just been blood, my fangs would have descended. But the rest of the gore turned my stomach.

The woman who'd been *entertaining* him lay with the back of her head touching the heels of her feet, her eyes slowly fading from life. A rattling breath slid from her throat, a gurgle that dragged on and on.

"General, I truly hope it is important and you aren't just...bothering me." Edmund sat at a small table and poured himself a drink. Fresh blood, by the smell.

I tore my gaze from the maid and turned to the King. There was no saving her.

Straightening my back, I tucked my hands behind myself and spoke to him. "You asked me to report anything out of the ordinary. I've been to the Boar and Blade."

"And?" He took a sip. Splatters of blood littered his face like pock marks, his upper chest too. I did not dare look further than that.

I cleared my throat and stitched my words together carefully. Choosing them so that they would have the right impact.

"There is a bet running that King Stirling was murdered. I thought you should know right away. If people are turning on your leadership already, suspecting you of murder, that would indeed be a difficult...situation."

He lowered his goblet and licked his lips. "We will proceed with the funeral as my advisors have set forth."

I dipped my head in his direction. "Of course. But a simple examination of the body by one of our healers beforehand would be enough to—"

"I will not desecrate *my* father further." Edmund said. Not with righteous outrage, no, he seemed...amused?

I stared at him and he stared right back, a slow smile sliding over his face.

Did he know that I knew he'd killed King Stirling? Was it possible?

"As you wish, Your Majesty." I bowed at the waist. "And what of the Boar and Blade?"

Edmund stood and swirled his mug as the maid gave one last breath, finally going silent.

"Burn the establishment to the ground."

I made myself bow again, knowing that I had to prove myself to him, to gain his trust.

So that when the time came, I could get close enough to pierce his filthy heart with my sword, and remove the snake's head from his shoulders.

CHAPTER 5

Sienna

The snow covered our tracks as we made our way to the Werewolf Territory, and that was a boon. But the three of us who'd fled did not have the clothing situated for the weather. Bethany, Will and I were wrapped in the thin blankets from the cabin. Now that we knew we hadn't far to go, Bee at least was riding double with Will, sharing in some warmth, but it was slow going.

Havoc would not allow anyone else on her back and so I rode alone, leading the lame mare along. Even slower than the rest, I couldn't help looking back over my shoulder every few minutes.

Feeling an itch between my shoulder blades, knowing that we were being hunted. If it had just been Edmund, I would've been less scared, funnily enough. But not knowing whether my leaving had finally triggered Dominic's monstrous side, it was the General that I truly feared.

For so many reasons, not the least of which were my complicated feelings when it came to the vexing man.

Lochlin loped ahead of us; his huge wolf's body clearly visible against the white of the snow. At least we had a guide. I wasn't sure I could have done us any good if I'd continued to try and lead us because as it stood, I couldn't feel my face.

Or my hands.

Or much of anything at all, now that I thought about it.

What felt like days passed before Lochlin shifted back to his human form and strode toward us. "Let me do the talking; we are at the edge of the territories."

Teeth chattering, I managed a nod, but doubted I could have spoken anyway. My body was numb from the crown of my head down to the tips of my toes. I might as well have sat naked on Havoc for all the good my clothing and the thin blanket had done.

A particularly hard gust of wind whipped around me and yanked my blanket free of my fingers. I just watched it go, unable to even reach for it.

Havoc pawed at the ground, and let out a long, low snort. I could hardly blame her. The wait was killing us all.

"Come on," Lochlin finally shouted over the wind. "The Queen will see us."

Bethany let out a cry of relief. Will squeezed her a little tighter. Havoc just moved forward the minute I thought about following Lochlin. But my fuzzy brain could barely comprehend that we'd done it. The Queen was allowing us to enter the Werewolf Territory. On some level, I knew I should be celebrating, but I was so cold. So motherfucking cold...

He led us along a narrow, winding path between thick fir trees that blocked out a good portion of the wind. All that did was allow me to realize that the chill was no longer due to the weather. It had settled deep in my bones, and I wondered dimly if it would ever go away.

"There, ride hard for the main structure, do you see it?" I blinked to find Lochlin at my side, staring up at me. "Sienna?"

I could do nothing but stare.

"Shit." He grabbed me around the waist and curled me in his arms. "Why didn't you say something?"

I did a slow blink. Say something? With frozen lips? He was an idiot.

Men were so dumb. All species of them. That made me smile.

"We have to get them to the keep, immediately!" Lochlin yelled, his arms tightening around me. His body heat began to warm one side of me and I closed my eyes. "No, keep your eyes open, Sienna!"

I tried, I really tried.

But the cold was so draining and that little bit of warmth seemed to be spreading through my limbs, inch by inch until I just sighed and didn't fight it anymore.

"Damn it!" Lochlin roared. There was movement around me. And then...nothing.

I floated in and out of dreams, out of darkness, and into light, then back into the depths of my mind.

Dominic was there, his eyes on mine, his hand outstretched. I wanted to take his fingers in my own, but I couldn't. I was going to find Jordan, I was going to leave. I'd done my part.

I'd gotten Will away.

Now it was my turn to escape.

A low moan rolled out of my throat as Dominic's hand ghosted over my face, his voice low and rumbly. "Lass, he'll kill me if you die."

Lass?

I struggled to open my eyes, feeling as if they had anchors tied to the lids. Slowly I blinked and was staring into Lochlin's face.

Sideways?

I shivered and he wrapped his arms around me. There was a warmth at my back. I slowly twisted my head to see Bethany behind me, snuggled up to Will. Below me was a thick, furred rug that enveloped me. A down filled blanket on top, light, but warm.

It took me a moment to understand.

Lochlin laughed as I whipped my head around to stare at him, open mouthed. "I'll not be telling Dom if you don't be, Lass. You're alive, and that's all that matters." He slid out from under the blanket, bare chested and...holy shit, built like a tank.

I swallowed hard and dared a peek under the covers. I still had some remnant of clothes on my body. Underwear and a thin tank top.

"You…"

"You were freezing, we had to get you warm. Best way without using magic is body to body. Especially with a shifter, lass. We throw heat like we have a furnace in our bellies." He laughed again and tapped his rock hard abs.

I looked away as he stepped into his pants and tugged on his shirt, giving him some semblance of privacy. Not that he wasn't worth looking at—if not for the fact that my body only seemed to throb for a certain vampire, I would have very much enjoyed looking.

Sitting up, I took in the space we were in. The room was large, twenty feet long maybe, and had a high ceiling with wooden beams across it that were covered in different hanging items. I didn't look too close after I saw the first skinned animal above our heads.

"You need to get dressed too, Sienna," Loch said. "You and Will."

Will stirred at the sound of his name, and sat up, blanket spilling down to his waist. Bethany shivered and he covered her back up, his hands trailing across her bare skin.

I raised an eyebrow at him. He just shrugged as if he couldn't help himself.

Within a few minutes, we had dressed and headed out of the room, leaving Bethany behind with a kindly woman, her face lined with years of laughter and smiles.

"Ach, go on now, I'll be looking after the wee girly." She'd shooed us out of the room, flapping her apron at us.

We walked the halls of the keep and I couldn't help but take notice of the difference between it and Blackthorne castle.

Rustic for sure, that was the first thing. There was a great deal of wood showing in the structure, it was less refined but clean. There were no fancy paintings or golden chandeliers, but huge sets of antlers with candles set into the tips hung for light.

More than that though, was the technology interspersed. I saw walkie talkies on some of the men's shoulders, and interspersed with the candlelight, there were actual lights—electrical—set into the walls and ceiling.

"We don't spurn technology like our neighbors," Lochlin said, seeing the direction of my gaze.

Will grunted. "We don't spurn it. Not exactly."

"No?" Loch laughed at him. "Where is your telephone, young Prince?"

"We use almost everything we have to create the sun shield in our territory," Will said. "There's none left for anything frivolous after that."

I stared from one to the other. "Wait. You mean you have a limited supply of electricity? How?"

Will glanced at Loch. "They have a hold on the electrical supply coming in from the mainland. Each of the other territories are allotted a certain amount each year. Our allotment allows for the shielding protection we created, that's it."

Lochlin nodded. "Correct. If you weren't such righteous bastards, maybe we'd share more."

There was no heat in their words, no animosity, more fatigue and facts.

Before I could ask another question, Lochlin swept a hand out to the room we'd stepped in. "My Queen, may I present—"

"No, you may not," a sharp voice, full of ice and steel snapped through the air. "We'll not make this like you've come bearing gifts, Lochlin of Clan Moonfall."

A woman crossed the room to meet us. She was dressed in what looked a bit like army fatigues, only her clothes were on the rustic side, like Lochlin's. Leather and fur adorned the edges. Her top was fitted, showing off the tight curve of her waist and the swell of her bust.

Her long dark hair was loose over her shoulders, intricate braids throughout, a few tiny bits of beads and feathers adorning it.

Her eyes were as sharp as her voice. "What have you dragged in, young Lochlin?"

Young?

Lochlin went to one knee. "They are—"

"We're hoping you can offer us refuge," I said, dipping into a curtsy. "Edmund killed King Stirling and would kill William here if given the chance. We fled to your territory in search of sanctuary, Your Majesty."

I realized I didn't even know her name.

As I stayed there in the deep curtsy, I waited.

"And you?" I felt her attention turn to Will.

"It is as she says, I nearly died on our journey here. I ask for time to heal. And if you must throw me out, then please keep the two women safe." Will's voice was nowhere near the jovial laughter that always seemed to hover at the edges. He sounded like a king for once.

A soft huff of air escaped her.

"How is it that you survived?"

My legs were trembling, but I would not step out of the curtsy. I couldn't. I needed her to let us stay, to give me time to find Jordan.

"Sienna here, and Bethany, who is still resting, fed me."

A hand snaked out and latched onto my wrist, yanking me out of the curtsy. I stumbled forward a few steps and instinctively pulled back, pulling the wolf queen off balance. She stared hard at me and I stared right back.

So much for being submissive and pliable.

Her eyes narrowed. "Why are you not resting also then?"

I blinked. "What do you mean?"

"You fed the prince?" She began to circle me, and I forced my feet to stay still.

"Yes, but it wasn't much—"

She adjusted her pace and slid around Will, sniffing the air. "You were poisoned with bloodworm, young prince. And it's still inside you, albeit dormant now. You should be dead."

He stiffened. "You can't know—"

"She does know," Lochlin growled. "Diana's nose is legendary. And it is what I also smelled on you, but I couldn't be sure."

I didn't understand why this was so important.

"It wasn't a lot of blood," I repeated. "Bethany gave him more than I."

The queen came back to stand in front of me. As quick as any vampire, her hand snaked out and she grabbed hold of my jaw. She wasn't hurting me, but she surely wasn't letting me go either.

Her nostrils flared, and she drew in a deep breath. Eyes fluttering, she gave a slow shake of her head. "Impossible. But, yet here she stands."

I didn't understand her words, or how they were related to me. "Your Majesty, please—"

She let me go and stepped back. "You are no more human than I am, though I doubt you even know yet."

My jaw dropped open, and I spluttered. "I assure you, I am. I've never—"

Again, she cut me off. "It is of no matter for this moment. We will discuss further at a later time. Lochlin, since you brought them to me, they are in your care, and they are your responsibility. Find them quarters and get them settled. I would speak to this one at length once she has fully rested. Have them situated and then bring them back for dinner."

The queen of the werewolves turned away from us without another word.

I looked at Lochlin who stood slowly, and he threw me a grin. "That went well."

"Did it?" William muttered. "She barely even acknowledged me." His eyes slid over to me as well. "It was you that had her attention."

I wrapped my arms around my middle, not liking the attention. "She is mistaken. Whatever it is she thinks I am, she's wrong."

I couldn't help but remember the words of the Duchess when I'd first arrived in the Vampire Territory what felt like a lifetime ago.

I know who you are, and more importantly, what you are."

CHAPTER 6

Dominic

The funeral was a tedious process, rife with long-winded speeches by career diplomats and aristocrats who were far more concerned about jockeying for position within this new regime than the death of the King. In fact, until the Duchess spoke, it felt more like a political campaign than it did a ceremony to honor the dead.

But when Evangeline stepped up to the podium in her black lace gown, she was armed to the teeth, and words were her weapon of choice.

"We are all gathered here to mourn the loss of the first of our kind, His Royal Highness, King Stirling. I'm certain there are a few originals still left among us with a similar tale of how they came to know Stirling, but I will share mine with you now."

Her eyes welled up but she blinked back the tears before they could fall.

"I was just a child, no more than five or six, when I had my first memory of it. The hunger. The deep, gnawing ache in my belly that would not be satisfied. It only took one ravaged goat for my father to set me loose in the woods and leave me there to die. When Stirling found me, it was months later. I was curled up in a barn, lonely, terrified and confused as I tried to survive despite wanting nothing more than to be dead. He'd heard rumors of a two-legged creature terrorizing the farmer's chickens and sheep, and he came to see if perhaps he'd found another like him. He gathered me up, and secreted me away, beyond the Veil to join the others like us. That day, he became my brother. A beacon that shined a light on the pathway of my life, then and ever since. But he was more than just my brother. He was also a leader. A leader who recognized that true strength meant ruling with a fair and even hand rather than an iron fist. Who valued tradition, but also embraced new ideologies that allowed us to thrive. Under his guidance, we came to an understanding with humans and found a way to live in relative harmony. Not only that, he negotiated a long-lasting truce with our werewolf neighbors that saved countless lives. But though long and prosperous, his rule was far shorter than it should've been."

She leveled a cool look in Edmund's direction, and I wondered if she was going to challenge him to a duel right then and there. Instead, she bestowed a loving smile on him before continuing.

"In his infinite wisdom, our new king—may the gods protect him—has chosen to cremate my brother for fear that this new version of bloodworm that has awakened from hibernation might have the ability to spread even once its host is dead. Still, I fear that my brother's death might have been due to a slithering creature of another kind entirely. And, despite our differences, I'm certain we can all agree...If there is a snake in our midst, we must set our personal politics and agendas aside and band together to remove its head before more are harmed."

She lifted her head then, looking every bit the royalty she was, and raised her voice in what could only be described as a rallying cry.

"*If there is a snake in our midst*, we must recognize that, even if it behaved as some of you may have wished upon this occasion, it is still a cold-blooded, self-serving creature. Unpredictable. Ruthless. Without conscience, loyalty, or care for what is best for our people as a whole." She raised one trembling fist high in the air, words raining like thunder. "*If there is a snake in our midst*, we must root it out with single-minded tenacity, and then exterminate it, like we did the bloodworms. As if our very existence depends upon it. Because, mark me, if we do not, we are surely doomed. Are you with me, my brethren?"

There were some rustlings and whispers as people tried to read Edmund's body language, but I had to give it to him. He looked as calm as could be. And, soon enough, a chorus of "Aye's" echoed.

"Are you with me?" Evangeline demanded again.

The chorus grew louder. "Aye!"

She glanced over the crowd and nodded slowly before lowering her hand and laying it over her heart. She turned toward the pyre behind her, where King Stirling lay swathed in white gossamer. "Brother, you will be missed. And know that your sons and I will not rest until we know the truth. If vengeance is called for, it will be ours."

With that, she swept off the podium and made her way toward her seat in the front row. She held Edmund's gaze the entire time.

Your move, young nephew.

He'd gone through with the burning of the body, but there were rumbles in the crowd and it was immediately clear his decision was not a popular one.

Even now, hours later, as our hunting party rode southeast like the hounds of hell were nipping at our heels, I couldn't help but shake my head in awe at Evangeline's cunning. That woman was braver than the most battle-hardened of men. She said all the things so many of us present wanted to say to Edmund without saying them at all. He could have her killed for her insolence, of course—and maybe he still would in the days to come—but not without major repercussions. She hadn't named him. Hadn't accused him of anything, or been disrespectful, but she'd affirmed the suspicions of those who had questioned the King's manner of death, and planted doubt in the minds of those who hadn't yet thought to question it.

If something happened to her now, it would only add to the evidence that fuckery was afoot.

It was a brilliant parry, to be sure. I just needed to lay him low before he exacted his revenge on her. And there was no question of it. Edmund might have appeared to be calm and unaffected, but he was seething with rage. One way or another, the Duchess would pay.

I swore under my breath. The women in my life were bloody courageous, but also vexing beyond comprehension. Between the Duchess's little rebellion, having to browbeat my mother into saving her own neck, and Sienna's lack of obedience, I was at my wit's end. God save us all if the three of them ever joined forces. I'd sooner face an army of Vanators riding the most blood-thirsty of Hunters.

The one female not hellbent on sending me to the brink of insanity rode up beside me.

"I've tried to get close to him at various points, but Frank hasn't left his side," Scarlett said, gesturing to the man in question who was deep in conversation with Edmund.

Frank Eleazar was an older nobleman who had been part of Stirling's team of advisors, and one of the few who Edmund had allowed to remain on the council when he'd taken over the day-to-day responsibilities of running the kingdom. In the days since our father's passing, the two had grown thick as thieves.

Frank was a skilled, respected statesman and an even better swordsman, not to mention a powerful vampire, to boot.

Separating them was an imperative first step to a successful ambush attack.

"There's several hunting shacks scattered over the next five miles," Scarlett continued as we rode on, gesturing eastward. "If they've stopped to rest, it will be around here. Hopefully, they'll have come and gone. Smells like the snow is going to start again soon, and we can try to talk him into setting up camp for the night. Then we'll make our move."

The unexpected winter weather—something that had begun cropping up randomly more and more since the fall of the Veil—in the midst of what should be our late summer was a double-edged sword. It hopefully bought Sienna and Will more time to get to safety, but it also added another level of concern. Sienna was an excellent horsewoman, but I doubted the same could be said for her maid. And by all accounts, my brother had been knocking at death's door when he'd left.

Had they succumbed to the snow and ice? Had they stopped at this very hunting shelter and stayed, unable to go on?

I spurred Ares into a full gallop, his massive hooves sending out a spray of ice and snow around us as I pulled ahead of the rest of our 20-person entourage.

If the trio was in a shelter ahead, things would devolve very quickly. Edmund would order all three of them executed immediately, unless he was smart enough to keep one of them to torture, and find out who assisted them in their escape.

Either way, there was an all-out melee on the horizon. The question that remained...Of those present, how many could I secure on my side?

Scarlett, to be sure. And at least the three men she'd selected from our army. That made five, plus Will, Sienna, and Bethany, assuming they could be of any help at all. Against Edmund and his fourteen men, chosen from his camp of loyalists that he used for protection when engaging in unsavory dealings or needed dirty work done and didn't want our father to learn of it.

Not ideal odds by any means, but with Scarlett's skills, my men's elite level of training, and the amount of skin I had in this game, I didn't hate our chances. A steely sense of calm settled over me as I mentally prepared for war.

The scent hit me before the shelter came into view.

Blood.

Sienna's blood.

A sea of red swam before my eyes and I barely restrained a bellow of fury.

"Get a hold of yourself, General."

Scarlett's whip-sharp command broke through the haze, and I realized I was pushing Ares so hard, he was foaming at the mouth.

"Feigning rage is one thing. Allowing it to truly take hold is another," she cautioned as we arrived at the shelter, the two of us leading the pack.

I dismounted and drew my sword in one motion, leaving Ares to his own devices. As I approached the door, it only took one sniff of the air to determine that the runaways had already vacated the premises.

Thank the gods.

That meant they had all been alive not too long ago. Whether Will stayed that way remained to be seen.

I kicked the door open and stepped inside, assessing the cramped space around me.

The remnants of a recent fire smoldered in the hearth, a pile of stained, woolen blankets piled on the floor in front of it. The scent of blood was even stronger now, and a low growl reverberated in my throat.

"Interesting. Seems as if the ladies decided to assist the young prince in his healing," Edmund observed. His tone was chilly, but there was also a devious gleam in his eyes as he studied me. "I wonder if he fucked his food. What do you think, General?"

I didn't make any effort to hide the fangs that had broken through my gums as I spoke. "Doesn't matter. He will die by my hand either way."

"We'll need to find him first, though, won't we?" Edmund replied, cocking his head, the last of the cruel humor leaving his face. "If they escape our borders, we will have a serious problem on our hands. You realize that, don't you?" he demanded.

"I do."

He stepped toward me until the toes of our boots touched. "Are you the General of my Army? Sworn to protect the crown at any cost?"

His hot, fetid breath washed over my face, and it took all I had not to head-butt him into next week.

"I am."

"Then you'd better figure out how we catch up with them tonight, because the Duchess's little speech has the villagers feeling restless. They want a snake? A scapegoat to blame our father's death on? They shall have one." Spittle formed in the corners of his mouth, and his eyes were filled with something close to madness. "You will provide me with the traitor William's head on a pike to parade around the halls of Blackthorne castle by daylight tomorrow, or yours will take its place. Is that understood?"

"Yes, Your Highness."

I understood completely.

We wouldn't be stopping for the night, and I had twelve hours to come up with a plan to murder Edmund and his men.

Challenge accepted.

Because Sienna was out there somewhere. Either vulnerable, freezing, and on the run. Or somewhere safe, warm, and possibly in the arms of my younger brother.

And both of those scenarios made me want to howl with fury.

CHAPTER 7

Sienna

Hot water swirled around my calves as I stepped into the massive, copper bathtub and let out a groan of relief. Unwittingly playing the part of the salami in a vampire/werewolf sandwich had warmed me up some, but a chill had settled deep in my bones from days of damp and cold. The steamy, scented water was like pure heaven.

I lay back, letting the heat envelop me in its embrace.

Things had seemed so bleak just a few hours before, and now, it seemed like we might actually have a chance of surviving this cluster-fuck. Who would've thunk it? Certainly not me, despite the false bravado. But here we were, in Werewolf Territory, the three of us wholly intact.

Which reminded me, Will was still recovering and would likely do so more quickly with another serving of blood.

My blood, to be exact.

But why?

The Queen's words floated back into my mind and I tried to shove them away, along with the Duchess's. These enigmatic women spouting their cryptic observations like a pair of low-rent fortune tellers at a backwoods carnival were getting on my last nerve. I might be "magic" but I wasn't a fucking mind reader.

Say it or don't say it, for gods' sake.

I let out a frustrated sigh and sank deeper into the tub, but my mind was far too busy to relax. That was fine. I'd use the time before supper to plan, then.

Priority number one?

Locating Jordan.

I'd blown my chance at doing recon when we'd first entered the Werewolf Territory by succumbing to hypothermia. That meant I'd need to gain the Queen's trust so she would allow me to move as freely as possible so I could get the lay of the land. For all I knew, Jordan could still be twenty miles away. Which, in this weather, might as well be a thousand. So how to get intel on Jordan's whereabouts without leaving the keep?

Bethany.

Bee was the key. If you needed to find out what was really going on in Blackthorne Castle, no one knew more than the servants. They were so often almost invisible to their mistresses and masters, so they not only heard conversations they shouldn't, they also dusted the skeletons in their closets, and swept the dirt off the places the bodies were buried.

"Hey Bee!" I called, sloshing as I stood and reached for the massive towel I'd been provided.

She stepped into the bathroom and shot me a questioning glance. "Yes?"

"Can you do me a solid?" Without waiting for her to reply, I wrapped the towel around my still-dripping body and continued. "I need you to rub elbows with the servants. Maybe even try to get into the kitchens, if you can."

"To what end?" she asked with a frown.

I hated to lie to her, but I also had no choice. If I told her I needed her help finding Jordan so we could plan our escape, she'd surely shut me down. She'd tell me I had a death wish, and that the two of us would never make it out in one piece.

And she'd likely have been right. But that wouldn't stop me from trying. I settled for a partial truth.

"I need to find out where my friend Jordan is, and if he's okay."

She narrowed her blue eyes and studied me intently.

"That's it? You just want information, and then you're going to leave it alone?"

"I just want to know that he's safe."

A white lie, at most. Because the fact remained that, as a pair of humans on the wrong side of the now-defunct Veil?

Safety was an illusion.

She nodded slowly and took a step back. "Fine, then. I'll head to the kitchens now and offer my assistance...see what I learn. But I'm not making any promises!"

"I'll take it," I said, following her out of the bathroom and making my way to the fur-covered bed in the center of our shared quarters. "I can dress myself and get ready, and I'll meet you downstairs in thirty minutes."

She stopped and held my gaze for a long moment.

"Don't do anything stupid, Sienna." With that, she exited the room, leaving me to watch her go as I swallowed past the sudden knot in my throat.

I was a victim here. There was nothing to feel guilty about. From the start, I'd made no bones about my motivation. I would do whatever it took to find my friend and get us back home.

Together.

I cared about Bee, and would never do anything to intentionally hurt her, but she was a willing cog in this twisted machine. If she wanted to stay among these monsters while they warred for supremacy, bully for her. I was finding Jordan and getting the hell out of here as soon as I possibly could.

Dominic's face shimmered to the forefront of my mind, and I sucked in a steadying breath.

He was a misstep. A mistake. And as much as I liked and respected Will, I'd done more than most would to help him. So long as I fed him one more time, my conscience would be clear. As for Bee, I had to hope that she would understand. If not right away, then someday. She would forgive me, or she wouldn't. There was nothing to be done about it.

Who knew? Maybe she'd be glad to see the last of me. Then she would have Will all to herself instead of being jealous over some connection with him that I could neither stop nor control if she wanted him to live.

Clinging to the thought, I dried off quickly and got dressed.

The clothes that had been provided for me were in the same design as those the Queen herself had been wearing. Fitted, fatigue-style pants that were slung low over my hips, a fitted long-sleeved shirt and a fur vest that went over top. Snuggly wool socks and a pair of black combat boots completed the outfit, and for the first time since I'd been picked up and dumped off at the pens, I felt something close to normal. My stomach let out a long, loud growl and I managed a grin. A juicy steak and I'd be strong as ever.

I made my way down the stone steps, following the scent of roasting meats into a massive dining hall. Despite the thirty plus seats surrounding the perimeter of the rectangular table, only three chairs were taken. The Queen at the head, a much older man with gleaming, dark skin to her right, and Will to her left.

The queen waved a hand at me. "Sienna. Come, sit."

I made my way to the head of the table and took the seat she indicated, next to Will.

"Sienna, this is Lycan. The former king and my dearest friend and advisor. Lycan, this is the creature I was telling you about."

I pursed my lips, biting back my response.

Creature, my ass.

The older man studied me like I was a specimen under a microscope, and I barely managed to keep from squirming.

"Pleasure to meet you, lass," he said finally, shooting a furtive nod at the Queen.

More subterfuge.

Perfect.

"You look much better," Diana observed with a nod. "I take it you were able to get some rest, then?" she asked.

More like I was able to get my head together, but I nodded.

"I did, Your Majesty, my thanks."

A million questions sat, perched on the tip of my tongue, the first of which was what the hell she thought I was, if not human. But coming here and grilling her at her own dinner table was a bad look.

Less vinegar, more honey, Sienna.

Before I could say more, the pleasantries were cut short as a trio of servants stepped into the room, each carrying a covered tray. It took me longer than it should have to realize one of them was Bee. I tried to make eye contact with her to see if she'd gotten any info, but her eyes were downcast as the first of the servants set her tray down and lifted the cloche with a flourish.

"Lollipop lamb-chops on the bone with a shallot and red wine jus," the young maid said before stepping back with a curtsy.

My mouth watered as I eyed the perfectly cooked meat.

The second servant moved to the table. "Roasted venison served rare with a blackberry, cracked peppercorn reduction," she said as she presented her tray.

That dish looked as good as the first and I waited with bated breath to see what Bee had in store for us.

She stepped forward and set her tray on the table directly in front of me.

"Parsnip puree, candied sweet potatoes, roasted cabbage, and a saute of wild mushrooms in a cream sauce."

As she stepped back, she stomped on my toes.

"Jesus," I hissed as a shot of pain snaked up my leg. What the actual fuck—

"So sorry, m'lady! Clumsy, as you know."

But she wasn't, and the almost-manic smile she aimed at me didn't quite reach her eyes.

"Prince William, I know your tastes lie...elsewhere, but I hope you can enjoy some of these offerings?" she said, retraining her overly-bright smile on Will, who looked more confused than anything.

Okay, so she was pissed. And rightly so, I realized with a start. I'd basically relegated her to the kitchens, yet another reminder that she and the man she loved were from different worlds and destined to be apart. And now here I was, sitting next to her man, while she served the two of us like we hadn't all been in the same trenches together not six hours before.

Shit.

"I still enjoy the taste of good food," he said, turning to assure the Queen of the same with an appreciative smile. "And it looks and smells delicious."

"Nonetheless," Diana said, pursing her lips. "Once we're done here, it's probably best if you feed again and get a good night's sleep before we meet tomorrow. I have some ideas about how we might be able to help one another, and all those of the Veil. We'll need you sharp-witted for those discussions." She turned to face me. "Needless to say, your presence will be required as well, Sienna."

"I can feed him," Bee piped in, her cheeks coloring as Diana blinked at her, nonplussed.

"You are but a human, girl. Why would he feed from you with Sienna here?"

The queen looked genuinely confused, and I knew that her careless words weren't intended to be hurtful. But the sickly look on Bee's face and the way her bottom lip trembled was all the evidence I needed that they had, indeed, hurt.

A lot.

"I apologize, Your Majesty," Bee said in a rush before dipping into a deep curtsy. "I'll head back into the kitchens and take my supper with the staff." With that, she wheeled around and scurried back toward the door.

Part of me wanted to run after her, but I knew I couldn't. People like Diana, and even Will, didn't understand how the rest of us lived. Servants, humans, the great unwashed masses...as kind as they might be to us, we were beneath them.

For whatever reason, they held me in higher esteem, and if I ever wanted to figure out why, I needed to remain a welcome guest at the table. That didn't mean I had to feel good about it, though.

My sins were adding up fast. The sooner I could get back to the right side of the Veil, the better.

"Please, eat," Diana said, gesturing to the spread before us. "Lycan, your favorite lamb dish."

"I appreciate you, my child," he replied with a grin before loading up his plate as the two chatted easily.

I forked up a pair of lamb chops and was on to the parsnips when I felt an elbow in my side.

"Is she alright?" Will whispered. "Do you think one of us should go in there and talk to her?"

I shook my head and leaned in close. "We need to stay here. Bee will be fine." As soon as I was gone.

Diplomacy was a tricky thing, especially between species with a beef as old as time and Will leaving to check on a maid was not a good look.

"When in Rome, you do as the Romans do if you want them to trust you. I'll talk to her later and explain."

Will nodded reluctantly and began fixing himself a plate.

"Please forgive me for my tardiness, Your Majesty," a familiar voice boomed.

I looked up to find Lochlin striding into the room, an apologetic smile on his scarred but handsome face.

"I was stopped a dozen times en route," he explained, taking the seat next to Lycan and reaching for a lambchop with his fingers. "Some of the alphas are questioning why we have two humans and a vampire royal in our midst without assembling for a vote."

He tore into the chop with strong, white teeth, devouring it in one bite before setting the bone on the table.

"Why?" Diana replied, her dark brows rising high on her forehead. "Because I said so, that's why."

Lycan patted her hand gently.

"You know how these things work, love. They are creatures of habit and tradition. They prefer it if it feels like a democracy. Schedule the assembly and do what you always do, and have done to me for decades."

"And what, pray tell, is that, wise one?"

The old wolf winked as he forked up a roasted carrot. "Talk circles around them until they think it was their idea in the first place."

Diana's lips twisted into a fond smile. "Fine. I'll humor them. Set a time for the day after tomorrow and let the packs know, Loch."

I shifted in my seat as I chewed on that information along with a piece of venison.

What if it wasn't as simple as all that? What if the packs came together and voted to have us ousted? Or worse?

I needed to find Jordan, and I needed to do it fast.

The thought had barely crossed my mind when he walked into the room, a pitcher in hand.

"Ale, Your Majesty?"

I inhaled sharply, and the chunk of deer meat lodged in my throat. Bending at the waist, I tried to cough, to no avail.

"Our guest is choking!" the Queen shouted.

Panic shot through me, as much from the shock of seeing Jordan as from the lack of air, and I shot to my feet and backed away from the table.

"Should I hit her back or–"

A pair of arms circled my waist and then–

"*Gack!*" The piece of meat flew out of my mouth and landed on the stone floor a few yards away.

"There you go, miss."

Gasping, I turned to find Jordan staring back at me, that familiar, goofy smile wreathing his handsome face.

"Ceecee," he whispered, eyes widening in surprise.

I threw my arms around him in a desperate bear-hug.

"Thank you, oh kind stranger, for saving my life! I owe you a debt of gratitude," I cried in a booming voice. Then, I pressed my lips against his ear. "Pretend we don't know one another. Meet me at midnight, at the top of the stairs. If we can't find a place to speak alone, I'll pass you a note that will explain everything. Don't ask questions, just nod if you understand, Jordan."

Please, Gods, let him understand.

I held my breath, my prayer like a litany. When he finally nodded, I almost sank to the floor in relief.

"Well done, young man," Diana said.

I turned to face the table as she stood.

"What was your name again?"

Jordan stared at me for a beat too long before turning his attention to the queen.

"It's...um, it's Jordan."

"Yes. I remember now. From the pack Killian. Your quick actions are much appreciated. You can be certain I will tell your alpha of this noble deed."

Jordan beamed at her and nodded.

"Thank you, Your Majesty."

She nodded and waved him away.

"Take the rest of the evening off. We can pour our own ale."

Jordan bowed and then exited the room without looking back. Legs still shaking from adrenaline and relief, I took my seat with a grateful sigh.

Maybe it was because she felt sorry for me because I nearly choked to death on venison. Maybe it was because she realized I'd had a long day already. But, for whatever reason, the Queen allowed the rest of the meal to pass in a haze of food, drink, and small talk. An hour after nearly meeting my end, I was seated at the vanity in my quarters, still reeling from this miraculous turn of events.

We'd been here less than a day, and I'd already found Jordan. I just needed to come up with a plan to get us out of here before the packs were assembled.

Or Dominic and Edmund found us.

I shuddered at the thought, and then pushed it aside.

Focus on the positive.

I toyed with the beaded bracelet on my wrist that I'd made to track the passing days. There was still plenty of time to get Jordan out of here and to the ship that would take us home.

The door swung open and Bee stepped into the room, her expression chilly.

"Hey," I said, turning to face her. "I'm really sorry about the–"

"There's nothing to be sorry for," she cut in abruptly as she yanked the apron from her waist and tossed it on the floor. "It was fine. I'm fine."

She definitely wasn't.

"Look, I shouldn't have even asked you to do that. You should've eaten dinner with us at the table."

"Your friend Jordan lives with a family about two miles from the keep," she said as she made her way toward me and took the hairbrush from my hand. "They're part of the Killian pack and word is they're not a cruel bunch."

I didn't have the heart to tell her that I'd already found that out myself.

"That's amazing. Thank you so much! I can rest much easier now."

She didn't reply as she began brushing my hair.

"Did you eat something?" I asked gently.

"I had a head cheese sandwich and a bag of crisps, thank you."

"I tucked a couple of lamb chops in my pocket for you," I said, pointing to the napkin-wrapped parcel sitting on the vanity in front of me.

"No, thanks. I'm full." She continued to brush my hair in silence for a few minutes and then finally said, "How did it go with you? Does the Queen seem sympathetic to our plight?"

"She does. The dinner actually went really well. Diana is much nicer than I'd have expected the Queen of the werewolves to be," I mused thoughtfully. "Ouch!"

I turned and glared at Bee, who stared back at me with wide-eyed innocence.

"Sorry. Was that too hard?"

"A little, yeah."

I rubbed at my stinging scalp and turned back to face the mirror. She didn't need to be doing my hair at all, given the fact that she wasn't technically my maid anymore, so I wouldn't complain. But bloody hell, she'd yanked at that knot like it owed her money.

"I'm done in any case," she said with a sniff as she set the brush down and picked up my butterfly hairpin. "Just going to put it back up in a loose bun so it doesn't get knotted in the night, and–"

A sharp pain shot through my skull, stealing my breath.

"Godsdammit, woman!" I howled, standing up so fast, the stool beneath me flipped on its side as I faced her. "The foot stomp, I get. I deserved that. But I said I was sorry. What else do you want me to do?"

"I want you to not be so smart, and funny, and beautiful," she shot back, tears pooling in her eyes. "I want you to be a regular human being, like me. But noooo...you've got to have magical blood, and now not only does the man I love need you, the Queen wants to be your new best friend, and I'm still just dumb old me, good for brushing hair and emptying chamber pots...nothing more."

I took both of her hands in mine. "You know it isn't me he wants, don't you?"

She stared back at me and shook her head. "I don't know anything anymore, Sienna."

"He stares at you all the time when you aren't looking. And even when he drank from me, I know he wished it was you. When you left crying, he wanted to run after you. If he didn't have feelings for you, he wouldn't have cared at all." I gnawed at my lip and shrugged helplessly. "I don't know what I am, or why my blood helped him. But I can promise you, it's no picnic being talked about like a creature in a zoo of curiosities."

She swiped her forearm over her nose and nodded. "I know. It's got to be really confusing. I'm just...Sienna, even if you're right. Even if he does want me, what does it matter? We can't be together. Not just because he's a vampire, but because he's a prince. We're worlds apart. We'd have a better chance if he were a cat and I was a mouse."

"Do I need to slap you upside the head again or what?" I demanded, scowling at her. "Since when did we become the type of women who just give up? Aren't we the bitches who confronted and survived the Hunters?"

"I guess." She shrugged, and I gave her a little shake.

"Aren't we the women who escaped a horde of vampires, rode through a bloody ice storm, and risked our necks entering werewolf country?"

"We are," she said, her voice a little stronger now.

"Don't tell me that now is the time to get all meek on me. That this–seducing a prince–is where you draw the line?" I let out a snort. "Say it isn't so."

Was I seriously encouraging another human to make a move on a vampire?

But, damn if there wasn't something that seemed precious between them...

She scrunched her eyes in a dubious squint. "So you think I should seduce him, then?"

"I do. We'll go in together to feed him, as the Queen requested. I'll go first, but then I'll slip away, and you offer yourself as dessert...in more ways than one."

Her cheeks flamed, but a wide grin spread across her face. "I supposed I could try."

"Sit!" I said, uprighting the stool. "We'll get you looking fresh and lovely and find you a sexy nightdress. Operation Seduce a Prince is in full effect."

As I brushed Bee's hair and listened to her chatter excitedly, I tried not to think about the growing nausea in my belly.

I *did* think that Will and Bee belonged together.

And I did think that she could find her happy ever after with him—assuming we didn't all die a gruesome death either by werewolf or at Edmund's hands. Plus, the fact that she would now be otherwise engaged with Will as Jordan and I plotted our escape didn't hurt.

The guilt did, though.

I'm so sorry, Bee.

CHAPTER 8

Dominic

At the edge of the woods, in the territory between vampires and werewolves, I stood with Edmund's contingent. Even if the scent of our quarry wasn't still thick in the air, the snow and ice had finally let up. Now, the tracks of three horses and a werewolf were clearly visible by the light of dawn.

I'd failed.

But they had not. They'd escaped and made it into Werewolf Territory, with the help of a wolf I could only assume was my old friend, Lochlin.

A strange mix of relief and fury coalesced in my gut. They'd made it this far. But my woman was still out of reach, a fact that made my blood run hot.

Scarlett and her steed pulled up beside me, and I could sense her body shaking.

"Run," she whispered. "He has not caught up yet, you have time. Go."

I stared at the tree line and then at the horizon to see the true sun rising beyond our borders.

"The sun would kill me long before I found shelter." My voice was empty of emotion.

I knew my fate was sealed.

The sounds of horses approaching through the crusted snow turned us all around.

"Contact the Vanators," I breathed to Scarlett. "Get them everything they need to end him. Put the plan into effect. You have the forged documents."

The skin around her eyes was tight as she looked at me. "Dom, please—"

"I am not going down without a fight," I said. "But I have to know that when I am done, gone to dust, that there is someone still trying to stop him. Trying to put Will on the throne."

"Why would you care if you're dead?" she breathed the question as Edmund and his lordlings came into view.

I didn't answer her, but I knew the reason went beyond my mother, beyond Will and the duchess.

Sienna would not be safe, not as long as Edmund was alive—he knew now that she meant something to me, and that was enough for him to continue to hunt for her. I refused to consider what that meant; That I was willing to put her safety above my own, perhaps even above my own family.

"I am growing soft," I whispered.

I dismounted, patted Ares on the neck, and pulled my sword as I took a few steps in front of Scarlett and my horse.

Edmund's face darkened as he reined in his mount. "And now the truth is here for all to see. Not that I didn't suspect. You think me a fool, General? I know you favor Will, and I know that you despise me. I wanted to see how far you would go in trying to convince me that I was the one your sword belonged to." He let out a heavy sigh as if he were truly disappointed. "I will admit, you almost had me fooled for a moment, with thoughts of that redhead being fucked by Will. Your response was...not like you. I was almost proud that you'd finally started behaving like one of us. Alas, it was short lived. Back to the Boy Scout you've always been, hmm?"

I stared up at him and gripped the hilt of my sword until the wood haft groaned.

"Edmund Blackthorne, you are the snake our aunt spoke of. You killed our father to secure your seat on the throne. It is my right and obligation as the General of the Vampire Army to remove you of your duties. And your head."

A gasp rippled through the soldiers and the lordlings around Edmund. His eyes narrowed and then a slow smile slid over his face. "All to put yourself on the throne?"

"William should be king," I growled.

"And if he is dead? You would then be king. How convenient for you to kill me and then find out that Will is gone, pretending all the while to be the grieving brother. What was it you said?

You'd spit William's head on a pike yourself? In fact, you roared it through a fit of jealousy for all to hear, if I am correct. Tsk, tsk, General. What a plot you have woven, rather sloppy if you ask me. To kill our father, then blame me? All for power."

Those around him shifted uncomfortably in their saddles. He was far more refined in his words than me. Gods be damned, I should have learned more from the duchess about politics and fancy speeches.

"You were all witnesses to his words regarding William, and his admission that he wished to kill me in order to take the throne. Bind him. We will bring him back for a public execution on the grounds of high treason and the murder of my father, the king."

The party began to dismount, albeit some reluctantly.

"And what of William?" Frank said.

"We'll deal with him once we've given the people their snake on a platter...if the young prince is not dead already. Seize the General, now!"

"I will die before you take me," I snarled, raising my sword.

A cry behind me.

A blow to the back of my head so hard that the world went dark and I slumped face first into the snow.

"I'm so sorry, Dom, but I cannot watch you die like that," Scarlett murmured, her voice in and out of focus as I struggled to make my limbs move. She'd slammed the point of a staff right to the base of my skull, ringing my bell so hard that it was several hours before I truly came to.

It was still cold, more so because I was arse-deep in snow. A campfire crackled in the distance and I could hear the low drone of talking.

I took a quick stock of my body, a searing pain coursing through me as my breath hitched in my chest. Looking down, I could clearly see the markers of four wooden stakes that had been driven into my upper body. The deep red of the dragon blood tree was no mistake on Edmund's part. I tried to take a deeper breath, but my lungs were pierced on at least two of the stakes. Shallow breaths were all I could manage.

One stake had been jammed perilously close to my heart. I could actually feel the wood brush up against it each time it beat.

There would be no quick easy escape for me now.

We'd stopped to rest. After a long night of riding, of searching for signs of Sienna and Will, the horses needed a break.

I was well away from the others, my arms and legs bound back around a thick tree. My fingers were numb from the cold and the tension in the chains on my wrists. I lifted only my eyes to sweep the area, to try and see what I had at hand to aid my escape. At least Edmund hadn't poked my eyes out.

Not much for aid, as far as I could tell.

Scarlett sat right next to Edmund, his one hand pawing at her thigh while she stared straight ahead, motionless.

As furious as I was with her, I understood why she'd done what she'd done. I might've done the same in her shoes. But that did not change my predicament, or the fact that I was currently skewered like a shishkabob.

The lordlings stood in various positions around Edmund, trying to curry favor no doubt. My soldiers were working around the camp, feeding horses, keeping an eye on the woods. We must still be riding along the border of Werewolf Territory, and being attacked was not unheard of this close to it.

One of the lordlings stood, grabbed a mug and headed my way.

Frank Eleazar. Bastard. He had been Edmund's loudest supporter, hailing him as the king we needed, strong, vital, and worthy of the crown.

"General, I thought you might be awake by now," Frank said as he approached.

"You were my father's council long before you were Edmund's," I growled, my breath wet with blood gurgling up my throat. "Traitor."

"Quite the contrary, I believe you are the traitor here. Edmund has made it abundantly clear that your death is imminent. He knows you long to put William on the throne. Or worse, yourself." He crouched down in front of me and pressed the mug to my lips.

I turned my head, the only act of defiance I could manage at the moment.

He lowered his voice to a tone that I could barely hear as close to him as I was. "Come now, Nicky. You would not want to be so weak that, at a moment's notice, you could not flee? The stakes will be a problem, but not as much if you drink up."

I turned my head back to him and stared, not entirely sure I'd heard him right. Why would he use the nickname given to me and used solely by the Duchess?

The old statesman smiled and held the mug to my lips again. I drank, shocked at the amount of blood mixed into the mead, the coppery tang sweet and invigorating along with the thick honey in the mead.

Frank sat back on his heels as I drained the mug dry. "There, that's better, yes?"

"Make sure he drinks all the sedative!" Edmund yelled.

I gagged and spat to the side, but it was too late. I'd swallowed it all down. I glared at Frank, a wave of hatred washing through me.

"You are a real bastard. And my father trusted you."

He dipped his head slowly, staring into the empty mead mug, his voice low again, barely breathing the words.

"I...your father was a good man, Nicky. A good man. I believe that he was plagued for years by someone trying to kill him. And in fact, I have two maids who saw Edmund go into his chamber moments before he died. I am quite certain he was murdered. By Edmund."

Why was he telling me this now, as he did the bastard's bidding?

I stared at him, waiting for the sedative to kick in.

"Lower your head some, you must pretend it is working. I will not be able to free you until tonight, you must be ready." Frank reached up and patted my cheek, like one would with a child.

Shock.

I could not have been more shocked at what I was hearing. Frank was not with Edmund?

I wobbled my head to the side and then back up again. "You are not—"

"I despise the snake," Frank said, "I loved your father as a friend, a good, loyal friend. And I would do what I can to see that William is on the throne."

"Thank you," I murmured in relief, letting my head drop, so that my chin touched my chest.

I sucked in a sharp breath and Frank cuffed the side of my head, raising his voice.

"I will not have you speak of our king that way, traitor!"

Once more seeing stars, the open wounds from the stakes in me throbbing from the hard movement, I watched as he strode away and handed the mug to one of the soldiers.

"Be sure to wash it thoroughly, along with the mixing pot, we do not need one of you falling off your horse."

I lowered my head, pretending to be sedated as my body trembled and shook. Even not piercing a vital organ, the dragon blood wood was slowly poisoning me, sapping my strength.

After ten minutes, two men came to release me, and lift me bodily across Ares' back, where they tied me, belly down, across the saddle. I couldn't help the groan that slid out of me, the stakes driving in deeper.

"I don't know, Jack, I don't like this. He's our general." That was one of my soldiers, Rafe.

Jack, another of my men, sighed. "We don't have a choice. If we did, I'd be setting the general loose. I don't like our new king, gives me the shakes when he looks at me."

Rafe tied my wrists loosely. "If the General says that he's the snake, then I believe him."

A tiny burst of pride rolled through me. My men still trusted me. But I still didn't dare move and let them know I was not sedated. It would only put them in danger.

The day rolled on and, when night came, we were still a half day's ride from the castle and back to the first hunting shack, where Will and Sienna had taken shelter. My body ached and sweat dripped from every part of me. If the stakes were not removed soon, I was going to be even worse than useless.

I'd be dead.

"Make camp here," Edmund shouted. "I will have the cabin, the rest of you sleep where you can. We leave at first light."

Snapping his fingers at Scarlett, he led her back inside.

I watched in disgust but couldn't move to save her. My limbs were going numb now, and it had nothing to do with the cold. I could taste the sharp clean bite of the dragon blood wood at the back of my throat.

I had to find a way to get us both out of here.

A moment later, I was hauled off the back of Ares and once more tied to a tree. The camp was made up quickly, the soldiers and lordlings stamping down the snow around them, building a fire, setting a large pot in the middle. There was laughter among the lordlings, but not among the soldiers. They were quiet. Subdued. Sitting amongst themselves. This far away from the Werewolf Territory, there was no need for guards.

Frank bent over the pot and stirred it, the liquid sizzling as it hit the hotter parts of the blackened pot. He held out his hand and Rafe passed him a bowl. He ladled some of the soup in, and tasted it. I squinted, watching as something fell from his sleeve and into the pot, shaded from the others by the angle of his body. He gave it another good stir.

"Tastes as good as it's going to. Go ahead and serve yourselves," Frank grumbled as he scooped up two more bowls.

Rafe and Jack, they didn't move forward, but sat back with their heads together.

The lordlings and other soldiers though, they tucked right in. Frank took two bowls to the cabin, and knocked on the door with a boot tip.

"Your Majesty, some food?"

The door was flung open and a naked Edmund yanked the two bowls from Frank without a word, then slammed the door shut.

I caught a glimpse of Scarlett on the bed, also naked, her eyes somehow finding mine in that brief moment.

I swallowed hard.

I would have to choose. Scarlett or Sienna.

No, I would save them both. But how? That was the better question.

An hour ticked by and each of the lordlings and the soldiers slumped, one by one. All except for Rafe and Jack.

The pair of them looked around, seeing everyone asleep.

Frank stood and motioned for them to come to him.

"Listen to me." He led them across to where I was tied to the tree. "You two will go with the General and bring back the rightful king. Do you understand?"

Rafe's jaw dropped and Frank nodded, shoving them toward me.

"Do not argue. There needs to be someone to blame for the sedation and his escape seeing as he is useless, stuffed full of stakes. And you two are it."

Jack spluttered and Frank clapped a hand on his shoulder.

"The General has been right all along. Edmund killed our king. Now, get gone. All three of you."

"How did you know they wouldn't eat?" I asked as Jack and Rafe untied me.

Frank smiled. "I told them not to. That I heard them discussing how they didn't agree with what Edmund had done. As punishment, no food."

I stared at him, realizing how deftly he'd played his hand.

"Perhaps *you* should be king, Frank."

The older man laughed. "I find myself in need of another bowl of soup. Bring back your brother Dominic. For all our sakes."

"Scarlett," I said. "I'm not leaving without her."

Frank grimaced. "She's fine, General. He won't hurt her, and you don't have time to save her."

Loose from my ropes, I lurched forward, Rafe and Jack catching me, holding me up.

Frank shook his head. "You can't protect her now. You need to think of the good of all of our people, not just the one. She's strong. She'll manage."

I went to my knees, the world wobbling. "Not leaving her behind."

"You force my hand, Nicky," Frank sighed, turning to face Rafe and Jack. "Get him out of here. Don't pull the stakes until you are close to the territory edge."

"No!" I grunted the word, my lungs rattling.

But it took nothing for Rafe and Jack to manhandle me. They shoved me onto Ares' back and Rafe took the reins. I could barely clutch the front of the saddle, blood now dripping from my lower lip.

Frank turned and ladled himself a bowl and began eating it.

"Mount your horses," he said to the young soldiers.

There was no choice given to me. Ares leapt forward, jerked by one of the boys. Before I could even throw myself off the horse's back, the two young soldiers were racing away into the night, dragging me with them.

I'm so sorry, Scarlett. Please forgive me.

Through the forest, Rafe and Jack picked up the pace, following the path that Edmund's hunting party had put into the snow.

"General, why did Lord Frank free you? He seemed to be loyal to Edmund."

"He did what he had to do to gain his trust, it seems. Not everyone believes Edmund's lies," I explained through the haze of pain that was growing with each step of Ares' hooves. "Which is the only reason we are alive. For now you are traitors too, along with me. For that, I'm sorry."

After that, silence reigned as we made our way as fast as possible back the way we'd come. At this pace, the horses would get us into the werewolf territory before the sun rose, but not by much.

The night rolled over us, and we rested the horses as best we could, the soldiers running beside them at several points. Jack and Rafe never complained, though I felt their fear as clearly as the cold slapping at my face.

As dawn approached, we again reached the edge of the two territories.

"Here, let me get the spikes out," Rafe said.

Blood leaked down my shirt, out of my mouth and nose. The pain was consuming my thoughts to the point that I would have willingly let them cut my head off if given the choice.

The stakes came out with squelching sucking noises, but I didn't care. The pain receded immediately as soon as they were gone.

I took a slow, deep breath, testing the wounds. While they were not healed, they were healing fast.

I looked over my shoulder, toward the clearing and hunting lodge I couldn't see. Knowing that my friend was still there. I would find a way to get her out. I had to.

"We go on," I said the words with almost as much difficulty as if the stakes hadn't been pulled.

I urged Ares to keep going, through the last of the trees between the two territories.

Jack and Rafe kept pace, still silent.

We'd ridden a solid two miles into Werewolf Territory before we were taken.

"Hold your hands up," I said to the boys, "eyes down, do not make eye contact, keep your hands clear of weapons."

"Yes, General," they replied in tandem.

The werewolves who approached us did so with dizzying speed and violence. I held my hands up, did not make eye contact and spoke only one thing.

"I wish to be taken to the royal keep!"

"What the actual fuck is this nonsense?" growled the werewolf on the left. I knew him.

"General, please. It's imperative that you do as I ask, for the safety of your kind as well as mine," I said, keeping my eyes down. "Rather quickly, if you don't mind. I've not any desire to change my skin tone."

General Whalen grunted. "An influx of vampires is not a good thing in my book, but it be up to the Queen what to do with ya."

An influx...

"Will and his party are alive and in the keep, then?"

"No more chatter, let's go."

Bound up once more, we were dragged through the snow in haste.

Right to the werewolf stronghold, to the throne room and out of the weather. Pushed to my knees, I kept my head down and waited.

Footsteps.

The sound of laughter and a voice I knew. My head jerked up as Sienna stepped into the room with a striking raven haired woman, a circlet on her head. But it was Sienna who held my gaze.

Sienna, and the pretty young man she leaned forward to kiss on the cheek.

CHAPTER 9

Sienna

Hand in hand, Bethany and I went to where Will's chambers were situated. I knocked on the door and gave Bee a look. "I'll feed him quickly, like we planned, then you take over."

She nodded, her cheeks bright with color. Her hair was swept up off her shoulders with a few ringlets escaping, as if by accident, showing off her neck.

A thin night dress of ivory, and a simple overlay of a shawl in the same tone and she looked a bit like a bride going to her first night with her husband. Not a bad image to put in William's head.

"Come," William called out. I squeezed Bee's hand, and we stepped through together.

William stood beside his bed, his tired eyes barely glancing our way. "What do I owe the honor of two beautiful women coming to visit me? Surely I would remember if it was my birthday?"

Even under the weather, he still couldn't curtail the charm.

I smiled at him. "You look like shit, and even Diana has noticed. She's asked that both Bethany and I feed you again."

His baby blues widened. "Why don't you cut straight to the point then?"

I pursed my lips. "I have things I need to do, so I am going to feed you first. Then Bee here will do her share."

Will shot a look to me and then to Bethany before doing a solid double take. "Bee?"

She curtsied to him. "Yes, of course, Your Majesty. I cannot make you your favorite cocoa here, but I can do this for you."

Will held up both hands, which trembled slightly. "I do not think it necessary."

I lifted an eyebrow. "I'm not going to be the reason you die now, when Bee and I have nearly paid with our own lives to save your ungrateful ass."

"Exactly. What she said." Bee nodded.

We'd already agreed that he wasn't getting out of feeding from us, though for different reasons.

"Dominic is already going to be furious with me as it is. He would kill me himself if I didn't make sure you survived." I crossed my arms. "I'm not about to end up at the point of the General's sword."

Will's mouth quirked. "Are you so sure of that?"

It was my turn to blush. "By order of Diana, you are to take blood from both of us. End of discussion."

He sighed and sat on the bed. "Do you understand what you're offering?"

Bee snorted. "You do recall that we've both fed you already? That in the cabin you were dying most certainly, and it was Sienna and I who made sure you lived?"

He wasn't looking at me anymore, his eyes had landed solidly on Bethany. "I never want to hurt you, Bee. I never want to have you suffer, not for anyone. Certainly not me."

As Bee went to him, I pulled the butterfly hair pin from the back of my chignon knot. I already knew from last time, it was deadly sharp.

I pressed the tip to my fingertip on the opposite hand, drawing a single, crimson bead. For whatever reason, he didn't need much of my blood, and that was just fine by me.

I trailed behind Bee as she took Will's hand and laid it across her heart.

Me, I wasn't so graceful. I stuffed my finger in his mouth. "You aren't getting flowers from me tomorrow."

His eyes rolled into his head as he clamped his mouth around my fingertip, sucking hard.

I grimaced and fought not to pull back. "Count, Bee."

"Right, to sixty?"

"Yes." That was what we figured would be enough. Or hoped, based on the minimal amount I'd fed him at the cabin.

"Fifty-eight, fifty-nine, sixty," Bethany said and I tried to yank my finger back.

Tried and failed.

Will's free hand shot to my wrist, and he growled.

At me.

I would not panic, I would not panic, I would not—

"Bee," I yelped her name as I fought to get free, panic quickly grabbing hold of me, tighter even than Will.

"I'm trying." she moved between us, placing herself in his line of vision and blocking me completely. "Will, look at me!"

She slapped him hard, and his mouth popped open. I stumbled back and scrambled to my feet. My finger was bleeding all over the place but I didn't dare put it in my own mouth. I wrapped it in the edge of my skirt and held it tight.

"I'm so sorry," Will said, shame filling his eyes. "I...have no idea what came over me."

"Just go, Sienna." Bethany looked over her shoulder at me. "I'll be okay, I don't have...whatever you have in your blood."

I started moving toward the door. "Are you sure?"

"I won't hurt her," Will said. "I would rather die than hurt her."

Truth, it rang in his words and that was enough for me. I let myself out of his room and hurried down the hall to the suite that Bethany and I shared.

Shutting the door behind me, I leaned on it for a moment to catch my breath. My finger ached and on a quick look down the blood had soaked through my makeshift bandage.

Will's reaction had been very much like the one in the cabin, only he'd been weaker and we'd been able to subdue him more easily.

I made my way to the bathroom where actual real plumbing existed. I flicked on the tap to cold and let my finger stay under until the water was no longer pink, but clear.

The ache in my finger though, it remained.

I closed my eyes and a flash of Dominic's face filled my mind, of him taking my hand, drawing me close, sliding my finger into his mouth, the heat of his lips and tongue a balm to the tiny wound. I struggled not to gasp, because it felt so very real.

Worse was the tremor it caused to run through me, from my finger all the way to my lady parts which were suddenly throbbing in tandem with my finger.

"Fuck," I whispered, bowing my head and leaning against the sink.

It did not take much for me to feel as though Dominic were there, his body naked and wet in the tub, his hard cock pressed up against my inner folds. A groan slid through me, and I worked my uninjured hand down my side, and under my skirt. I just needed relief, I just needed a way to forget him—

"Well that didn't fucking well work!" Bethany yelled as she slammed through the main door.

I yanked my hand away from myself and turned to stare at her out in the main room.

"What happened?" Yup, my voice was breathy, far too breathy.

She spun and looked at me. "You alright?"

"Fine. What happened with Will?" I fought to get myself together.

Bethany paced the room, ringing her hands as she circled. "It started out okay. I mean, he kissed me."

I blinked and then strode across the room. "That's good, though!"

"I know, I know, but then he pulled me into the bed, and then...and then he just said he couldn't. He couldn't do that to me." She collapsed at the side of the bed and covered her face with her hands. "I don't understand him, it was like...heaven kissing him. Everything I'd dreamed of and then some, he...he was so hard, Sienna."

I didn't think she meant just his abs either.

I sat down beside her. "Then we just keep trying—"

"No, I don't want to. It's bad enough that he turned me down, but he said...he said that we could never be together for real because he will soon be king. That to be with him as anything more than a dalliance I'd have to be a vampire or I would be in constant danger from those who would resent a human having such power in their world. I'd do it, too. For him, I would become one of them, but vampires are born, not created. Even if all that weren't true, I could never give him an heir. Babies between humans and vampires are unheard of since the Veil fell. It's truly a lost cause."

Her sobs filled the room and I carefully wrapped my arms around her as she cried herself out.

She sniffled and then slumped. "I hate men."

I couldn't help it, I laughed. "Well, they're pretty terrible. I can see why we castrate so many of the other male animals...dogs, horses, cats."

Bee let out a soft laugh that dissolved into tears again. All I could do was hold and whisper falsehoods to her.

"It will be okay, Bee. If Will isn't the one, then that means there's someone better, someone who will love you for you. Please don't cry, he doesn't deserve your tears, my friend."

That did nothing to soothe her pain, I'm sure, but there wasn't much more I could do. In the end, I helped her into bed early, and prayed she would sleep deeply. Because my day was far from over.

I still had a secret rendezvous to attend.

. . . .

Midnight could not come fast enough. I paced my room, watching the one clock hand tick ever slower toward the hour. Bethany slept soundly in her bed, unaware of my pacing, her sobs having tired her out completely no doubt.

Time, nothing to do with it, and so my mind rolled back through what I was going to have to do in the coming days and weeks. I looked at the beaded bracelet on my wrist. Thirty-six days left. Too many to leave the werewolf stronghold yet. I would have to find a way to stay longer, to prep our flight from Werewolf Territory and then...back through Edmund's kingdom. My fault for letting the captain of the boat tell me where to meet him, and not the other way around. He'd said he'd only pick me up on the southern edge of the territories, and then I'd had no idea where the layouts were, so I'd agreed to it.

"Blast," I whispered as a cold rush of true understanding rolled through me. The boat was coming into the harbor below the vampire's castle, just prior to dawn in thirty-six days. How the fuck was I going to get past Edmund, with Jordan in tow? Sure, he might be dead by then, but I rather doubted he'd go down easy.

One step at a time, girl, one step at a time.

The clock ticked and it was five to midnight. Good enough for me. I strode to the door, wrapping the thick wool dressing gown tighter around my waist.

I crept through the door and closed it softly behind me. Placing each slippered foot carefully on the rough-hewn floor, I made my way down the hall. The top of the stairs came into view, a statue on either side, each one a massive werewolf crouched as if ready to launch themselves down the stairs and into battle.

Moving with care, I tucked myself in behind the one on the left, where I could see both the hall and the stairs.

And there I waited.

Time ticked by, and I began to count the seconds, minutes and after thirty, I knew that Jordan wasn't coming.

Disappointment flared and I forced myself to recognize that he might not have the ability to move freely. That he might be as caged as I had been in Vampire Territory.

I ran a hand over my face and froze as the sound of footsteps up the stairs reached my ears.

Chewing the inside of my lip, I held myself back.

"We cannot go to war," a rumbling voice said. Lycan? "It would put too many lives in danger. Lives that have peace here."

"I know that," Diana answered, her voice…hollow. Sad. Lonely? Why was I thinking lonely? "But the girl, she is not human, Lycan. The Duchess wrote to me of her, when she first arrived for the Harvest Games. That she should arrive on our doorstep requesting our aid? I think it no coincidence. The question is, what do we do with her?"

Lycan snorted. "Evangeline is ever sending those that need safety here, you know that."

"I do," Diana said. "Baran would have been dead as a child had she not sent him to you. Now look at him, our General, and one of our greatest fighters. Perhaps this girl will prove equally useful."

Their voices faded and I thanked whatever gods that were listening that I had not been sniffed out.

Useful? I didn't want to be useful to the werewolves any more than I wanted to be in the Harvest Games with the vampires. But...to get Jordan out, what would I do?

That answer was simple.

Anything.

I waited for their footsteps and voices to completely fade, counted to sixty, then slipped out of my hiding place and back to my room. I tucked myself into bed and stared up at the ceiling. Stars had been etched into the paint, flickering with some unknown light. Stars that I did not recognize. Even the sky here was a fantasy in this world of alpha territories.

I rolled onto my side and stared out the window, into the darkness beyond, steel filling a resolve that had not failed me yet.

If I could play a game for the vampires, then I could play a part for the werewolves.

The next morning dawned far earlier than my eyes and aching head wanted. I had laid in bed for a long time, unable to shake the worry that I wasn't going to be able to get us out of here.

Rising ahead of Bee, I knew I needed to find Jordan. He'd been helping serve us the night before, so my best chance was the kitchens. Pressing a kiss against Bee's temple, I slipped out of our room and down toward the sounds of pots and pans and cooks cursing.

No one tried to stop me, no one did more than glance in my direction. I was just another human, doing her duties as a maid.

At the main entrance to the kitchens I paused for a moment, steeled my nerve, and let myself in.

What had to be the head cook looked at me. "Ya need something, lass?"

"Can I help serve this morning? A young man named Jordan saved my life last night. Least I could do would be to help him with his duties." I smiled, meaning every word.

"Ach, you are a sweet thing, aren't ya?" She came round the counter and patted my cheek. "Jordan love, ya gots a new friend here!"

I turned as Jordan approached. The scar above his temple was not as angry as it had been. But the results of the head injury were still there.

He smiled. "Ceecee. Sorry I didn't meet you last night. I slept past my alarm."

I reached out and took his hand. "That's okay, let me help you."

Which is how I ended up with a jug of fresh squeezed apple juice in one hand, and Jordan clinging to my free hand.

"Are you okay?" I whispered as we made our way toward the main dining hall.

"I am. I love it here, Ceecee! I can't wait for you to meet my family, they are so good to me. They adopted me!" He flashed a badge on his shirt, a K etched into it. For Killian no doubt.

"They don't hurt you?"

"Oh, no, never! They love kids! I'm just one of the new kids they adopted!" He grinned wide, his eyes guileless. He hadn't a deceptive bone in him before the accident, and even less after. I couldn't help but notice that he had filled out, his skinny frame now leanly muscled, his cheeks pink with health.

A bittersweet sense of grief rolled through me. Leaving was going to be tough for him, but it couldn't be helped. Just because his captors weren't cruel to him didn't make it right. Besides, he couldn't possibly understand how tenuous his safety was in this new world.

We reached the head table and I set down the jug, turned and cupped his face in my hands and kissed him on the cheek. "I love you, Jordan, always."

"I love you too, Ceecee." He butted his head against mine. "But I gotta work now. You go eat!"

He pushed me toward the table where Diana and Lycan waited. But that was not what caught my eye.

No, it was the man on his knees in the dining hall. His name slipped from my numb lips.

"Dominic."

Chapter 10

Sienna

For a moment, I was unable to move as emotion threatened to overwhelm me.

He was alive. That alone was enough to make my legs weak with relief. The fact that he was here and the expression on his face – some terrifying mix of longing and fury – had a sizzle of fear snaking up my spine.

"Escort the ladies upstairs while I deal with the prisoner," Diana commanded.

I was summarily ushered away and, although I couldn't see Dominic's eyes, I felt them burning two holes in my back as I left.

"If you keep it up, you're going to chew that lip right off," Bee murmured an hour later as she watched me from her perch on the edge of my bed.

"I just don't get how this happened," I said, shaking my head in confusion. "Dominic was captured infiltrating Werewolf

Territory, but where is the rest of the hunting party? Were they killed or did they escape?"

Even as I said it, I knew the latter wasn't possible. As much as the man got under my skin, if he didn't want to be caught, he wouldn't be here. Which meant he'd allowed himself to be taken. That still didn't answer the dozens of other questions rolling around in my brain.

"He didn't just walk away," Bee reasoned. "So either there was a massive battle between Dominic, Edmund and his men, or he escaped in the night."

The takeaway? Edmund might already be dead and Dominic might only be seeking audience with Diana to get us back.

A shudder rocked me from head to toe as I again thought of the look in his eyes when he first saw me.

If this was a rescue mission, he'd done a good job of disguising it. If looks could have killed, I'd be nothing but bones right now. There was no doubt about it, he was furious with me. Had my disobedience caused something inside him to snap? Did he feel betrayed that I spirited his beloved little brother away without him?

Or was it something else?

The wound on my finger throbbed, and I stuck my hand in my pocket.

"Enough of this, then," I said, tamping down my rising fear. Sure, we'd been sent away summarily the moment Dominic was led in...

But Diana hadn't said we had to stay here. At least, not specifically...

"We have way more questions than answers. I'm not going to sit here and stew while we wait to be summoned."

Bee let out a low false laugh. "And why would you? Now that you and Diana are going to be special, magical besties you should just go down there and—"

"Enough!" I wheeled around and glared at her. "You are my bestie, okay? You are the one constant since I've been dragged to the hellhole rife with monsters. I don't love Diana. Hell, I barely know her. I love *you*, Bee. But right now I'm going to need you to stop being a whiny bitch because we have way more important things to take care of. Do you think you can do that for me?"

She blinked at me and then opened her mouth like she was about to argue, but I held up a finger.

"Just a nod or a shake, please."

She snapped her mouth shut and nodded reluctantly.

"Excellent. And you're right about one thing. I should go down and at least see if I can speak with Diana." I removed my hand from its pocket and held it up. "Can you see if you can find a small bandage? I think it's finally stopped oozing and I want it to look as unobtrusive as possible."

She stood and made her way to the bathroom before stopping to face me. "For what it's worth, I love you too, Sienna. You're the best friend I've ever had, even though you're bossy, impulsive, seem to have a death wish, and you irritate me at times."

"Well, I don't know if the last parts needed saying but thanks..."

I trailed off as I realized she was already in the bathroom rooting around in drawers and I was talking to myself.

"Okay, then."

I had to admit, after my latest interaction with Jordan, the declaration of love was nice to hear. Not that Jordan didn't care for me anymore. I knew he did and always would, but the dream I'd had...my whole reason for being here was in ashes. I'd risked life and limb, thrown myself into a pit of vipers, all to save someone who didn't want to be saved.

Maybe Bee was right. Maybe I did have a death wish.

I thought of Jordan's little monogrammed K and let out a sniff. Just because an indentured servant was treated "well", if it hadn't been his choice to come, and he couldn't choose to leave, did that mean it was okay?

But he looks happy.

Happiness was relative, though. Jordan was a simple person with simple needs, and an optimist to the core. He could find happiness anywhere, so long as he wasn't being subjected to cruelty. As his friend, the person he trusted most in this world to take care of him, it was my duty to secure his freedom so he could live life on his own terms. What if he wanted to become a carpenter? Or owning his own farm in the hills someday?

I ran my thumb over the beads on my bracelet and shook my head grimly. There was still time.

And I wasn't giving up on him yet.

My knee kept bouncing up and down of its own accord as I glanced at the clock for the hundredth time. I was seated in the Queen's study, awaiting her arrival, and had been for nearly an hour. The wait was killing me.

When the door finally swung open another twenty minutes later, I was halfway through counting the books lining the walls.

Seven hundred sixty-three, so far. Most of them non-fiction about the history of creatures behind The Veil. I'd already made a mental note to ask Diana about borrowing one on vampires.

"I planned to call for you once I'd dealt with the matter at hand, Sienna," the Queen said as she swept in, her smooth brow furrowing as she shot me a chilly glance.

"I know, and I'm really sorry. I was just driving myself crazy with worry up there and hoped that maybe—"

"You could hurry me along by inserting yourself where you weren't wanted?" she finished with a short laugh. "Maybe you are human, after all."

Ouch.

"I humbly ask for your forgiveness, Your Majesty," I murmured, bowing my head to make sure I looked the part.

"Ha! Save it, Sienna. We are far too alike for me to be swayed by your false meekness. Tell me, what is it that you need to know so badly that it is you who summoned me?" she asked as she took a seat behind the ornate desk across from me.

Given the amount of time I'd been waiting, I probably should've been prepared for that question, but she'd disarmed me with her candor.

"Well," I said slowly, shifting uncomfortably in my chair. "I guess the most important thing...is Edmund dead?"

She pursed her lips and shook her head. "Edmund lives. As do the rest of his hunting party, I fear. According to your General, they stopped for the night and a friend to the cause helped him escape. Edmund knows he defected, but was unable to pursue him. If Dominic is to be believed, he is here to reunite with his brother William, and hopes to form an alliance with us with the shared goal of removing Edmund from the throne."

My brain had stuttered around the "Your General" part, but once I was caught up, I nodded. "If what I know of Dominic is true, that all tracks. He loves his brother Will fiercely. I don't think he would do him harm."

Diana cocked her head as her expression turned to one of sympathy. "You've lived among them for but a month, and you think to know them? That you understand them? If I told you what I've witnessed those creatures doing...to others, but worse, to their own? You wouldn't sleep another night through the remainder of your life." She pushed her chair from the desk and moved to stand. "If the purpose of this meeting was to convince me to release him and for us all to become fast friends, you're wasting your time and mine."

Ignoring her, I plowed onward. "He's nothing like Edmund."

She paused and looked up from her papers. "He does have his father's eyes. Still, he's one of them nonetheless. No...I've sent word to the Duchess Evangeline asking if she can corroborate his story. Until I've received a reply, he and the two men he brought with him will be separated, and he'll be treated with extreme caution. I've already raised the ire of my people by accepting you lot. William is known to us as a diplomat, and Evangeline has vouched for him in the past, so I can at least somewhat justify giving him refuge. But welcoming the black sheep, bastard of the family into our midst? One of the most powerful vampires alive, who specializes in war and stratagems, and has sworn fealty to the evil King as his sole protector? A virtual Trojan Horse?" she let out a shrill laugh. "They'd be calling for me to be the one in chains."

I wished I could've argued with her, but she was right. I just had to hope that the Duchess was still alive to send her response.

"Can I see him?"

The words were out before I'd even thought them through, and I didn't try to retract them.

She studied me for a long moment before replying. "We've taken every precaution. He's chained and behind multiple locked doors, with two soldiers on watch at all times. But if you wish to speak to him, it's at your own risk. I won't be sending my men in to be slaughtered if he should decide to take you hostage, or worse."

In other words, I was on my own.

Was she right? What if I didn't know the real Dominic at all?

The memory of his mouth on mine...and other places, sent a hot rush of blood to my ears.

No. I had to use my brain to make this decision, not my body.

Did I think Dominic was capable of hurting me?

My heart gave a squeeze as I tried again, reframing the question.

Did I think Dominic was capable of physically hurting me?

Only if you ask him to, a little voice inside my head replied.

"I'd like to see him, please."

Because I needed answers. Because I couldn't stand the not knowing. Because I needed to see him, face to face, one on one.

Because, what the hell?

It wasn't like the little voice in my head had ever been wrong before...

Ha ha ha.

CHAPTER 11

Dominic

Thoughts of Sienna, with Will bent over her, sinking his fangs into her supple neck, drinking...feasting...had plagued me night and day since she'd gone. Even when I was shackled and labeled a traitor, planning my next move, the thoughts never left me. They rankled, like a swarm of angry bees in my mind.

The possibility of my brother—my *blood*—taking what was mine had been bad enough. But to willingly allow myself to be captured in enemy territory, dragged to the Queen's Keep in chains, only to see Sienna kissing another man?

I let out a roar so loud, it shook the rafters.

"So... you're saying maybe I should come back later, then?" a low voice called.

I stared into the darkness and realized there was a pair of booted feet just visible in the narrow sliver of light coming from beneath the heavy door.

"Sienna?" I growled, wondering if my mind was playing tricks on me.

"If I come in, are you going to kill me, General?"

Despite the scorching hot rage pouring through my veins, I managed to keep my tone low and even as I replied.

"I will not."

But I had a feeling it would be a close thing. The woman knew how to push my buttons, and I was in no mood to be trifled with.

The door swung open on squeaky hinges and a familiar silhouette filled the space.

"It's all right. You can return to your post," she said, presumably to a guard just out of my line of sight.

There was a long pause before his reluctant reply. "Alright, then. Knock...or scream when you're ready to come out, Miss."

A moment later, the door closed and the sound of the iron bolt sliding into place echoed through the near-empty room.

Heavy footfalls sounded and then all went quiet but for the sound of Sienna's quiet breathing.

Diana had done me the kindness of giving me a windowless room to minimize my discomfort in the bright sunlight of day, but in that moment, I hated her for it. Despite my enhanced night vision, I couldn't make out Sienna's features in the near pitch-dark.

"Let me see you," I commanded.

For once, she didn't argue with me as she flipped on the light switch and then turned to face me.

If I had been worried about her physical well-being, her appearance made those worries disappear. She looked amazing, decked out in the clothes of a warrior, and damned if the sight didn't make my loins quicken. She was pink-cheeked, well-fed, auburn hair in a knot to showcase that swan-like neck. A neck I currently wanted to close my fingers around and squeeze until she put me out of my misery.

All the fear and desperation I'd felt the past few days morphed into anger.

"Why did you leave when I commanded you to stay put?"

She looked up at me, a challenge in her eyes. "Why did *you* think you were the boss of me?"

"Damn you, woman! All I'm trying to do is keep you alive, but you seem dead set against it, and fight me at every turn."

"And thank the gods I do!" she shot back angrily. "You should be praising me right now. Bee and I are the only reason your brother still walks the earth. If I listened to you, he'd have choked on a growing bloodworm already. Lord only knows what Edmund would have done to me and Bethany if we'd stayed! Staying alive isn't my only priority, you know. I have people that I care about as well."

"Bethany?"

She nodded reluctantly. "Yes. And another person."

I'd thought I'd withstood all the rage my body could handle before I snapped and did something truly monstrous, but apparently I was wrong. It took all the discipline I possessed to remain calm, and I was shaking with the effort.

"The scrawny boy you were kissing when I arrived?"

"Yes," she admitted with a defiant glare. "That's my friend, Jordan. He's the reason I'm here. Hell," she added with a harsh chuckle, "he's the whole reason I even allowed myself to be captured by the Collectors in the first place."

I stared at her in silence as I took a moment to process her words.

"You allowed yourself to be—Bloody hell, Sienna. Are you saying you sacrificed yourself for this...friend?"

"I didn't sacrifice my—"

"You were minutes away from being chum until I stepped in."

Yet she cared for this Jordan *so* much, it was apparently worth the risk. I couldn't help but wonder, would she find that pretty young man so pretty if she had to put him back together like a jigsaw puzzle?

That question and a dozen more leapt to my mouth, but then I smelt it. Faint...barely a whisper, but it was there. A familiar scent.

My *brother's* scent.

"Did he drink from you?" Even to my own ears, the query sounded more like a threat, but I was long past caring.

"Jordan?" she asked, squinting at me in feigned confusion.

"Don't toy with me, Sienna. You know exactly who I mean."

"What? Are you asking...like, did Will drink from me?" She wet her lips and held up a calming hand. "Look, Dominic, it's complicated. He was very ill, and—"

"Enough!" I leapt toward her, quicker than the human eye could see, until the chains jerked me to a stop just a foot away from her. To her credit, she flinched, but didn't back away. "I can smell your fear, woman. And I cannot in good conscience tell you it's unjustified. But you will answer me." I lowered my voice to a silky whisper and stared into those golden eyes. "Did. He. Drink from you?"

She didn't need to reply. It was written all over her guilty face.

White-hot fury coursed through me, obliterating all thought as every muscle in my body flexed. The iron chains that bound me groaned and then snapped, and an instant later, I had her pinned against the wall with my body, one hand around that pretty throat.

"I told myself it was just a ploy. A strategy to help me fool Edmund into letting me lead the hunting party to find you. But I'm hard pressed to come up with a reason I shouldn't lock you in this room, run him down like a rabid dog, and tear him limb from limb."

Her soft body was flush against mine and even in my fury, I wanted her. It was all I could do not to hoist her high against that stone wall, tear those pants off and bury myself inside her.

Reclaim her until she sobbed my name and Will was nothing but a ghost of the past.

Which still wasn't out of the question.

"Think, Dominic," she whispered, her lean throat muscles working against my hand as she swallowed hard. "Use your head instead of whatever it is you're thinking with now. William is your baby brother. The brother you cherish and love. The brother you'd give your life to protect. I did what I knew you would want me to do, if you allowed yourself to let go of this macho bullshit."

I let out a harsh laugh and dipped low to press my forehead against hers. "How I wish it was as simple as that. We aren't wired like you, Sienna. A casual fuck is one thing. But this...what lies between us? There is no undoing it. And once I take you...truly take you, you'll understand because then you will own me like I own you."

"No one owns me."

"Keep telling yourself that," I murmured as I loosened my grip on her throat and slid my hand lower, tracing her collar bone, cupping one full breast.

"Dominic," she gasped, leaning into me, her hips nestling closer to mine.

"That's right. Say my name," I hissed before nipping lightly at her bottom lip. My fangs extended but I didn't pierce her skin. That would come, but not today. Not like this.

I pulled away, just far enough to give myself room to slide a hand under her shirt. When my fingertips met her bare nipple, I let out a groan, but I couldn't afford to lose total control.

"Tell me...did he bite you?"

She stilled and I almost lost her until I slid my free hand between her thighs.

Hot. So fucking hot down there...

"Did he bite you?" I asked again, sliding my hand up and down in a slow drag.

"Yes...no. I—" she broke off and let out a gasp as I ground the heel of my palm against her clit. "I cut myself and let him feed from there."

I nearly howled with relief.

"Your neck?"

"My wrist. My finger," she added, her breath hitching as I began to move my hand faster, harder. My cock was like a tire iron pressed against her belly, and the ache in my balls was worse than any torture, but I still needed one more answer before I took her.

"Did it feel good? When he fed...did you like it, Sienna?"

Her head was tossed back now, cheeks flushed, eyes wild with need.

"No," she said, holding my gaze as she breathlessly rode my hand.

"Why not?"

"Because…" she gasped as I tore the front of her pants open with the flick of my wrist and covered her bare pussy with my hand. She bucked against me and spread her legs wider, drenching my fingers in wet heat. "Because he wasn't you!"

With a satisfied growl, I pulled my hands away, laid them on the wall behind her, and pressed my mouth to her throat.

"Please, Dominic," she gasped. "D-don't."

I scraped the very edge of my fangs over her silky skin and she shuddered against me, her nipples pulling into tight buds, branding my chest.

"Do not mistake me, Sienna. I *will*. But not until you beg me to."

The distant thump of footfalls sounded in the distance and I released her. Backing against the opposite wall, I draped the chains around my forearms to look as if they'd never been off.

Sienna remained there for a long moment, slumped against the wall, pulse pounding so loudly I could still hear it more than a dozen feet away. But as the bolt slid open, she straightened and quickly righted her clothes, covering the torn zipper with her shirt.

I took one last, long look at her, cock throbbing. I wasn't satisfied. Far from it. But I'd gotten the answers I'd been seeking, and for now, it was enough.

"Done now, Miss?" the soldier asked as he opened the door.

"I am, thank you." She cleared her throat and shot me a haughty glance before turning to face my captor again. "But you're going to need some thicker chains for this one."

Witch.

"The one thing I can't get my head around is why, if your goals are aligned with Sienna and William's, you didn't make your escape with them. Can you explain that to me, General?"

The Queen eyed me dubiously as she circled the room, making sure she gave me a wide berth. Not like I could get to her now even if I wanted to. Thanks to Sienna, even a vampire Houdini couldn't escape these new chains. But at least they'd brought me a chair to sit in. I settled against it now and shrugged, already irritated with the conversation despite the fact that it had only been a few minutes long. The only good thing that had come of it so far was her assurances that Rafe and Jack were fed, sheltered and unharmed.

I had enough guilt weighing on me after leaving Scarlett behind.

"I wish I had the answer, Your Majesty. Edmund had me close by his side in all the turmoil. There was little time to save Will, and I have to assume the Duchess got them out the moment the opportunity presented itself. I wasn't there, but if I had been, I'd have gone with them."

She stopped strolling and stared at me long and hard.

"Look, I'm sorry, but maybe I could speak to Lycan?"

The second I said it, I knew it was a misstep. Politics was so much worse than war.

Her eyes were icy as she took a step closer. "Lycan is no longer king. The transfer of power happened months ago. Apparently, you didn't get the memo."

"I wasn't trying to go over your head, I just meant that he could vouch for me."

Maybe. I'd had dealings with the King over the years, and while we weren't long lost friends, there was a mutual respect between us.

"He knows you're here, and while he did tell me that he rather likes you, he also told me you're a very dangerous man. Your kind has already caused turmoil in my territory. I won't add to it by allowing a wild card into the mix."

"What about Lochlin? We've been friends since childhood. He can vouch for my character."

"Lochlin is too kindhearted for his own good. He's already used his credits on your brother and his companions, and even that was a stretch." She shook her head slowly, shrewd, dark eyes attempting to stare right through me. "No, you'll remain here until I receive word from Evangeline. You'll be treated well. I'll have a bath and some food sent up for you when I leave."

"Why the Duchess? What is she to you?"

She considered that carefully before replying. "We've had an annual correspondence for many years. Women in power trying to work together and ensure the men in power don't cock it all up royally, as you're wont to do."

I wished I could argue with her.

"If Edmund holds the throne, it will be nothing but chaos and bloodshed. Stirling was ill for a long time, but he still was able to keep him in check. With my father gone, there would be no end to his cruelty."

Her eyes flashed fire. "You've no need to tell me of Edmund's cruelty. A good leader studies her enemy. I know more about your kind than even you do, I'd wager."

"Maybe. But I've been at his side for a very long time. I know how he thinks, and I know how to defeat him. We have the same goal. I'm telling you, Diana. If we work together, we can—"

"*I'm* telling *you*. I'll make no further plans until I've gotten word back from your aunt. End of discussion." She turned and strode to the door before turning back. "And you'll address me properly. I'm not one of your mates at the pub."

I tried to keep the smirk at her little power play from my face as I tipped my head in a solemn nod. "Yes. Of course, Your Majesty."

She rapped on the door and called for the guard when I remembered something else I'd wanted to ask her.

"Can I see my brother?"

She let out a long-suffering sigh.

"I suppose it's possible, if William is well enough and wants to see you. But I need to work out the logistics with my soldiers. You can't be close together, or even in the same room." She pursed her lips. "Maybe with glass separating you...I don't know, I'll need to think it through. I have to do some damage control within the packs so I'll be busy in the next day or so, but I will try to arrange something soon."

"And Sienna? I have some other things I need to talk to her about."

Diana shrugged. "Sienna isn't a prisoner here, or a threat to me. She can come and go as she wishes."

What Sienna wished remained to be seen, but so far, it had been a productive day. I was still alive, and armed with more knowledge than before. Now, all I could do was wait...

And dream of an auburn-haired, golden-eyed witch who had cast a spell on me that there be no untangling myself from.

CHAPTER 12

Sienna

I paced the confines of my room, unable to stay still, my body still on edge from my encounter with Dominic. I snorted at myself.

Encounter.

As if that could encompass the moments I'd spent with the overbearing general and the way he made me feel.

That time in the tub, the sensation of his slicked, hard body against my own as the water lapped around us. My breath caught and my steps faltered and my lashes fluttered.

The cell, only hours before, his hand possessive and claiming as he pressed it hard against my pussy, the ache that even now throbbed with the need for more—

"What in the world is wrong with you?" Bethany looked over at me from her seat in the window. "You've been pacing like a caged tiger all day."

I struggled to breathe past what just the memories of Dominic did to me. I needed to focus on something else. Need and want, they were all tangled up in me and they were making me foolish.

I looked at the sky, the color leaching from the clouds as the sun slid away. "I'm just out of sorts."

"Oh, I can see that. Anything you'd like to tell me about?" Her eyes flicked over me. "You know, like why your zipper was ruined and you had to change into your skirt?"

A flush slid up over my skin, images of Dominic's face as he pinned me to the wall and ripped open the front of my pants to get at my body. "Are you going to tell me what happened with Will?"

My question for a question caught her off guard and it was her turn to flush. "He turned me down, I told you that."

I arched a brow at her. "And? There was nothing more?"

Tears filled her eyes as she turned to look out the window. "Fine. You have your secrets, and I'll have mine."

I sighed, feeling like a shit. Bee was, in many ways, as trapped as I. Even if she hadn't thought about leaving. I scrunched my face up thinking about trust and friendships.

About Jordan and leaving.

Bloody hell. I did trust her, and there was no time like the present to spill my guts.

"It's not a secret, Bee, I just...I don't plan to stay. I plan to go home and that means that getting involved with anyone is stupid. For me."

"What?" Bethany did a slow swivel in her seat, her tone incredulous. "What the bloody hell are you on about? How exactly are you planning on getting out of here? Catching up a Hunter and flying across the ocean?"

I saw more than surprise in her face. Mixed in with a sort of resigned grief, there was also a thread of hope. I shot her a quick smile. "You want to come with me?"

Yup, talk about throwing caution to the wind.

She stood and hurried over to me. "Are you serious? How?"

Now or never, I either trusted her or I didn't. "I have a boat coming in," I glanced down at my beaded bracelet, "A little over a month from now. We have to be back to the harbor at Blackthorne Castle, and then yeah, you, me, and Jordan can get out of here."

I ignored the sick sensation in my gut as the memory of his smiling face flitted through my mind.

Her eyes widened and she put her hands to her mouth, as understanding dawned. "You...you came here to rescue him? The boy?"

I nodded, not surprised she put two and two together so quickly. She was smart, it was why she'd survived so long here in the territories.

"Yes. I...let myself be captured, I thought I was being taken to the werewolves, where he'd been scooped. None of that matters now, Bee, I'm trusting you with this secret. And if you want to come, then you can come with me. With us."

Maybe a part of me was worried about going alone. Because while I hadn't given up on Jordan, whenever I'd seen him he looked happier than he'd ever been—even with me. More than that, he didn't look scared. Something that I'd seen on his face every day on the streets. I shook my head. No way. I wouldn't believe he'd choose to stay here over coming with me. Jordan was a prisoner. He wasn't happy. He just *thought* he was. There was a difference.

I let Bethany ask me questions about how I'd secured the boat, how I'd gotten in the way of the Collectors, all the things. I answered every question, while in the back of my head, all I could think about was Dominic.

No matter what distraction was in front of me, it was not enough to push him out of my thoughts.

"Are you listening? I said we need to prepare for the journey back then," Bethany said. "Better than we prepared for coming here, for sure. We should get good amounts of food, maps, extra clothing...*warm* clothing. The horses of course. Maybe proper weapons?"

I nodded, trying not to think about leaving Dominic behind without ever feeling his mouth on mine again. "Yes, absolutely. We should start slowly, so no one notices anything missing. If we start squirreling away items now, we can fly under the radar. A block of cheese here, a missing knife there..." I spoke automatically, with only half a mind on Bee. Damn that man and his intrusion to my life.

She nodded and grabbed her cloak, obviously invigorated by the task. "I'm going to take a walk, just see what I can see. Get a lay of the land. Maybe you do the same?"

It was a good idea. It gave me something active to do.

"Yes, I'll head to the north end," I spoke without thinking as I grabbed a cloak and slung it around my shoulders.

Bee stared at me from where she stood, hand on the door, her eyes assessing. "You mean the dungeons?"

Again, the heat flushed up to my cheeks. I could only imagine how red my skin was. I'd not even thought about what I was saying. Before I could even try to deny it, she grabbed my shoulders and gave me a light shake.

"Get him out of your system, like I did with Will. Whether he turns you down, or takes you up on the offer, get it done with and let it be. They don't want a human, not for a long-term partner, Sienna. I know that. Will made it very clear. And Dominic isn't in any better position than his brother is to take on someone who isn't a vampire. You know that, right?"

Her words struck the mark, one that bled and ached a little.

A part of me knew though, she was right. If I could get him out of my system...fulfill this fantasy, maybe I could focus on what I needed to focus on...namely getting me and my two friends out of this place.

"Bee, I—"

"Go." She gave me a shove. "And don't stop until he regrets ever making you want him."

A laugh slid from my lips as her words wrapped around me. Make him regret it? Make him regret ever getting under my skin? Regret ever purchasing me from the auction? Regret ever making me want him as she said?

I'd danced more than once to make a man burn with desire, I'd paid mine and Jordan's bills every month doing just that.

Picking up my pace, I hurried toward the north end of the keep, eager in a way I didn't want to dissect.

Down the two sets of stairs to the dungeon I went, ideas flowing already, of how exactly I would make Dominic suffer.

The same guard was on duty as the night before.

"Do they ever let you rest?" I asked.

He grunted. "Shift work is a right bitch. You want back in to see the prisoner? We got bigger chains on him now."

I nodded. "Good. And yes."

"Your funeral," he muttered. "But remember, I ain't coming in if you scream."

I smiled up at him and winked. "Perfect. In fact, I'd prefer that you not even peek in should you hear me scream."

His jaw dropped as I stepped past him and into the dungeon cell, shutting the door behind me.

Dominic sat on the only stool in the room, arms at his sides, his head slowly lifting. There was no way he could have missed my exchange with the guard.

"Sienna." He rumbled my name, the sound of his voice cascading across my skin and making my body tense.

Damn him. This was supposed to be about me making him suffer, not the other way around.

I didn't say a word. There was music in my head that I let flow through me as I stepped into the room further, close enough to him that I knew he couldn't reach me, but that I was tantalizingly almost within reach. The beat in my mind was a steady pulse that had me moving in time to it. Trailing my hands from my upper thighs, over my torso and to my breasts, then to my shoulders.

"What are you doing?" he growled the question, but I heard the uncertainty and lust in his words.

I just smiled as I did a slow turn, giving him my back as I let the cloak off my shoulders pool to the ground at my feet.

I was no longer wearing the pants he'd torn the zipper on, but a loose flowing skirt that fluttered as I turned. Bending at the waist, I took hold of the bottom edge and pulled it up, sliding my hand up my calf and upper leg as I turned again, flashing my thigh. Bending again at the waist, this time facing him, I went down slowly, flicking my hair forward so that it slid over his lower body.

His breath hitched. But he didn't tell me to stop.

I slid my hands back up over my legs, to my waist where I slowly undid the three buttons holding the skirt up. Wriggling my hips in time with a music only I could hear, I slid free of the skirt.

Dominic leaned forward in the chains so fast that they creaked dangerously. His mouth was an inch from my left breast.

I laughed and stepped back, even though all I wanted to do was lean into him, to let him clamp his mouth over my nipple and drag me onto his lap.

No, I was going to make him suffer the way he'd made me suffer. More than that, I had the power here, it was my decision how this played out.

Just like it had been my decision to get into the tub with him.

It was a madness, I realized as I stripped slowly for him, shedding each piece of clothing until I was dancing wearing nothing but a thin pair of panties, my hands sliding over my body, hiding myself from him. A madness born of being alone too long, of being traumatized, of him waking a need in me I didn't want nor had asked for. That was the only thing I could think to call it as I swayed and spun, my body brushing against his knee, or his thigh, his chains keeping him from touching me at will.

The creak of the chains drew my eyes up. He was staring at me, his chest rising and falling a little too fast, a bead of sweat sliding down the side of his face. His voice was hoarse. "So you *are* trying to kill me then?"

His words broke the spell I'd been weaving not only around him, but around me. I stared at him. No regrets. I didn't want a single one once I'd left this place and I understood that was what Bethany was trying to get me to see more than anything else.

That I might not have this chance again. Or maybe more than that, I might not be brave enough to take this chance again.

"Do...you want me?" I whispered the words. Half question, half plea. What if he said no? What if like Will, he turned me down as he tried to keep me safe.

Then I would walk away, I knew that.

I let my hands fall as I walked toward him, my hair sliding over my upper body. His gaze never left my face, not even as I slid myself onto his lap. Very slowly his hands came up and he set them on my waist at the edge of his chain's length.

Bastard could have reached me the entire time! I blinked and he smiled. "You seemed to be enjoying yourself, I didn't want to interrupt."

My lips twitched and then dipped into a frown. He hadn't answered my question, and despite what I felt pressing against my thin panties, I wasn't going to assume anything.

I started to pull back, but he was faster than me. His lips were right at the edge of mine. "More than anything, Sienna. I want to fuck you until you have no breath in you left, because you've screamed yourself hoarse."

That was when I should have left. Should have kissed him and ground my hips over his cock and then left him blue-balling life.

Shoulda. Coulda. Woulda.

No regrets is a funny thing. I didn't want to look back and wish I'd seen this through when I was old and gray and reminisced about the adventures of my life. I wanted to be able to say I'd fucked this General until we were both senseless.

"No touching. Promise me," I whispered.

He frowned. "I can't touch you?"

"Not this time. Promise me." I smiled.

His frown deepened. "You want to torture me? Then kill me?"

"What a way to die." I looked up at him from under my lashes.

I waited until he let out a low sigh. "Gods above, save me. I promise."

A shiver of anticipation slid through me. Before I could change my mind, my tongue darted out on its own volition to taste him, and I shifted my weight a little, pressing my hips against his at the same time. He growled as our lips connected, the chains clanking as he tried to get his arms further around me, then he paused and held back. He lowered his hands to the edge of the chair and gripped it.

"Very good, General," I whispered as I shimmied a little more, pressing my breasts up against his thin shirt, the texture of it making my nipples pebble.

His jaw flexed as a tremor rippled through him, but he was true to his word. He didn't lift a finger.

I pulled his shirt open and slid my hands over his torso, watching his face as I let my hands wander.

"Why no touching?" he asked as I dipped my hands lower to the waist of his pants.

I didn't answer him as I worked the buttons open. I knew the reason, even if I only ever admitted it to myself.

His cock all but leapt out of his pants as I worked to free it. Sliding a hand down, I gripped him lightly. The sound of his teeth grinding made me smile and I dared a quick look at him from under my lashes.

His lips were parted, fangs showing as he watched me sliding my hand down his shaft, slowly. Velvet wrapped steel, that was what he felt like.

Going up to my toes, I lifted myself over the tip of his cock and slowly lowered myself a mere inch.

"Goddess," he groaned the word out and the chair creaked as the muscles in his forearms flexed.

"Don't break the chair, General," I whispered. Working myself up and down on the tip of his cock, I watched his face as he fought to hold still. As he fought the urge to touch me.

My body begged for me to slide all the way down, to take him all in. Before we were interrupted again.

Placing my hands on his chest for balance, I slid down another inch.

My body ached for his touch, for his mouth on my nipples, or his fingers to brush against my clit. But this moment...this was my show.

Another inch, then another. I held my lower lip between my teeth as I slid *finally* all the way to the base of his cock, feeling him so deep in me. I just held myself there, letting my body adjust.

"Sienna," his voice was broken on my name. "I can't...hold on."

I looked up at him, his eyes tight with the strain of doing just that—holding on. "No? I should hurry up?"

I swiveled my hips so I could find that perfect spot, pressing against my clit as I began to ride him.

The wet, slick heat between us only intensified as I rode him. Head thrown back, I leaned into it, knowing that this was it, this was the one moment I'd have with him. I wobbled on my toes and his hands shot from the sides of the chair to my calves, steadying me.

His breath came in hard gasps, a growl on the edge of it as I kept up my pace, steady, finding that sweet spot for me.

I was so close. Maybe I whispered that, I don't know. In the haze of need, my breast brushed up against him and he dipped his head, mouth circling my nipple. The heat and pressure of his lips was all it took to finally tip me over the edge.

The orgasm that had been building slowly swept up like a tsunami, rolling over me so that I screamed and bucked against his mouth, my pussy clenching his cock over and over as my body fluttered and climaxed around his.

His hands swept up around me, catching me as I slumped against him, his own muscles tremoring as I laid my head against his chest and the world went dark as I passed the fuck out.

CHAPTER 13

Dominic

Sienna's breathing was slow as she rested against my chest, her body warm and languid after her...workout.

A smile flitted over my mouth as I ran my hands over her back, playing across her muscles. A soft sigh slid out of her and she snuggled closer to me, her cheek pressed close to my neck. I breathed her in, trying to memorize everything about this moment.

I didn't understand why she wouldn't let me touch her, but...it was sexy as fuck watching her ride me to completion, to see her take her pleasure and allow me to be a part of it. My cock twitched, still deep inside of her as the images replayed in my head. She stirred and lifted her head, and I couldn't help myself, I held her a little tighter and she burrowed against me with another deep sigh.

Selfish, it was completely selfish of me to try and keep her there. But I wanted a few more minutes of this connection with her.

Because as long as Edmund was alive, as long as I was a prisoner, it wasn't fair to even pretend there was something between us that could survive.

A fist on the door, the boom of it rocketed through the room and Sienna all but leapt off me. I groaned as she slid fully off my cock.

"Time's up!"

Her naked body, fully on display, panties askew, and hair wildly mussed. I could have drank in the sight for hours.

"Sienna, we should talk—"

"Nope." She scooped up her clothes and jerked them back on with a speed that told me it wasn't just the first time she'd danced for someone, but dressed rapidly after. How many men had seen her like that? Hurrying to get clothes on, hurrying to leave a small room?

A flickering anger burrowed through me. One that she had to dance for strangers for money, maybe even had to fuck them. Two, I didn't want her dancing for anyone but me ever again, and that was not something I could even make sure of which sent fury racing through my veins.

Dressed, she all but ran to the door, once there she paused and looked over her shoulder.

She opened her mouth to speak and my heart constricted at the thought of her saying goodbye.

But she closed her mouth and slid out of the door, gone like a dream evaporating with the morning light. As if she'd never truly been there.

If not for the smell of her on my skin, she could have been just that.

I tucked myself back into my pants as the guard slipped into the room and sniffed the air.

"Lucky bastard."

I glared at him. "Do not even think of touching her."

The guard snorted and held up his hands in mock surrender. "Not even for a second would I consider it, General."

He moved through the room to check my chains. I didn't attack him, though I could have grabbed him and broken his neck before he had time to scream. If I'd wanted to escape, it would have been so simple.

That's what the wolves' new leader didn't understand. I didn't need to be put in chains, I was happy to stay where I was to get the help William needed. My jaw ticked tight as I thought of my brother, of his scent on Sienna.

"I want to speak to William," I said to the guard as he moved to leave the room. "Ask Diana if I can speak to him yet."

He shrugged. "I'll send the request up the pipeline."

The door slammed and locked behind him with a heavy clunk.

I stood, not moving from my spot in the center of the room while I waited. I let the events that had brought me here wash over me, filter through my mind, and fill me up with purpose.

With everything on the line, my only hope was that Scarlett was able to reach the Vanators, and that they would in turn be willing to take on Edmund.

Did I truly believe that they'd be able to kill him? Perhaps not if they were not being guided by Scarlett, but with her help, she'd secure them a way into his inner circle. She knew his patterns as well as I did.

If anyone could make sure they succeeded, it was my second in command.

I could still see her eyes through the cabin door...

An hour ticked by before footsteps had me lifting my head.

Footsteps I knew like the back of my hand, so there was no surprise as William opened the cell door. His grin was as quick and light as ever, but there was a strain around his blue eyes and it was clear he'd dropped some weight.

"I see they have you in the premium suite again, General." He flinched as the door slammed behind him. "Though I rather think that you should have asked for the satin sheets."

I glared at him, smelling Sienna's blood on him. I leaned against the chains, stretching them as far as I could. "You drank from her."

William's eyes softened. "Oh, you poor, poor bastard. You've got it bad too, eh?"

I growled and he had the nerve to fucking laugh at me. "William, brother or no—"

"I never bit her, Nicky. I don't even remember the first blood she gave me, but it was from her wrist, and had nothing to do with my fangs. And this is according to the girls. Because I don't remember fuck all about it. I was mostly dead, to be fair."

I stared at him, knowing his tells when he lied and none of them were showing. He slumped against the wall and slid down, his eyes closing.

"Even coming here now was exhausting. The bloodworm is still in me, you know. That bastard poisoned me before I left the castle."

Bloodworm.

"What the fuck, how are you not dead then?"

He laughed, though there was no humor to it. "That seems to be the question of the day. Something about Sienna's blood is healing me, and frankly, it is keeping her in good standing with Diana too. She is intrigued by the girl."

I stared at him, remembering the taste of that one drop of Sienna's blood on my tongue, the way it had felt...magic.

"She's the reason I'm alive," he said quietly. "But I still need her...blood that is." He amended the last quickly as I tensed again. "The doctors here seem to think another feeding or two from her and the worm will be dead."

The words were in the air, but I was struggling to understand. "Bloodworms don't die once they're in a host."

He nodded. "I know."

"Ever."

"I know."

The ramifications of this were far flung. The bloodworm that had feasted on our kind for years was now being choked out by a human's blood?

He ran a hand over his hair. "Why could Edmund have not been such a raging cunt?"

It was my turn to laugh. "He always has been, and you expect him to change for the better now that he's wielding more power?"

Will sighed. "I just wish that life were different. I love her, you know."

I moved so fast I don't think even I knew I was at the end of my chains until I felt the strain on my wrists.

Red rage flowed over me, and I wasn't sure I could have stopped if not for the fact that I was in fact, tethered to the wall. "She's mine."

He blinked up at me. "Good thing they broke out the big boy chains for you, seeing as I was speaking of Bethany. I can smell Sienna on you, Nicky, I know you fucked her. She's not my type, not at all."

It took a moment for the words to penetrate through the haze of anger, slowly draining it off. "The maid?"

"Yes, she's...I got her out of the Harvest Games she was in, and as a maid. Because she was safer that way. An-phony wanted her too. I think only because I'd shown interest."

I shifted back to my chair and sat down. "You love the maid, and I am—"

"Fucking the magical girl everyone is trying to figure out?" His mouth quirked up. "Maybe that will get you out of chains faster?"

I rolled my eyes. "Doubtful. Diana does not like me."

"You're the General to Edmund the Awful, there's a lot to not like." His face was pale as he sat there, as if just talking was fatiguing him. "I only point all this out because if you have not come to the conclusion yet that fucking Sienna is a bad idea, I want to help you get there. She's not any safer in your arms than Bethany is in mine."

I stared at my younger brother, giving me advice that was not unwarranted, even if it was not wanted. "I know this."

"Yet you did it anyway?"

I shrugged. "I was chained, and she had her way with me. I wasn't about to complain."

His eyes widened. "Wait...what?"

I waved a hand at him, chains jangling. "You're right. We are a danger to both of them. They would have been better off put on a boat and sent back to the mainland."

He grunted as if I'd punched him in the balls. "Impossible, and you know that."

I did know that. As of yet, though, Sienna did not.

"See if you can convince Diana to speak with me again," I said, changing the subject. I did not want to think about Sienna going away or being hurt. Neither was acceptable.

"You think I haven't tried?" Will pushed up, using the wall for balance. "I'll try again, but you have to prove to her that you're trustworthy. And barring the Duchess showing up and speaking for you in person, I doubt that Diana is going to take anyone's word."

Well that was just fucking perfect. I'd made it here to raise an army to help support Will in his ascension to the throne, but I couldn't convince the one person I needed to that I was here for the right reasons.

I lifted my eyes to his.

"Then ask Sienna to speak for me. If the Queen is soft to her, let us hope she has that same magic with the wolves as she does with us."

CHAPTER 14

Sienna

"Can you pass the clotted cream, please?"

I watched, enveloped in a sort of surreal wonder, as Bee handed a cut crystal bowl full of fluffy, white cream to the Queen, who nodded in thanks.

Who would've thought, four weeks before, that I'd be seated at the dining table of the Queen's keep set in the heart of Werewolf Territory having a proper British high tea, while my vampire enemy/lover was imprisoned just down the hall?

Certainly not me. In fact, I shifted uncomfortably in my chair as I realized how wrong I'd gotten it all. I'd imagined the Territories to be a lawless, ruthless land of untold horrors. And, don't get me wrong, in a lot of ways they were. But then there were things...people...places that made me wonder...

Were they all that different than us? From humans?

We fought vicious wars and committed horrible atrocities on one another. There was slavery, and torture, and subjugation of women for centuries.

But there was also beauty, and kindness, and love. Surely, the same held true here?

"This is the best Victoria sponge I've ever eaten in my entire life," Bee announced before taking another hearty bite of the delicate cake.

Diana inclined her head with a smile. "I'll be sure to tell the chef. She'll be pleased to hear it." She stared at the tower of scones, petit fours and sandwiches before us and the smile slid from her face. "Usually, we have mixed berry tarts as well, but most berries have been in short supply since the weather has gotten so erratic..." she cleared her throat and shook her head, the furrow in her brow smoothing. "Well, there's nothing to be done about it today, at any rate. Let's just enjoy, shall we?"

I took a half-hearted bite of my smoked salmon blini and gave her a thumbs' up. "So good."

It wasn't a lie. The food was delicious, but my appetite was sorely lacking. After a terrible night's sleep, tossing and turning, replaying the evening before in my mind obsessively, I'd woken up on the wrong side of the bed. And, in the hours since, nothing seemed to improve my mood.

Bee had buzzed around, chattering endlessly about our escape plans. That should've been comforting, knowing that I wasn't alone in this quest anymore. Instead, though, it just made it all the more real. We were going to leave this place soon enough. If we failed, I'd sentenced all three of us to death or worse. If we succeeded, I'd never see Dominic again.

There was a time that would've seemed like the ultimate win.

Now, though? After feeling him move inside me...after knowing what it could be like between us? I wasn't so sure.

As I stared all my potential futures straight in the face, every one of them left me feeling cold inside.

Diana had clearly set aside her own earlier worries, because she was currently chowing down a sausage roll with a groan of pleasure. Luckily her eyes were closed, because when I spared a glance at Bee, she was shoving handfuls of pecans into her pockets.

I glared at her, letting my eyes bulge for good measure, and luckily she took the hint. We were going to have to have a serious talk about stealth or I wouldn't have to worry about coming up with an escape route. We'd never make it past the door.

"So, Your Majesty, I went for a walk about yesterday and noticed there weren't all that many craftsmen or shops nearby, and homes were scattered few and far between. Do the different packs each have their own keep, and is each like a little, self-sufficient city?"

I had to give it to her, Bee was nothing if not doggedly determined.

The Queen patted her lips with a violet-sprigged napkin and swallowed. "Each clan has its own keep, and in the center of them all lies our town square. We have loads of stores and artisan shops and the like. That said, yes, The Royal keep is self-sufficient and everything is made in-house, from our weapons to our stilton." She winked as she plucked up a morsel of the latter and popped it into her mouth. "Sienna, are you sure you don't want to try the battenburg? It's out of this world. Or maybe another cup of tea. I imagine you could use the caffeine after your...exertions last night."

It took a second for the teasing dig to penetrate, but when it did, my ears went white-hot.

"I don't—what did you—"

"Don't bother denying it. My quarters are right above the General's cell. I had to put a pillow over my head to drown the two of you out."

And here I was mentally dressing down Bee for her lack of stealth.

"Your Majesty, I do apologize. I have no excuse..."

"Oh, relax," she said with a laugh. "You aren't in trouble or anything of the sort. You're a grown woman with needs. You don't need an excuse or my permission." She leaned forward and held my gaze for a long moment. "But I feel the need to warn you. No matter what it might seem like at times, vampires cannot be trusted. Especially when it comes to love and loyalty. They will take what they want, whenever they want it, and cast you aside. Mark my words on that."

"Yet you trust the Duchess Evangeline?" Bee asked.

Diana's deep green eyes softened as she settled back against her seat.

"I do. But she is an exception to the rule. Hence my caution in moving forward until I hear word from her. Dominic is largely unknown to me. And until I learn otherwise, I have to go in assuming the worst."

I'd hoped to use our little meal to broach the topic Will had come to me about earlier that morning. Potentially trying to sway the Queen into changing her mind about Dominic, but that thought dried up and blew away like a husk in the wind. For whatever reason, she had a deep mistrust of vampires, and nothing I was going to say would change it.

Diana pursed her lips and shrugged.

"I know you must think me archaic and prejudiced in some way, but you must understand. I am responsible for thousands of lives. I can't afford to have my head turned by a handsome face, a bit of charm, or a glib tongue."

She shot a telling glance at Bee and then at me.

Ouch.

Very barbed point taken.

"It wasn't any of those things for me, if you want to know the truth," Bee murmured, fretfully toying with her napkin as she studied the table intently. "It was his kindness that drew me to him. When I was first brought in for the Harvest Games, I literally couldn't stop shaking. I must've looked like some pitiful chihuahua. When the cruel Earl DuMont seemed to take an interest, Will made it his business to help, pulled me from the lot and made me a servant. I truly believe I owe him my life."

"Ay, that may be true, Bethany. But do you owe him your heart? Because I can promise you this. He will obliterate it. They don't do monogamy, loyalty is scarce, and he is a royal. If he wanted to blow all that to hell and roll the dice, he'd have already done it."

The words were aimed at Bee, but I could feel the daggers land on me too.

"I'm so sorry, Bethany. But even if he does love you, it's only in his way, the same as a man might love a good steak. Now," Diana said, shoving her plate away, "If you can live with that...knowing there's an expiration date on their affections, and you want to partake? Go for it. Both of you. I won't stop you. But I feel it is my duty to warn you as one who's been betrayed by a bloodsucker more than once. It won't end well for you. It never does."

Despite the fact that Bee and I had basically come to the same conclusions on our own, having our suspicions confirmed felt like a real kick in the dick. I needed to get out of here. I needed to clear my damned head.

"Your Majesty, am I permitted to ride my horse for a bit today? The weather looks calm, and I could use the fresh air."

"Certainly. I'll have one of the servants take you down to the stables," she said, pressing a button on the arm of her chair. "Just make sure that you stay on the grounds of the keep and do not cross the moat. We're still on thin ice when it comes to the clans, and I don't want you bumping into the wrong wolf until I have secured everyone's support at the upcoming assembly."

"I understand." I nodded and pushed away from the table. "And thank you."

A moment later, the kitchen door swung open, and Jordan appeared.

My already battered heart skipped a beat at his guileless expression.

"Oh no...Are you choking on a chunk of meat again?"

I shook my head and then slipped my arm through his. "I am not, but it's a fair assumption. Actually, I was hoping you could show me to the stables?"

He shot the Queen a questioning look, and she nodded.

"Alright, then."

I remained silent until we exited the keep and began to make our way down the winding, stone steps to the lawn. It was only when a balmy breeze ruffled my hair that I realized how warm it was. Like a spring day in the Pacific Northwest back home. That, compared to the ice-storms and frigid temperatures that had nearly ended me just days before.

"What's the deal with the weather here, Jordan? Do they have proper seasons like us?" Surely they did. We shared the same earth, and we were equal distance from the sun...

"Apparently, they used to. It's been different of late. One day it's cold, the next warm. Uncle Paddy says it's something to do with the Veil coming down."

My hand twitched on his arm reflexively.

Who the fuck was Uncle Paddy?

"Who the fuck is Uncle Paddy?" I snapped an instant later, unable to stop myself.

Jordan slowed and scratched nervously at his chin. "He's, um, he's the elder in my clan, and that's what he likes to be called."

I could see the stables in the distance as I took a look around to make sure we were alone before pulling him to a stop. "I know they've not been unkind to you, and that was probably a huge relief when you first got here, terrified and alone. But Jordan, these people aren't your family. Me." I poked myself hard in the chest. "I'm your family."

My heart dropped to my toes when he wouldn't meet my eyes.

"Jordan?"

His nobby Adam's apple bobbed as he swallowed hard and finally looked down at me. "I know you are, Ceecee. But can't...can't both things be true?"

Oof.

What could I even say?

"Can I show you something?" Jordan asked softly.

I didn't trust myself to speak so I just nodded.

He perched his tongue on his upper lip as he rummaged through his pocket.

"The alpha for clan Killian was the only one who bid on me, and they're the best clan here, if I say so myself."

He held out a set of tiny figurines in his palm, each finely whittled. He plucked two from the pile and held them up.

"These are my parents now, Maya and Kavan. They push us pretty hard sometimes, but everyone who works for them gets treated like family. A wolf from another clan tried to mess with me one of my first few days, and my sister Elka—that's this one," he said, pausing to thumb a smaller figurine, "beat him bloody with a broom when she heard. When his pack leader came asking about it and saying he wanted to see me whipped for being a human and causing trouble, Kavan stood by me, even when it almost turned into a full on battle between the clans."

I gulped, a wave of anxiety running through me as I took it all in. The way he was talking, the shine in his eyes, the contented look on his face... had I really lost him?

I glanced down at the smallest piece of whittled wood in his hand, this one a little wolf. "And that one?"

He held it up, beaming. "This one's me. Or it will be. I'm still just a human for now, but Da says we're going to hold a changing ceremony once he feels like I'm physically strong enough to handle it. I've been training pretty hard, but he thinks it'll be a year or so before I'm ready. I think it will be sooner."

For a long moment, my brain couldn't compute the words he was saying. Not truly.

But when it hit me, it hit me hard. Jordan wasn't just a well-treated captive, he was a full on member of the Killian Clan family.

I fingered my beaded bracelet, heart aching. Had it really all been in vain?

"I love your figurines, Jordan," I forced out. "And I love you, too."

In the moment, though, I was officially at the end of my rope.

Between wanting a vampire I shouldn't and couldn't have, trying to save a loved one who didn't want to be saved, and fighting a war I shouldn't even be in, I was mentally, physically, and emotionally spent. Tomorrow was a new day.

Today...right now, what I needed was a saddle, my horse, an open field.

"What say you lead me to those horses now, okay?"

He let out a deep sigh of relief and ambled ahead, leading me along with him.

When we reached the stables, he handed me off to a bearded man dressed in jeans and a cowboy hat before rushing off. If wolves were as long-lived as I'd heard, this one was clearly pushing the century mark. Despite looking fit as any fiddle and a distinct lack of wrinkles, he fairly oozed a calm, almost zen-like wisdom before he even spoke.

"Hello there, lass. Name's Hamish. You must be Sienna."

"I am."

"I was on duty when you first arrived. Your Havoc is a wild one to be sure. You must be one hell of a rider," he observed with something like respect filling his eyes. "If you're wanting to take her out, I'll fetch her for you. Back in a jiff."

True to her name, I could hear Havoc kicking up a fuss inside the stable, but before I could go in and take over, I heard a low, threatening growl that chilled me to the core. By the time Hamish led her out, Havoc was saddled up and quiet as a lamb.

"You seem to handle her pretty well yourself," I observed lightly as I took the reins.

"Sometimes you just gotta know how to talk to them," he replied with a wink.

As someone who wasn't above intimidation when necessary, I had to give it to old Hamish. You had to use the tools at hand.

After getting some basic information about landmarks, I was on my way.

For the first twenty minutes when I should've been plotting escape routes, noting guard locations and potential pitfalls, I did nothing but ride. The wind whipped at my hair as my skirt blew wildly around my hips, but I didn't care. For those precious few moments, I felt free, even though I was anything but. It wasn't until I reached the moat around the keep that I slowed to a trot and started paying attention to my surroundings.

The royal keep was at a high point, and I could see the land beyond these grounds was vast...acres and miles of woodland in every direction. While I was sure I'd remember where to go once we crossed back into vampire territory, I'd been in the grips of hypothermia when we'd first gotten here. A map was an absolute must. Again.

I spurred Havoc on, moving along the perimeter of the moat. It wasn't very wide across, and would've been breached easily enough by a rowboat or even a strong swimmer. Hardly seemed like all that much of a deterrent if someone wanted to gain access to the royal keep grounds without coming through the way we had. I was still pondering that when something buzzed past my ear.

"What the hell?" I swatted the air as I looked around in confusion. It had been too large to be any bug I'd ever seen, but—

Thunk.

Havoc bucked and let out a squeal of outrage as I tried to maintain my hold on the reins.

"Shhh, shhh, it's alright, friend. You're okay," I whispered, laying a hand on her neck as I tried to make sense of what had happened. It only took a glance down to see an arrow pinning my skirt to the leather fender of the saddle to put it altogether.

We were under fire. Someone was shooting at us from the trees on the other side of the moat.

Adrenaline shot through me as I clicked my tongue and tugged Havoc's reins to wheel her around, back toward the keep. As she broke into a canter, I caught sight of a second arrow still trembling from where it stuck, buried in the ground a few yards ahead.

"Bloody hell. Keep going, girl!"

We rode hard for a mile or more before I felt comfortable enough to stop. Havoc was snorting and tossing her head, but I could sense it was from fear as opposed to injury. Still, I had to be certain. I slipped a hand beneath the fender of my saddle and let out a sigh of relief as I came in contact with soft, unmarred horseflesh.

With a snarl, I yanked the arrow hard, dislodging it from the leather and my now torn skirt.

I almost threw it on the ground but then stopped. It had to be from one of the werewolf clans Diana had warned us about, a near-fatal reminder that we were not wanted here by all.

Bastards. Couldn't we catch a break for even a moment?

I'd have to keep my guard up every second and tell the others to do the same. Because one thing was for sure. We might've dodged a bullet by making it to the Werewolf Territory before Edmund caught us, but that didn't mean we were safe.

As I raced back toward the keep like the devil was on my heels, I was starting to get the sinking sensation that maybe we never would be again.

CHAPTER 15

Dominic

It was long dark, and I'd about given up on her coming when the sound of her voice echoed down the hallway.

"I need to see him again."

When Sienna stepped into the room, I was already standing, too tense to stay seated.

"I wondered if you'd be back."

"I shouldn't be," she replied, her voice barely a whisper as the door closed behind her.

Her hair hung loose around her shoulders and she wore a long, woolen skirt. Just her scent alone had the blood rushing in my ears, but it only took a second to realize something was very wrong.

"Sienna? Are you alright?" I asked, moving as close as I could before the chains grew taut.

She nodded, wetting her lips as she focused on a spot behind my left shoulder.

"Yeah. Sure, I'm fine."

She moved closer and laid a hand on my chest, using it to push me backward until my legs hit the chair. Her scent was like an elixir and my cock stiffened instantly.

"Talk to me," I said, taking a seat as she hiked her skirt up and straddled my thighs, but stopping her when she went to kiss me. "Tell me what's going on."

"It's nothing. Nothing that anything can be done about, at any rate. Now are we going to fuck or are you going to continue to try and psychoanalyze me? Because if so, I can take my leave—"

"No." I gripped her hips and clutched her tight against me. Truth was, I'd take her any way I could get her, so long as she stayed. How far the great General had fallen...

I let one hand trail up her side, brushing against her breast before slipping into her hair and taking hold. Then, I slanted my mouth over hers. It started out rough as she gasped and crushed her lips closer, but I pulled back and gently nipped at her.

"Can't we take our time, love?" I whispered, tracing her bottom lip with my tongue. It was so full, so juicy, I deserved a medal for not taking a bite. Then I kissed her like I wanted to. Slow and easy, trying to show her without words that this wasn't just sex.

"Don't," she whispered brokenly as she pulled away, a suspicious shine in her eyes. "Don't be gentle. I can't bear it right now. Please, Dominic. Just take me."

I wanted to argue, but she arched her back, grinding those hips against me, and all I wanted to do was please her. I yanked the skirt off with the flick of my wrist, the sound of tearing fabric echoing through the room. When I slid my hand between her thighs, I expected to find a slip of cloth, and let out a groan when I encountered nothing but warm, wet pussy.

"Yess," she hissed, pulsing her hips toward me in a dizzying rhythm. I pressed two fingers inside her, plunging them in and out in greedy thrusts. With every movement, I imagined being inside her, that hot column convulsing around my aching cock. My fangs sliding into the tender skin of her neck like butter, sucking and fucking at the same time—

"I knew it from the start," I managed, releasing her hair and making short work of my zipper. I had every intention of fulfilling her wish. To take her, hard and fast like she wanted, but then she pulled away from me and dropped to her knees.

"Sienna..."

Her name was as much a plea as it was a warning.

She held my gaze with a half-smile. "I want to taste you."

My eyes drifted shut for a scant second before she batted the head of my cock with her tongue. Minutes passed as she explored me, teasing, licking, squeezing. It wasn't until my chains began to clatter and my hands were balled into fists at my sides that she began sucking me off in earnest. Her mouth was an inferno as she bobbed up and down, making a little noise in the back of her throat all the while, urging me on wordlessly in a way that had me at point break in no time.

"Enough," I ground out, tugging gently at her hair.

But the damnable woman wouldn't be moved.

"If you don't stop, I'm going to come in your mouth," I added, breathing through my nose, desperate to regain some control as the need continued to grind me down.

Sienna only sucked harder, her softly rounded cheeks going concave as she pulled me deep.

"By the gods, I always knew you were a witch."

I reached down to her blouse and popped off the first few buttons so I could close my hand over her breast. The nipple beaded against my palm instantly and she released my cock with a pop to let out a gasp.

Taking advantage of the moment, I lunged forward and lifted her up by her hips, setting her back on my lap.

She scowled at me and tried to wriggle away.

"Not fair."

"All's fair..." I left the rest unsaid, because I knew she was in no state of mind for declarations of devotion. Right now, she wanted pleasure to replace the pain. She wanted to forget where and who we were. And, for the moment, I would oblige her.

I lifted her away from my lap, adjusting her center until she hovered over my cock. My eyes were glued to the space between us as I lowered her onto my shaft, inch by inch.

"Ah, yeah," Sienna groaned, her nipples pulling tight as she threw her head back. "Fuck, that's so good."

I swallowed hard, trying to ignore the sound of the blood pulsing in her neck. Trying to stay strong and forget the sweet smell of it calling to me like a siren's song, just inches from my mouth.

"All of it," she murmured, pushing her hips against my hands restlessly. "Please."

I lifted my hips and pulled her down all at once, plunging deep until I was fully seated inside her. Her muscles leapt and twitched around me like a medieval torture device designed to drive me insane. For a long moment, we stayed that way as her body stretched to accommodate me, and then she started to move. Slow at first. A light, easy roll of the hips. Then faster, tits bouncing, cheeks going flush as she rode me up and down.

I watched through narrowed eyes as she gripped my shoulders for purchase. She was so fucking beautiful, it almost hurt to look at her, but I couldn't look away. I dipped my head forward, taking one taut nipple into my mouth and sucked. My cock was swollen to the point of pain, and the slow drag of her wet flesh clasping and releasing with every move was sending me to the brink, so when she began to whimper, I wanted to howl with relief.

"That's it love, come for me," I growled, taking her hips once again and using them to work her faster, harder. "Let me feel that tight little pussy go up in flames." She met my every move, riding me hard, slamming her hips into mine. My balls drew tight as hot liquid snaked up my shaft.

"Dominic!"

The sound of her screaming my name...the feel of her spasming around me like a fist...

"So good," I grunted as I pinched my eyes closed and let the sensation swallow me whole. I came in hot, heavy spurts, pinning her hips to mine as pleasure crashed over me in waves. I held her tight as she twitched and bucked against me, my name a chant on her lips.

For a long while, I held her close. Until her pulse quieted. Until my breathing finally slowed. The bone-deep satisfaction was so consuming, I nearly fell asleep.

It was only the wet warmth on my chest that finally had me stirring back to consciousness again.

"Sienna?" I pulled back and stared down at the top of her head. Chains jangled as I tucked a hand under her chin, lifting it so I could see her face. "Are you crying?"

Stupid question as the evidence of it streaked down her still-flushed cheeks.

"Ah, fuck. What's the matter...did I hurt you, love?"

Self-loathing tied a knot in my belly even as she shook her head.

"No. I mean, yes, a little, but in a good way. It's just—" she broke off and bit her lip before pressing on. "Everything is so fucked up, Dominic. Every time I think things might be getting even a little better, something bad happens. The constant pressure and fear and worry. I think I'm just so exhausted that my brain can't take it anymore." She let out a muffled chuckle. "Do you know I was shot at today, and it barely fazed me?"

"You were what?" I demanded, jerking upright so quickly, I nearly upended her from my lap.

Great way to soothe someone whose nerves were fried, Nicky.

I slipped my hands around her hips to steady her, and then tried again, in a softer tone. "What do you mean you were *shot at*?"

"I mean I was riding Havoc around the keep grounds and, when we reached the moat, someone loosed at least two arrows our way." She shrugged and swiped a hand over her running nose. "Luckily, they missed, and the only victim was poor Hamish's beautifully crafted saddle, but it was a close thing."

Way too close for my liking.

It took me nearly a minute to calm myself enough to press her for more details. "Did you get a look at the archer?"

"No. Although, they'd have to have been either extremely skilled or astonishingly cocky to think they stood a chance of hitting me from that distance. I haven't told Diana about it yet."

"*Yet* being the operative word, yes?"

If I was trapped in this cell while someone was taking potshots at *my* woman, at the very least, I needed to be assured that she would be better protected going forward. My cooperation depended on it. And Diana, Queen of Wolves, did not want to meet me if I was feeling uncooperative.

"As soon as she finds out, I'm going to be a prisoner all over again," Sienna muttered. "She's going to keep me indoors, or force a guard on me, and that's the last thing I want."

The hair on my neck bristled at her words.

She'd never tried to hide it. She wanted out from the get go. Somehow along the way, I'd convinced myself that she'd finally come to grips with the reality of life here. Hoped that she'd finally resigned herself to the fact that she belonged on this side of the Veil. Apparently, I'd been fooling myself.

I dipped my head low until she met my gaze. "If you run from this place, you will die, Sienna. Do you understand what I'm telling you? In this territory or mine, an unprotected female—or even a pair of you, if you've got your maid in on whatever cockamamie plan you've been hatching—you won't make it a day alone. You're being targeted now, even on the Queen's land, under her protection. Trying to leave is a suicide mission." I didn't dare tell her the rest.

That, even if they did manage to get away from this place, there was no going back.

Not now. Not ever.

"And staying here in a den of monsters is better?" she shot back, her voice trembling with outrage.

"I prefer you alive, so yes."

She stared at me, those golden eyes piercing me to the bone. "I'm not sure that's enough for me, Dominic."

A haunting, terrible image wormed its way to the forefront of my mind. Sienna, slung over the back of Edmund's horse, those eyes empty...lifeless.

Fury coursed through me, unchecked.

"Hate me if you must, but if you aren't going to tell Diana what happened today, I will," I snapped, tightening my grip on her hips.

"Don't bother," she said, pushing herself from my lap and tugging her skirt back into place. "I'm going to tell her myself, if only to protect the others. I can't very well have Will and Bee waltzing around like there isn't a threat around every corner, can I?"

She swiped the last of the tears from her face as she shot me a glare.

"But don't think that means I'm resigned to staying on this side of the Veil forever. Because the second I have even the slimmest chance of success, I'm in the wind. You can count on it."

With that, she made for the door, and it was all I could do not to tear my arms out of their sockets to follow.

Blast this woman for being so bloody stubborn, and foolish, and brave, and beautiful—

When the bolt at the door slid open a few minutes later, I instantly shot to my feet. "Sienna?"

"Relax, Romeo, it's just me," Lochlin said as he stepped into the cell and waved off the guard. "I had to beg to get to see you, and even at that, I only have a few minutes." He shook his head sadly. "I don't know what you did to our Queen, but she doesn't trust you any more than I'd trust a fart after a pot of beans, boyo."

I retook my seat with a grunt. "I don't think it's me as much as it is my kind, but whatever the case, we need to figure a way to get her past that, and fast. Sienna was out on her horse today and had shots fired her way."

Loch flinched and nodded slowly. "I'm disappointed to hear it, but not surprised. Word going 'round is that a couple of the clans aren't happy with the situation at all. I'm hearing calls for Diana's removal. 'Course, some of the more peaceful clans are happy, and hoping for an alliance as well. It's going to depend on how Diana handles them all at the assembly. Will be a good test of her skills as a diplomat and a strong leader."

"Until then, though, I need you to keep Sienna safe."

"Come on, Dom," he protested with a snort. "I'm already on her majesty's shite list for bringing them here in the first place. If I start skulking around here and keeping watch on your say-so, she's going to have me skinned and filleted."

I stared at him hard. "I'm not asking."

Loch's expression went dark. "And if I don't comply?"

"Then I tear the head off the next guard who brings me vittles and anyone else who gets in my way and I go find her myself."

He let out a long-suffering groan and raked a hand over his face in disgust. "I need to find some new fucking friends, that's what I think. Gods, man, why does everything have to be so fire and brimstone? You know that when you're not around, I can go years without talk of decapitatin' or getting hunted down like a rabid mutt?"

"Sounds boring," I said with a yawn. "And while you're doling out favors, I'm going to need you to help me come up with a way to get into the Queen's good graces. For all we know, Edmund's got the Duchess under lock and key or worse. She might never get Diana's message. There has to be another way..."

Because I could feel the noose tightening around my neck. Whether that meant Edmund would breach the border and come get us himself, or our respective "welcome" here was short-lived, we were running out of time.

"There might be something. I remember more than a decade ago, Lycan was in a similar situation with someone he felt could not be trusted..." Loch murmured, stroking his coppery beard in thought. "Yeah, there could be a way. But I can promise you this, old friend."

He met my gaze and shook his head slowly.

"You're not going to like it."

CHAPTER 16

Sienna

I sat on the edge of my bed with the arrow in my palm, rolling it across my fingers. The emblem etched into the metal tip was a single star with a cross set inside of it. I had no idea who the clan was that it belonged to, but whoever it was did not want me here. Or maybe just didn't want me alive at all.

Bethany was across from me, counting her damn pecans. "I think I can snag a whole bag of nuts today without getting noticed. I overheard one of the cooks talking about making pecan pie."

I nodded and mumbled, "Great."

But my mind was on the arrow, the danger that we faced...and then occasionally sliding back to Dominic and the feel of his body, of his hands and mouth as they wreaked havoc on my ability to think straight.

The arrow was the issue. I mean, yes, we planned to escape the territories. But making a run for it injured or being hunted—by yet another foe—was not going to make any of this easier.

For now, I put the arrow on the side table, then went to the door that led onto a small balcony. I needed cool air that would help me clear my mind and think straight.

Opening the door, I closed my eyes, fully expecting...not what came through. A wash of summer heat caught me off guard, like a slap to the cheek.

"What the hell...This weather is so strange."

Bee came to stand next to me. "Hard to believe we arrived in the middle of a snowstorm just a week ago, isn't it?"

A week already? I blinked several times, eyes watering from the bloody hot air that swept over my face. I found my bracelet by feel and counted the beads. She was right. We were down another week.

A knock on the door turned us both away from the balcony.

Bethany moved swiftly, flicking a blanket to hide her covert pecan counting operation, then hurried to open the bedroom door.

Lochlin stood there with a crooked grin on his face, deep hazel eyes twinkling. "Ah, there is my snuggle bug." He said bug like 'boog' and I couldn't help the laugh.

"Oh please, I don't even remember a thing, you needn't brag on my part."

He slapped a hand to his heart as he entered the room. "Wounded to the core I am, lass. But...even so I will do my duty and take you and the lovely Bethany for a walk to the water's edge."

I raised an eyebrow. "Guard duty now?"

He bowed at the waist. "Well, I did have to beg, but once Diana knew of our torrid affair, she granted me leave to guard your body with me own." He winked and waggled his eyebrows first at me, then to Bee. "Not one beautiful lady, but two if I'm lucky will be holding me to the ground, yeah?"

Bee blushed and blew a raspberry at him. "You realize that I know who you actually love? The cooks have told me."

His face paled and he stood up straighter, but he continued with the jesting. "Another strike to the heart. That you think I could love any but—"

She snapped her fingers, and I shot a glance from one to the other.

"I think she has you by the short hairs, Loch. You going to spill the beans about who the lucky woman is?"

He shook his head forlornly. "I am not worthy of any woman, so I live to serve."

Bethany snorted. "Doesn't mean you don't want to wham bam thank you maam with a certain—"

He clapped his hands together, cutting her off effectively. "I have a picnic basket of food, and, with Diana's permission, am taking you two lovely lasses to the beach. Unless you'd rather stay here? Cooped up on such a lovely day?"

I looked out over the balcony at the crystal blue waters of the ocean that lapped against the sandy beach. That should cool my jets as I doubted the water had warmed a great deal in just a few days.

The view I stared at could have been cut out of a magazine. The scene was so pristine, so beautiful, it was a setting out of a fairy tale.

"Fine. Lead the way, Lochlin." I waved at him as I turned, tipping up my chin as if I were indeed a high-born lady.

Bee linked arms with me, and we followed Lochlin and a second guard by the name of Deacon, through the keep and out onto the main grounds. The sun all but beat down on us and, after only ten minutes or so, my skin was prickling not only with salty perspiration, but the feel of an oncoming burn.

"The weather here," I said as we followed the two werewolves, sweat dripping down my spine despite the ease of the terrain, "Is it typically like this? Yesterday felt like spring, and now, today it could be high summer in the desert."

Lochlin and Deacon shared a quick look. "Nah, Lass. This is strange patterns. Changing more each year since the Veil fell. No one knows why."

Deacon gave a low growl. "Vampires, that's what be doing this to us. They've always coveted our lands, and our women, and now they are going to try and starve us out by killing our crops."

"Except that it's the same in the Vampire Territories," Bee replied with a sniff. "I've been there for five years, and each year the weather has grown stranger. They blame you for the changing patterns, you know."

Lochlin and Deacon shared another look, but once more it was Lochlin who spoke. "The weather is bad there too? You're sure about that?"

Bee nodded. "It's not exactly a state secret."

I guessed I hadn't been looking too hard, what with trying not to get my throat ripped out at the Harvest Games. It was interesting, though. Not that it mattered. We'd be gone soon. A month from now, we'd be back on the mainland. Living our lives. Free from weird weather patterns, free from the men who'd stolen our hearts.

We reached the edge of the beach where the soil shifted and mixed with the nearly white sand that spread out toward the brilliantly blue water. Even at a distance, I could see the shapes of fish swimming.

"Noteworthy," Deacon said. "Diana will want to know about that. Seeing as the vampire prince hasn't spoken a word of the weather patterns in his kingdom."

"Shit," Bee whispered. "I shouldn't have said anything."

I squeezed her arm. "I think it's fine, Bee. Will needs to be open too; this maybe will force his hand some? And maybe it will help Diana understand and trust him more."

We were right at the water's edge now. The sound of the waves sliding over the sand, back and forth, the bright call of the gulls above and the scent of salt in the air was enough to wash away some of the angst building in me.

"Today, for this moment, there is nothing we can do," I said as I kicked off my shoes. "Except enjoy the fact that we are alive. And we are safe." I reached to my waist and undid the long skirt.

"What are you doing, Lass?" Lochlin asked. "I thought you'd want to wait for some privacy before we picked up where we left off at our tryst the other night—"

"I'm going for a swim." I pulled the blouse over my head leaving me in a thin shift over my bra and panties. Still far more covered than I would have been in a mere bikini. "You coming in, snuggle boog?"

"Nope. I don't like the water," Lochlin said and he actually took a step back as if I would be able to drag him in if I tried.

"What he means," Deacon laughed. "Is that he can't swim. Sinks like a damn stone, as if he were fae or something!"

Lochlin laughed with Deacon but I saw his face tighten, just a little. That comment had stuck him like a hot pin. But why?

No, no more questions. There was zero reason to entrench myself any deeper into this soul-suck of a place than I already was.

Okay, maybe one more question...

"Bee, you coming in? Work on those muscles a little." I swung my arms around in a mock breast-stroke motion. The guys laughed, but I pointedly locked eyes with Bee when she looked like she was going to say no. She glanced out at the water, zoning in on the boats bobbing in the distance, and her eyes went wide with comprehension.

"Oh, fine, why the hell not?" She grinned at me a little too brightly but at least she'd picked up what I was putting down. How long since I'd last swam more than a few feet? Not since I was a child. I had no idea if Bee was a strong swimmer or not, and we were going to have to swim all the way out to an anchored boat once we got back to Blackthorne Harbor. Might as well see if we could do it or if we had to figure out a way to train between now and then.

Diana had inadvertently helped us get one step closer to pulling ourselves onto the boat in less than a month's time by suggesting this little trip down to the beach. I'd have to thank her later.

Maybe I'd send her a postcard.

Bethany stripped down to her shift and before either of the men could protest, the two of us ran full tilt into the water. My expectation that it would be cold still was spot on. The water splashed up my bare legs and I couldn't keep from squealing. Did I stop running? No, I did not. The screams just peeled out of me as the water rose above my knees, thighs and to my waist, at which point, I dove in.

Probably I didn't need to get my head wet, but the shockingly cold water over my face drove away a great deal of inconsequential things weighing on my mind. Things like would Dominic ever love me if I stayed, or would Bee, Jordan and I even make it back to Blackthorne Harbor without dying?

Nope, the cold water made sure I was thinking of only one thing.

Survival.

I burst upward, gasping for air even as I started swimming out deeper. Teeth chattering, I kicked my feet and plunged my hands into the water over and over.

"You're slower than a bloated walrus!" Deacon yelled.

I didn't care what he thought I looked like. I swam with my eyes on one of the nearest boats. All the way out to it, I pushed myself, muscles burning, the cold water sapping my strength. I didn't even know if Bethany was still close. I only knew that I was focused on the boat, on the grains of the wood making up the slats as I drew nearer.

"Hey! Where you think you be going?" Lochlin yelled from shore, still sounding rather close. I turned in the water and looked back. He was knee deep in the water. Bethany was right behind me, swimming hard.

"Not like I can swim to the mainland!" I yelled and then turned and continued swimming toward the boat.

"Sienna," Bethany groaned. "I can't go much further! The cold water is making my muscles cramp"

"I know. To the boat, just to prove to ourselves that we can," I called to her, teeth still chattering some.

The two of us pushed with all we had and made it to the boat. Then with zero grace, I grabbed the small ladder and hauled myself up a few rungs, hanging like a limp noodle. Reaching down, I helped Bee up behind me.

A face looked down and over the edge of the boat. "What ta fuck? I didn't order me no mermaids!"

"Just taking a breather," I gasped, soaking in the sun's rays and trying to thaw myself even a little. "Then we'll swim back."

"Fine, but I think all you women be crazy!" He shook his head and promptly disappeared.

Bee let out a giggle, but I heard the fatigue in it. I reached down and gave her shoulder a gentle squeeze.

"We need to do this a few more times over the coming weeks."

"It's smart." She let out a heavy sigh. "Let's see if we can make the return trip even as tired as we are. If we have to, we can float on our backs to take a rest."

She let go of her rung and was back in the water a moment later, paddling for shore.

"Thank you!" I yelled up at the fisherman, and then dove back into the water, forgetting just how cold it was yet again.

I dove deeper than I'd have thought to, something pulling me to the depths. A pang of longing slid through me, a hunger so deep it felt like I hadn't eaten in weeks. Weird, because we'd eaten breakfast right before we came down to the beach. Then again, swimming took the stuffing out of me.

I didn't realize how long I'd been under the water, maybe a minute, before I shook myself and swam for the surface, breaking through not far from Bethany who squealed.

"You scared the shit out of me!" she swatted some water my way.

I glanced behind her at her bottom. "No, I see nothing. Not a single shit."

"Oh!" She gave me a mock glare and then we were swimming slowly back toward the shore again.

Lochlin stood nearly thigh deep in the distance now, his hands on his hips, his face tight with worry as he looked toward us and then back toward the Queen's keep. Deacon sat on the beach, leaned back on his elbows. We were close enough now that their conversation was clear across the water.

"Let the girls be, Loch. They be having a good swim. And when they get out of the water, all that cloth will be draped tight to their wee bodies. A nice show it will be."

"Knock it the fuck off, Deacon," Lochlin growled.

Another hunger pang slid through me, and I found myself wincing with the pain of it. So very strange. When we were close to shore, I started reaching with my toes for the sandy bottom, my head bobbing.

"You're too far out to stand. Keep swimming," Lochlin said just as I found firm purchase.

I stood up, only waist deep in water and tried to mimic his accent. "Really? I'd say you be wrong, laddie."

He frowned and stared not at me, but down at my feet, eyes wide as his voice pitched low, to a whisper. "Lass. Look down into the water."

I did as he said and peered straight down. Almost indistinguishable from the water, the pale blue scales were not noticeable at first. The thick tentacle had to be at least six feet across, and I...I was standing on it.

"Kraken." I whispered the word that had wedged itself into my brain.

Bee was just ahead of me, bobbing and oblivious. As she turned to look back, Lochlin grabbed her arm, and all but yanked her out of the water and up the sandy beach where Deacon caught hold of her.

Which left the kraken and I still in the watery depths.

The creature was starving—I was sure that was what I'd felt earlier—and I was about to be its good morning meal.

I was wrapped up in a split second, yanked clear out of the water and high above the beach before I could take a breath. Lochlin lunged toward me, but was grabbed as well, his arms pinned tight to his sides.

Screams erupted from the beach, the air filled with terror. I should have been freaking out, should have been so afraid I peed myself. But as the tentacle spun me around and I faced the gaping maw of the creature that looked like some sort of massive octopus with a crocodile snout in the middle of its body instead of a beak, a wave of sadness rolled over me.

Alone.

Hungry.

Afraid.

Others gone.

Family. Gone.

I closed my eyes even as Lochlin was bellowing at me to fight. I had one hand free, and I set my palm against the thick scales wrapped tight around me.

"Not alone. Don't be afraid. I hear you. Put me and my friend down. We won't hurt you." I was speaking out loud, but the words reverberated in my head as well. The warmth in my hand and in my belly rolled through me and into the creature, calming its fear.

Not alone?

Family. Here.

"I don't know, but I can try to help you find them."

The thick muscles tightened around us, and again I knew I should have been freaking out like everyone else, but I kept my palm tight to the scales.

Slowly, ever so slowly, the beast lowered Lochlin and I to the beach.

Unwrapping Lochlin first, it hesitated with me, its tentacle trembling. Reluctant, it was reluctant to let me go because I was the first soul he had communicated with in months. I kept a hand on the light blue scales. "Not alone."

"Lass, Sienna, come away from it," Lochlin croaked my name, and I held up my free hand to him.

"He's hungry," I said, unable to look away from the eyes that were now locked on me from within the bundle of tentacles. "Are there like...some old cows or something we can feed him?"

Lochlin made a choking noise, but a second later, he splashed to the shore.

"Get me my axe!"

Me, I just stood there with my hand on the sea monster's thick tentacle, emotions whipping through me.

Others, the others were gone, all dead. Starved, the young ones first, sinking to the bottom of the ocean as the water grew too cold and then too hot. Food sources were scarce at best. Weeks since he'd fed last, coming into the harbor had been a last-ditch effort. Sensed the soul of one who might understand.

I swallowed hard, feeling the creature's fears as he clung lightly to me. He didn't want to hurt me.

"Sienna, come away."

And suddenly, it was Dominic's voice, calling to me...cutting through the cord attaching me to the sea monster.

"He's hungry. I think if we feed him, he will calm." I turned just my head to look at Dominic, seeing the sun glint off his sweating face. Blisters appearing on his cheeks.

He was well within reach of the sea monster now and closing in, sword in hand. "He is a kraken, deadly as they come, and I can't strike with you that close. Come away before—"

"He is alone and afraid and young," I said, seeing but not processing that Dominic was up to his chest in water, as the sun sizzled his skin, right before my very eyes. I was in a trance and I just couldn't shake it.

"How can you possibly know that?" His voice was getting weaker, but still he persisted. "Move, damn you!"

Frowning, I turned back to the monster at hand, knowing that he wasn't nearly as bad as some of the other monsters I'd met.

Not nearly as bad as Edmund or Anthony.

"Because he told me so."

CHAPTER 17

Dominic

20 minutes earlier...

"N o response from the Duchess yet, I assume?" I said from my new seat. The Queen of the werewolves had brought me up to a sitting room in her private quarters and set my chains into the wall. I couldn't help but wonder if the chains had been added just for the occasion or if they were there for other reasons.

"She has not sent word yet, and that is concerning to me," Diana sat across from me, her desk between us. Solid wood and charred around the edges like it had been in a fire at some point.

I frowned. "How long does she normally take to answer you?"

"Three days, never more, never less. She always has the same messenger as well." Diana's dark eyes flicked over me. "I'm of a mind to take you back to the edge of our territories and send you to look for her."

I kept my face still, knowing that she was leading me somewhere. One did not survive the vampire court without recognizing that you could and would be pushed in directions by those with more power than you. The trick was always to let them believe that they were doing the leading.

"Well, I'd rather not, seeing as my head would be on the first pike that Edmund could find."

Besides, I'd finally reunited with Sienna and Will. There was no chance of me leaving them again.

"Perhaps you would end up dead, but that's just as likely if you stay here. There are packs calling for your head now. If you were to bring the Duchess here and perhaps prove you are a man of loyalty in some way...maybe that would be worth your life."

It was as much as Lochlin had said the night before. The Queen would test me, which was fine. The sooner the better.

"You want to possess Sienna," Diana said, changing the subject before I could respond. Statement, not a question. "But you cannot truly love a woman. You aren't any more capable of it than any of your kind. Don't pretend otherwise."

Was she right? I'd never thought in terms of that emotion before so I wasn't sure, but I didn't like the direction this discussion was taking.

"I would protect her with my life. As I would and have done for my brother." I let out a grunt. "Can we cut to the chase? Why did you bring me up here? And why so damn chatty all of a sudden?"

Her smile was tight. "You're awfully cocky for a prisoner in chains."

Diana rose and went to the wide picture window. My chains allowed me enough room to stand and move beside her. The sun cast a long beam across my legs, but I barely felt the heat of it through my pants. My eyes were drawn to the figures hurrying toward the beach.

Bethany and Sienna with their heads together. Red and blonde. I cocked my head as Diana spoke again.

"I do not trust her any more than I trust you. But she is not dangerous like you, so it is easy to give her freedom. Though I think she has some...abilities...that I would like to understand better."

I swallowed hard, still tasting Sienna on my mouth. Were the two of them going for a swim? I watched, unable to look away as Sienna and Bethany stripped out of their dresses and ran for the water.

"What's going on here?" I growled.

"Sienna has claimed she is loyal as well. But I don't believe her anymore. She and her maid are planning an escape—as if I could miss the questions, the little bits of food and clothing being tucked away." Diana snorted. "Was she this obvious in your kingdom?"

I shook my head, my mouth going dry as they swam deeper. "No."

Diana tucked her hands behind her back and stared out the window. "Then she thinks less of us, that we can be more easily fooled than your kind." There was no mistake that the Queen considered that a slight.

"I doubt it," I said, trying to ignore the building sense of dread in my gut. "You give her freedom, and that would make you an ally in her mind. I am her enemy. I helped keep her caged." I spoke the words and knew that they were true, much as they grated on me.

"Well, I hope you said goodbye to her."

I jerked my head toward the Queen. "Why?"

"Because that boat there will take them back to the mainland, no questions asked if they make it on board," she said. "I want no one here that isn't loyal, that isn't trustworthy."

My guts climbed into my throat even as Sienna climbed the ladder. Bethany made it part way up with her.

"Free me." It wasn't a request, but Diana just stared at me, one brow arched.

"Free me," I repeated, louder this time, straining against my shackles. "You know what will happen if she tries to return to the mainland."

"You cannot stop her. It's full sunlight, General..."

I was through talking. I closed my eyes and gathered every bit of my strength, Sienna's face in the forefront of my mind.

I let out a roar and yanked with all my might. The very walls shook, a hairline crack creeping up the stonework, but the chains did not give.

"General, stop. If you go out there, you're as good as dead."

I yanked again, muscles straining as I fought for freedom.

"Stop this, right now," Diana shouted, standing in front of me and grabbing my chin in her hand. "You've passed the test. Look outside. She's already swimming back. I just needed to make sure that you weren't lying to me and that you were as loyal as they say."

I whipped my head toward the window and sure enough, Sienna and Bee were already nearing the shore once again. But a dark shape appeared behind them, so large, it could've been the shadow of an oil tanker.

Diana froze and the sudden silence between us was absolute. I'm not sure either of us was breathing as the scene below us changed from one of political posturing to life and death.

The creature that swam through the depths was barely visible, even from up high as we were. Body and tentacles were covered in a coloring that made it perfectly camouflaged as it reached Sienna.

"Dear Gods," Diana whispered, but I barely heard her as the creature wrapped around Sienna, and lifted her from the water. I thrashed against the chains, pulling for all I was worth, but already knowing it was not enough. Sienna herself had made sure that I was heavily bound, not knowing it would mean her death.

"Diana, free me!" I roared the three words as I spun back to the window. Sienna was still high in the air and now so was Lochlin.

"You can't save her, General!" she yelled back, her eyes wide with horror. "No one can stop a kraken!"

We locked eyes for all of a split second and then she strode to my side, her hands on the cuffs at my wrists and I was free. I grabbed her sword resting on her desk and ran straight for the window, bursting out of it and free falling to the ground three stories down to land in a crouch.

There was no time. Not with the heat of the sun blasting at me like a fucking furnace. It would take minutes at best before I was toast.

Screams lit up around me but I focused on only one thing.

Getting to Sienna.

My eyes watered as I ran, the sun blistering every part of me that was exposed, but I didn't stop. Couldn't. I hit the water and Sienna was there, the tentacle still near her. I raised my sword, barely able to see.

I pleaded with her to come away but her voice was dreamy, out of touch. As if she were not really with us.

"He is alone and afraid and young." Her body seemed to sway toward the kraken even as she looked at me. But I don't think she was truly seeing me.

"How can you possibly know that?" I demanded, holding my hand out to her. Time, I was running short of it, feeling the sun eat away at me. "Move, damn you!"

"Because he told me so."

There was nothing to do for it. I dropped the sword, leapt over the tentacle and grabbed hold of Sienna, hauling her out of the water and up the beach.

Hands were on me in a split second, pulling me even as I dragged her. I let out a hiss as my skin peeled away in sheets beneath those hands.

"Dom!" Lochlin's voice was right there. "Christ on a donkey, man! Are you insane?"

I could barely think straight. All I could do was hang onto Sienna and try to keep moving, stumbling back toward the castle.

"Here, you dumb shit!" Lochlin snarled and a moment later we were under the cover of a tree, the shade hitting what was left of my exposed skin like a rush of ice water. I couldn't help the groan that slid out of me.

"Dominic!" Sienna's voice curled around me, no longer out of touch.

I managed to open my eyes, feeling myself sliding, feeling myself...drifting. The agony I'd felt before was only on the periphery of my senses now, which was bad. Pain meant you were alive when you were injured. No pain...that did not bode well at all.

I lifted a hand.

"Sienna. I...don't leave." Gods above and below, was that truly me? Begging a woman to stay with me?

"I'm here, I'm not going anywhere." She bent over me, whispering softly to me. "Dominic, how do we help you?"

My lips twitched, but that sent a shiver of discomfort through me, the skin crackling around my mouth as I moved. Not good. None of this was good.

"Just stay."

I closed my eyes, feeling darkness sweeping up and over me. A darkness I had escaped for many, many years. Death was coming for me, I could feel it pressing against my body in all directions, laughing at me. All the battles I'd faced, all the danger I'd escaped, and I was dying over a woman.

Her wet hair fell forward and brushed against my face. "Dominic, please."

Her whimper cut through me and wanted to tell her that I'd stay, that there would be no going. That I would hold her forever. But really, it was bound to happen. Either I would die, or she would, and we'd be parted. She was human, I was a vampire. I could never keep her forever.

"Shh, shh." Her lips were against the side of my face, so gentle. They should have hurt, but they felt...good. Cooling.

There were so many things I wanted to say to her, so many things I wanted to do, but there was no time left. If I had known the night before, I would have told her how I felt. What I wanted and, for the first time in my life, dreamed of. My tongue was thick, and I could not speak. But that spot at my temple, it spread, the sensation of cooling on my blistering skin soothing and easing the pain until a sigh slid from me. My final thoughts were of Sienna and how easily I could answer Diana's question now, just minutes after she'd asked it.

If this was not love, I didn't know what was.

CHAPTER 18

Sienna

"**W**hat the hell was he thinking?" I hissed as I rose and stepped back from Dominic's bedside.

"You keep asking me that, and I don't have an answer for you," Will murmured, still standing vigil in the corner of the room as he had been for the past three hours. "I can only imagine he saw you out there and wasn't thinking at all. He just...acted."

My legs were trembling with fatigue, and I could barely think straight, but that didn't mean I wasn't going to kill Dominic when he woke up.

If he woke up.

A shaft of pain lodged itself in my chest as I chased those thoughts away. Surely, a little sunburn wouldn't fell the General of the Vampire Army. He was invincible, damn it. Or near to it, anyway...

As I spared him another glance, though, I couldn't help but flinch. Who was I kidding? This was no mere sunburn. Our planet's closest star had nearly roasted Dom's flesh from his bones before we'd managed to shield him. The only reason he hadn't died on the spot was because I'd done...

Something.

I still wasn't sure what. Laid my hands on him, and babbled words that had no meaning. Rocked back and forth like I was in a low budget remake of the Exorcist as some strange and terrifying force flowed through me, turning me inside out. And when I'd awakened, I'd found myself in this room in a cot beside Dominic's bed with a headache worse than if I'd spent the night with Jose Cuervo and several of his meanest friends.

As for Dom? Well, he was recognizable now instead of resembling something you might scrape off the bottom of a grill at a Fourth of July barbecue. According to Bee, I was a real Florence Nightingale.

The question was, had it been enough?

"Maybe my blood?"

"You're already so weak from the energy you expended healing him. Let's give it a little more time."

"What if he doesn't have more time?"

"He's not getting worse, his color is good. I think he just needs some rest. He's going to pull through this."

I'd spent enough time with Will now to know that he was the eternal optimist. Still, in my deepest of hearts, I prayed that he was right. If Dominic died trying to save me from a kraken I could've walked away from all on my own at any point, I'd never forgive myself.

I tried in vain to think back on my time with the creature, but it was all so fuzzy. Like I was in some sort of fugue state. I remembered hearing Lochlin calling for me....knew Dom was there, on some level, but I couldn't marry my perception with my memories. Couldn't think critically or grasp that him being in the sun like that would kill him.

"I wish he'd just wake up, already. Even if it's just to yell at me."

"If he wakes up, it's only because you saved him, Sienna."

Bee's low voice had me turning my head toward the doorway where she stood peering in.

"You should've seen it. I still can't believe it. I watched his flesh heal, right before my eyes. Muscle and tissue reforming. Charred skin turning pink with life." Bee eyed me with something close to awe...mixed with fear. "It was a bloody miracle."

I stared down at my hands, still in disbelief.

How?

Sure, I'd healed Havoc, and helped Will with the bloodworm sickness. But this?

This was something else entirely.

Bee cleared her throat and stepped fully into the room, pointedly ignoring Will.

"Anyway, I just came back in to tell you that Diana wants to speak with you in her study as soon as possible."

I nodded, and she melted away, leaving me and Will alone with Dom again.

"After the shit-show out there, I can only imagine she wants to be debriefed." I was surprised she'd given me this long before sending down the royal summons.

"Why don't you take a hot bath, have a quick bite to regain your strength, and then go speak to her? I can watch over my brother."

I hesitated, eyeing him suspiciously. "Okay, but promise you'll—"

"I'll come get you the moment he awakens," the young prince cut in with a weary, half-smile.

I didn't want to go, but hovering over Dominic, watching for any hint of movement like some sort of ghoul wasn't helping the situation any, either. Besides, I needed some answers and could only hope the Queen would provide them.

Sparing one last glance at Dom, I headed out of the room to my chambers. Bee was there, sitting in a chair beside the window, staring out into darkness.

"I feel like I'm losing it, Sienna."

I had to strain to hear her, and then wished I hadn't. I just didn't have the bandwidth to navigate her existential crisis right now.

"It's going to be okay, Bee. It was a scary day and—"

"They've all been scary days since you came!" She turned her teary blue eyes on me and shook her head. "One after another. It just doesn't stop. And I'm right there beside you, like some numpty, rifling through Hunter leftovers looking for some girl whose fate is none of my business, and running from the Vampire Prince straight into Werewolf Territory, only to be tossed into a kraken's lair so the Queen can test your powers." She stood and pointed a trembling finger straight at my chest. "But the thing you don't get is, I don't have any powers, Sienna. I'm just me. Bethany, the maid. A human, of flesh and bone, and I don't think I can almost die again without completely losing my mind. It needs to stop. You need to stop."

Some part of me wanted to deploy my defense mechanisms. Hit her with a, 'Damn. Tell me how you really feel, Bee.' Strike back with some straw man argument, or protest how none of this was my fault. But how could I when she was so freaking right?

"I'm sorry."

"I know you are. You always are," she mumbled, the anger seeming to drain away as she moved toward me and lowered her hand. "And I'm not even mad at you. Not really. I just need some space. From you. From Will. From everything while I come to grips with exactly how fragile and useless I am in this world. I've asked Diana if I could have a room in the west wing of the keep and she agreed."

Her words struck another blow to my already aching heart. My one friend in this place besides Jordan didn't want to be anywhere near me. I pulled myself together.

"Bee, please. I don't care about the room change or the rest of it, but you're not useless. You can't possibly believe that."

She rushed past me to the door and then turned. "I'll pack up my things when you leave to meet the Queen."

Then she was gone.

In a perfect end to a perfect day.

It was only in the tub a short while later, when I was wiping away the last of the grime and salt water, that something she said came back to mind and sank in the second time around.

Tossed into a kraken's lair so the Queen could test my powers? Surely not...

But as I thought back to how our morning started, I couldn't shake Bee's words.

Lochlin, strolling in out of the blue, offering up a picnic at the queen's request, taking us straight to the shore on a stifling day. I shot up, sending water sloshing onto the floor.

"That bastard! He knew!"

I barely took the time to dry off before yanking on the pants Bee had mended along with my shirt and vest. Then, I pinned my wet hair into a knot and raced headlong down the corridor, not stopping until I reached Diana's study.

I rapped twice but didn't wait to be invited in. She was sitting behind her desk hunched over a leather bound tome, but looked up in surprise as I entered.

"Did you set me up?"

Twin flags of anger unfurled on her cheeks and she straightened.

"Close the door behind you, and mind your tone."

I turned and yanked the door shut with a satisfying crack.

"Did you set me up, *Your Majesty*?" I asked again, but sweetly this time, with a tooth-gritting smile.

She blew out a sigh and waved for me to sit, which I did.

"I didn't set you up. I..." she waved at the air casually, "orchestrated a scenario in which I could assess both your mettle and Dominic's sense of loyalty. You both passed, for what it's worth."

It was only my soul-deep exhaustion that kept me from leaping over the desk and testing *her* mettle as I stared at her in horror.

"We could've died. All of us. Me, Bee, Dominic, Lochlin...He *agreed* to this?"

Diana studied a spot on the wall behind me, having the grace to look mildly chagrined. "It wasn't supposed to happen like that. You were supposed to go for a swim and Dominic was supposed to see you heading for the boats. That was all. Loch and Deacon were there to save you if the cold got to you or the swim became too treacherous."

"And the fucking kraken? You just thought you'd cross your fingers that he'd be all chill with that idea?" I demanded incredulously.

"There's never been a kraken in those waters," she shot back with a glare. "They're a deep-sea creature. I have no idea what it was doing so close to shore. Besides, there hasn't even been a sighting of one in the past decade. I thought they'd gone extinct."

At least I could confirm that part of her explanation was likely true. The kraken itself had told me as much. But I wasn't sure that absolved her of wrongdoing.

"You knew that if Dominic saw me in trouble, he'd come for me. Into the sun, unprotected. Now he's lying in that room in some sort of coma, and I'm—" *Don't cry. Don't you dare cry right now.* "And I'm sitting here listening to the woman who claimed to be my ally tell me this was on purpose?" I bit my lip and struggled to control the tenuous hold I had on my emotions. "Did you see what it did to him? Can you imagine the agony, Diana?"

Apparently, I wasn't the only one all up in my feelings, because she stood up and swiped the books off her desk in one motion. "I don't need to imagine it! I've felt it's equal, alright, Sienna?"

She leaned over the desk so far, I could feel her breath on my face.

"So spare me the lecture on agony, and for the love of the gods, watch. Your. Tone."

Her energy was dangerous, as if she were on the edge of wolfing out on me. Fuck, that was the last thing I needed. Once more, I pulled up my big girl panties and bit out words that I'd have rather shouted at her.

"Roger that."

I zipped my lip and threw the key away for good measure. When she finally sat down again, she ran a hand over her still-neatly coiffed hair.

"I know it didn't work out as I planned. I wanted to see how he reacted to the idea of you escaping, knowing the journey would be fraught with danger. I tried to stop him before he leapt out the damned window, but the kraken definitely...complicated things. This wasn't for naught, though."

"Because we passed?" I asked, trying to keep the sarcasm from my voice and failing.

"That. And also because the assembly of the clans is set for tomorrow afternoon. Word will spread about this like wildfire. It's already begun. The story is passing from clan to clan, and soon the whole territory will know. You're not just some human who was dumb enough to get caught up in a sweep. You are something else. Something special. And so long as you're alive, Dominic and his brother will remain by your side. Loyal to you. Loyal to our shared cause to take down Edmund and restore The Veil."

When she said it that way...

"Okay, so some unintended potential good came of it." Now it was time to see if the tiny bit of hand she'd given me held any sway. "But nothing like that can ever happen again, Your Majesty. If Bethany, Will, Dominic, or myself are ever put in a situation like that again, our association is over. Are we clear?"

She looked like she wanted to argue, but then just nodded her head.

"I've learned what I needed to know. If I need something further from you all, it will be done with your knowledge and permission."

The next request was dicier. "As for the kraken... He isn't evil, you know. He's just lonely and hungry. I wonder if you can maybe have some food set out for him? He might be the last of his kind, which is tragic. And he's probably much safer to have around if he's well fed."

Diana's nostrils flared but then she nodded wearily. "I'm not one for luring deadly sea monsters to our shores, but I'll set something up to help as safely as I can, and I'll warn the clans to avoid swimming in the harbor for the time being."

I let out a shuddering breath of relief. "Thank you. And, now, for the million dollar question..." I sat forward, on the edge of my seat. "If I'm not human, then what the hell am I?"

She was quiet long enough that I wasn't sure she would answer me. The tension rose and flowed in the room, tightening around my neck until I thought it would strangle me before she finally spoke.

"I've spent the past few hours consulting book after book, and I have to admit it." She shrugged her lean shoulders, clearly frustrated. "I'm stumped, Sienna. A healer? A conduit for animals to be heard? I can't find record of anything like you."

Which explained the reprieve. Diana had been busy herself trying to untangle what had happened today. Both out there on the water between me and the kraken, and here afterward as I'd healed Dominic.

"So I've called in someone to help."

As if on cue, the door swung open and crashed into the wall.

A blur of movement that I couldn't follow.

Dominic was on the Queen in a flash, the letter opener from her desk pressed to her neck before my eyes could even detect his motions.

"Give me one reason I shouldn't kill you right now, you crazy bitch."

CHAPTER 19

Dominic

"Dominic!" Sienna cried, rising to stand, I could see her just out of the corner of my eye.

Will came rushing into the room and skidded to a stop as he stared at me in horror. "Bloody hell, Dom. Put down that blade and step away from her."

I shook my head and held my ground. "She allowed Sienna into the harbor with a fucking kraken."

Will swiped at his nose, which was still bleeding from where I'd cuffed him when he tried to stop me. "Your Majesty, please forgive my brother. That prolonged time in the sun has clearly addled his mind. He knows not what he does."

Despite the blade at her throat, Diana appeared remarkably calm, which only enraged me further.

The Queen held my gaze, sounding more annoyed than afraid as she replied. "Still, it's easy to see who inherited the diplomatic gene from your father. And the brains, apparently."

I let out a grunt as something poked me in the belly, hard.

"Did you really think yourself so much faster than me, so much stronger that you could just rush into my private space like an enraged bull and put a knife to my throat without suffering the same fate you had planned for me, General?" she asked, her voice deceptively soft. "Right now, I have a Glock g-17 nine-millimeter pistol cocked and pointed at your sweetbreads, but I can easily change targets and blow your fucking balls off, if you rather."

The gut was one thing, but the threat to my balls had me wincing. No point in being hasty... Sienna was here, and seemed both physically unharmed and calm enough, thank the Gods. Maybe I should at least hear Diana out.

I slowly lifted both hands in temporary surrender.

"Good. Now what say you take a seat, and we can pretend your kind aren't bloodthirsty savages and try to talk this through, hmm?" she cocked her head, brows raised in question as she regarded me the way one would a five-year old in the midst of a temper tantrum.

She laid the gun on the desk before her, and I followed suit, setting the wickedly sharp letter opener beside it.

"Apparently, I should've ignored my sympathies and chained you again, despite your grisly injuries," Diana observed lightly as I took a seat in the chair beside Sienna, and Will selected the one closest to the door. "In my defense, I didn't expect you to be quite so... energetic this quickly, even with Sienna's amazing healing powers."

The last thing I remembered was searing, white-hot pain and the sound of muffled voices, barely audible through what was left of my ears as I was dragged through the sand. Then, it was like time ceased to exist. No dreams, no nightmares, just an empty void in my memory, until I sat up in a strange bed to find Will staring at me.

"You did this?" I turned to Sienna, who had retaken her seat, and stared at her. "I'd have known if I drank from you. How?" For the first time since I lurched back to consciousness only a short time before, I looked down at my hands. Gone was the blackened skin and melting flesh. It wasn't just better. It was as if it had never happened. "How did you do it?"

She shook her head and wrapped her arms around her waist. "I wish I could answer that. I have no idea. It's like, something takes hold of me, and I get this weird surge of energy—I honestly can't believe you're standing here right now. It was so bad, Dom. I was sure you were—" she broke off and let out a hiss as she faced Diana again. "There's got to be some information about this. Somewhere in all these books that you just haven't found yet, or maybe in one of the other Territories? The fae know a lot about...magical shit or whatever, right?"

"We'll get to that soon enough. Let's catch your General here up to speed before he blows another gasket." Sienna nodded reluctantly, and the Queen continued, "I do apologize for how things unfolded. It wasn't my intention at all. Lochlin suggested a test of loyalty as a way to expedite matters. I agreed. In order to ensure he didn't spill the beans, what with his own affections being split and you being childhood friends and all, I decided to do it sooner than later."

I already figured most of that out, but that didn't explain how she'd rolled the dice with Sienna's life by allowing her to enter the water at all if there were krakens in the area.

"She didn't know the kraken was in the harbor. And he shouldn't be. They're nearly extinct," Sienna added, clearly sensing that Diana's explanation so far was doing nothing to cool my anger. "Loch and Deacon were there to help in the event something did go wrong, sparing you the sun exposure. She couldn't have known it would be something they couldn't help with."

I chewed on that for a long while, and the room was silent but for the ticking of the grandfather clock in the corner of the study.

"Dom?" Will prodded gently. "I know you're still pissed, but the well-being of all the wolves in this territory rests on Diana's shoulders. If the shoe were on the other foot—"

"Spare me the glad-handing, brother. I'm lucky I even have a foot to speak of. Do you know I felt my boots literally melding with my ankle bones from the sun out there?"

Sienna swayed in her seat, cheeks going pale, and I sucked in a steadying breath.

"Alright. Okay, let's say you did what you had to do, Your Majesty. Can I safely assume that you won't be...testing us any further?"

Diana folded her hands primly on the desk in front of her. "As I already explained to Sienna, I have the information I needed. If I need anything else from you, I'll ask. Are we good here, General?"

Good was probably overstating it, but I was past the point of fantasizing about ways to kill her, so I nodded.

"Excellent. Now we can talk about my guest." She bent low and plucked a large, leather-bound book from the floor, dusting it off with a glance at Sienna. "When you first arrived, I sent word to Myrr, the Oracle of The Veil, begging for an audience with her. I wasn't sure she would come, but I got word from my guards at the northern border that she's en route. She should be here any time now. If anyone can tell us more about Sienna's magic, it's her."

Will and I exchanged a glance. The Oracle of The Veil was a relic who lived in a hut near the ruins in the most central part of the Empire of Magic, just north of the wolves. For centuries, her prophecies held sway over everything from commerce and political matters, to wars and alliances. Her last accurate prediction had been the falling of The Veil fifteen years ago.

Since then?

Nothing.

Given the lackluster decade and a half of underbaked guesses, and words of hope that felt more like platitudes than prophecy, I didn't share Diana's confidence in Myrr's ability to solve the riddle of Sienna's powers. But there was no Plan B at the moment, so I wasn't about to argue.

"It's probably best if you go and prepare for her arrival."

I was about to ask what she meant by that, but then followed her pointed glance at my naked chest. When I'd come to, I'd been wearing nothing but a pair of pants that were nipping at my ankles they were so short. My own clothes had disintegrated in the fire...

Except the boots.

I shot a look at Sienna, still not sure how she'd managed to fix that. Or fix any of me, really.

"Right. If you can send something up to my room in my size?" I said, turning my attention back to Diana.

"I'll have someone get right on it."

I stayed seated but Diana stared at me expectantly.

"You and your brother are free to go now. I need to fill Sienna in about Myrr before she gets here."

I'd been hoping to get a few minutes alone with Sienna myself, but that clearly wasn't going to happen any time soon. She seemed off. Not herself at all, and who could blame her? It had been a traumatic day for her and all I wanted to do was scoop her into my arms, carry her to bed and hold her for a while.

Instead, I stood and joined Will, who had made his way to the door.

"Thank you, Your Majesty," he murmured, bowing deeply. "I truly appreciate you not shooting my knobhead of a brother, and again, I apologize for his behavior."

Diana was already focused on showing Sienna something in the book she was holding as we closed the door behind us and started down the corridor.

"You don't need to apologize for me," I snarled under my breath as we walked.

"Oh, how I wish that were true, brother mine," Will muttered back. "I can't wait until we're both back to full health so we can spar again. As happy as I am that you survived, it seems your face is in desperate need of punching."

"Better bring a friend."

We jawed back and forth that way until we reached my new bedroom, which, upon further inspection, was a huge step up from the previous one. An actual king-sized bed, a window with a view, and no shackles.

Clothes were already waiting for me on an armchair in the corner, which was only slightly disturbing, as I made my way toward the bathroom to take a quick shower. The burning had stopped, but the stench of roasting flesh clung to me and I couldn't wait to be rid of it. If only I could rinse away the memory of seeing Sienna in the grasp of that kraken, I'd be right as rain.

I stopped and turned to face Will. "What say once Myrr leaves, we raid the Queen's liquor cabinet and get piss-drunk?"

It was only then that I realized he had a haunted look about him and the only color on his face was the spot of blood that had dried under his nose.

"I'm trying to keep up with your mood, but I'm struggling right now, Dom."

"Everything is fine. We're all alive, aren't we? That's better than the oddsmakers down at the Boar and Blade would've pegged us for a week ago, right?"

Will cleared his throat and nodded. "Right. You're right. It's all fine." He turned to go and then stopped. "If you could make sure the next time you run out into the blazing sunshine that I'm not around to witness the aftermath though, that'd be super."

By the time I got down to the great hall a half hour later, Will and Diana were already there, seated side by side in front of a massive, octagonal table.

I took a seat across from them, and eyed them expectantly.

"Where are the others?"

"I made Sienna at least try to get down some soup and Myrr is—"

"Here and accounted for!" a rusty voice called moments before a stooped figure entered the room. "Greetings, young ones."

Her face was hidden by the black cloak she wore, but there was no mistaking her jerky gait.

We all stood by tacit agreement as she made her way slowly toward the table. Will pulled out the chair beside Diana, and the crone took it with a murmur of thanks. She unbuttoned the front of her heavy cloak and pulled a whole roast chicken from beneath it and set it on the bare, oak table with an oily *thump*.

She shrugged off her cloak and turned to Diana. "I hope you don't mind, child. I snitched a snack from the kitchen. It's been ages since I've had any meat besides possum, if you can believe it." She faced me and closed one milky eye in a broad wink. "I don't get out much anymore."

I'd seen paintings of her when I was a child, and heard tales of her over the years, but nothing could've prepared me for Myrr in the flesh. Her skin was crackled like aged parchment, and it was a surprise that she could see at all. But the thing that hit me hardest was the way her neck and back were misshapen and twisted beneath her shift dress, like the gnarled limbs of a mangrove tree.

"Hot as all the be-damned out there, Princess. Doesn't bode well for the future generation at all, does it?"

Diana tried not to stare as she nodded her agreement, choosing not to correct Myrr on her title. "It does not, Your Eminence."

The Oracle let out a cackle as she unceremoniously tore a leg off the bird. "You don't need to bother with all that anymore, dear. My ability to see the future has long been extinguished. My guess is because The Empire has no future to see. Which is fine by me. I've been here long enough. Maybe too long, according to some." She sank her teeth into the chicken with a contented sigh. "I'm glad I stuck around for this, though. Is that rosemary I detect?"

Diana and Will exchanged a worried look, and it was all I could do not to laugh. In a week where nothing had gone right, on a quest where nothing had come easy, they both still managed to convince themselves that *this* was going to be it. The one thing that went our way.

Adorable.

"I...I think it might be, yes," Diana said carefully. "Would you like me to send for some mashed potatoes as well? Maybe some glazed carrots, and bread?"

Myrr clapped her greasy hands together with glee. "That would be lovely, thank you."

Diana pressed a button on the arm of her chair and less than a minute later, the requested food arrived. Myrr ate with relish as the queen attempted to get some answers.

"There is a young woman. Her name is Sienna, and she has powers like I've never seen before. I am hoping you can help us understand what she is capable of."

For the next ten minutes, we all took turns filling the Oracle in on anything we knew about Sienna. The bits and pieces Will had picked up on their journey here, the stuff she'd told me, and everything Diana had gleaned from their conversations since she arrived. She just finished explaining about the kraken when Myrr sat back and let out a long, loud belch.

"A feast, and a story. I'm blessed today, indeed. But I can't help you," she said, eyeing the empty plate before pushing it away with a sigh of regret. "I'm as mundane as the fowl I just ate. I can remember the past just fine, but the future...even insofar as if I'll make it to tomorrow, is a mystery to me as much as it is you."

Diana pursed her lips and laid her forearms on the table, leaning forward. "Alright, then something from the past, maybe? Surely, there's been someone...something like her?"

Myrr's only reply was a shrug of her lopsided shoulders.

I lifted my head suddenly, scenting the air.

Sienna.

"I'm so sorry I'm late, everyone," she said as she swept into the room. "I was feeling a bit weak but I'm much better now that I ate something. You must be Myrr," she continued as she reached the table and caught sight of the Oracle.

If she was off-put by her appearance, she didn't show it. It was Myrr's reaction that caught my attention.

Gone was the impish smile and the carefree banter. She'd gone stock-still and was staring at Sienna like she'd seen a ghost. The eyes that had been milky blue began to swirl, turning a crystal-clear shade of bottle green.

"*The first of five keys, to bend the land, to break the trees and steal the sand.*

Then shall the path lay bare before, once more to walk between the doors.

Of death and life, of sun and rain.

Should one of five fall, then shall the world's heart be in vain."

CHAPTER 20

Sienna

The Oracle's words kind of reverberated through the room, as if the misshapen old woman had set off a bomb rather than just muttered a few lines of prose. The bomb, if you will, left everyone silent for a good ten seconds, a long time when all eyes are on you.

"Keys to what?" I managed to get the words out, though just barely.

Myrr blinked, her eyes almost owlish now as she stared at me. "Fucked if I know. It's been so long since a prophecy has come through me, I can't believe I was able to give you that much."

Beside me, Dominic tensed, his energy spiking, and I was surprised he kept his mouth shut. Or maybe it was just that Diana beat him to it.

"I think...that perhaps now is the time to rest, Sienna. It has been a long and trying day for everyone involved." Her eyes swept over me as she motioned at me with her chin to move me along. "We will discuss this tomorrow morning."

The Oracle sniffed and took a few steps closer to me so that I could smell the wild scents rolling off her. Greenery and soil, the bite of a sharp wind, they seemed to be what held her together. "Rest, indeed."

Just that. And yet I felt the threat behind the two words as clearly as if she'd shouted them at me. *Rest now for your time is coming to be put to the test.* Look at me go, I could be an oracle myself, thinking in rhyme.

Without a word, I spun on my heel and left the room as if it was my idea and not Diana's. Mostly because I didn't want anyone to see the truth of it. That I was fucking *snockered* beyond reason and that Myrr's stupid prophecy had seemed to sap the rest of what little energy I had.

"Sienna," Dominic called, and my feet slowed without any conscious thought from me. The hall wobbled and fuzzed as I did a long slow blink. I put a hand out and caught myself against the rough-hewn wall.

"Dominic, I cannot fight, or argue, or...anything else with you right now," I slurred the words as if I'd been drinking. Or as if I were sick and fighting a fever.

"We need to get you to bed." He wrapped an arm around my waist without an invitation and all but lifted me from the floor as he led me down the hall. My head lolled and rather than fight it, I let myself melt against him.

"You're the injured one," I said, managing to look up at him. He was clean now, and didn't smell of burnt clothing or...flesh.

His skin was pale, a bit pink in places that I could see, but it was almost as if there was no injury to him at all. As if the sun had never seared him to the bone.

And I'd done that.

I was the key to something...that I didn't want to be the key to.

A tear trickled down my cheek and his eyes shot to me immediately. "Don't cry, starshine, don't cry."

"Starshine?" I stared up at him.

His lips curved, softening his hard features. "The most beautiful light that exists, for it brightens even the darkest moments. It brings hope to the hopeless. You are...starshine. Of that I am certain."

My lips wobbled and the tears flowed faster. Why couldn't he just keep being a macho asshole? His words, his gentle touch, the energy rolling off him. I didn't want to feel like this, not for him. Not for us.

He half carried me down the hall to a room that was not mine, and let himself in. A large bed across from us was draped in black curtains, the room's windows were done in the same.

"Here." Dominic set me on the bed, then bent to one knee. For a weird panicked moment, I thought he was going to propose. I mean, after everything that had happened, what could cap off a day so strange, so unexpected? But he didn't pull out a diamond. He just pulled my boots off, one at a time, cupping my ankle gently, his fingers sliding down to my heels.

I couldn't stop the giggle that escaped me. He looked up, eyebrow quirked. "My lady?"

"Nothing, just...my mind is tired and you on one knee had me worried."

Worried.

What would I have said if he'd asked me to marry him? No. Of course I'd say no. I was leaving, eventually. He was a vampire. And he never would have asked. It all was impossible, and that in itself stole the giddiness from my body.

"You need to sleep," he reminded gently, helping me swing my legs into the bed.

"Stay with me," I was looking up at him, his profile outlined even in the shadows of the room. "Not for...I just don't want to be alone. Please."

Dominic didn't waste time answering. He just slipped in beside me, pulling my body tight to his. "I will not argue." He kissed the crook of my shoulder and kept his mouth there, as if breathing me in.

A part of me wanted to give him shit for running into the sun, to rescue me. Because...well because I didn't want him risking his neck to rescue me. Not ever. But I'd need energy for that conversation, to give him the tongue lashing that he deserved. There was not even the energy to ask him to have Will check on Bethany, to make sure she was okay.

Instead, I rolled in his arms so I could tuck my face into the crook of his neck and breathe in his smell.

"Sleep, starshine, and we will talk later." He kissed my forehead and I let out a long sigh, all the tension leaving me as I sunk into the sleep my body so desperately craved.

I wish I could say it was dreamless and restful—the two things I needed. But I wasn't so lucky.

I blinked and was standing in the middle of a daisy field. The flowers bobbed and danced in the wind, brushing against my fingertips, they were so tall. I did a slow turn. The daisies went as far as I could see, all the way to the edge of the blue sky. I was wearing white, a loose boho gown that flowed around my body, the sleeves were sheer and billowed to where they were tied at my wrists.

The scene was beautiful and serene and yet I felt nothing but a bone deep fear as I stared out across the vast sea of flowers bobbing and dancing in the wind, not a care in the world. I took a step and the ground beneath my feet shivered. The sky flickered as the sun dimmed and clouds rolled toward me from far in the distance.

Storm winds whipped toward me, flattening my dress to my body, the smell of fires heavy in the air. I lifted a hand to shade my eyes as the daisies around me were blown back, as if the storm would remove them from their stems by sheer force. I took another step and another and another, straight into the storm.

The daisies around me were starting to fall now as I walked. Some being blown free, some laying flat to the ground. Some shriveling up. They were breaking under the sheer force of the weather, petals and stems, leaves and roots being torn and thrown about.

I blinked.

Between one second and the next, everything changed. The daisies were no longer daisies, but bodies.

Bodies dashed to the ground, broken and discarded as if they had been thrown there by some giant playing horseshoes. The smell of blood, of viscera and fire whipped around me, infusing every part of me.

I blinked and the body at my feet was Bee. Her blue eyes empty, staring sightless and accusing.

"You did this. Always sorry. But always your fault."

"No, no, no, no," I whimpered as the bodies began to take shape in more detail, clothing faces I knew. People I cared for. I turned, trying to get away. But they were all around me.

Will. Jordan. The Duchess. Diana. Lochlin. Deacon. The stable boy, Timmy. Myrr. And...Dominic. His lifeless eyes stared up at the empty sky, his throat slit and dried blood, black as night, coating his too-pale skin.

The scream that crawled up my throat caught as a shard of lightning leapt from the sky and touched down amongst the bodies around me. They lit as if they were tinder dry kindling, flames erupting from every direction. The edge of my dress caught at the fire, but didn't light.

I tried to back away, shielding my face, barely able to see now through the smoke and the flames.

Why didn't I wake up? I *knew* in my heart that this wasn't real, that I was dreaming. But I couldn't seem to pull myself from it. I stepped back, stumbled over a body and went down in a tangle of dress and limbs that were not my own.

One by one the bodies melted away, gone, and I scrambled back to my feet.

A voice whispered through the air. I couldn't tell if it was male or female.

"You will fail if you stay, their world will burn, and it will be *your* fault. Their deaths will be on *your* hands."

Another bolt of lightning slammed into the ground at my feet, throwing chunks of earth around me, driving me back a step as a second bolt shot straight through me.

I did scream then, thrashing and fighting to stay alive as the electricity pumped through me, as if it would burn me from the inside out.

"Sienna, stop, stop, you're safe!" Dominic's words were as insistent as his hands that he clamped on my arms, holding me tight to his body as I shook and struggled to breathe. "A dream," he said, pressing his lips to my forehead. "Just a dream."

He said it was just a dream, but I could *feel* it under my skin, could *feel* the truth of it the same way I could feel the kraken's hunger, or Havoc's pain when she'd been attacked. A shuddering breath escaped me, and I clung to him a little tighter.

If I'd had any doubt that I needed to leave, to escape this place, there was none left in me now. With or without Jordan, with or without Bethany, I had to get away. To save them all.

Eventually, I did fall back asleep, but it was restless and fraught with dreams of the regular kind, though they were no less disturbing. Reliving the moments where I thought Dominic would die, reliving the kraken's fear and loneliness. So when I woke with a start the second time, it was of no surprise to me that I was still tired.

Dominic was sitting on the edge of the bed, pulling on boots.

"What's happening?" I sat up, touching my head and feeling the beginnings of a new headache there, begging to be unleashed on me.

"I'm not certain. An attack maybe," he said, "I can hear guards running, weapons being drawn."

An attack.

Like the storm from my dream?

I couldn't help myself, I grabbed his arm. "No. Don't go, Dominic."

He turned and looked at me, his eyes thoughtful. "You say that like you know something?"

Shivering, I didn't let go of him. "Something bad is coming. Something that...will kill everyone."

He lifted his hands and cupped my face, drawing me close with a gentle kiss to silence me. "There is always danger,

Starshine. Always. I cannot turn from it. Stay here, I will check it out."

Before I could protest, he was gone, his vampiric speed sending him out the door in a blur.

I swallowed hard, my throat dry as if I'd been breathing in the flames from my dreams. I wasn't about to let him go into this alone and I threw myself out of bed, barefoot, and ran for the door.

Which left me colliding with Bee in the hall.

"Did you hear?" she gasped. "She's come!"

I took a step away from her, as if just by touching her I would cause the fate from my dream to become real. "Who?"

She grinned. "The Duchess!"

My jaw dropped and I found myself running with Bethany as fast as we could through the halls toward the main part of the keep. Why did I think things would be better with the Duchess here? I wasn't sure that they would be. But...she had been the first to peg me as something 'other' and I trusted her. More than I trusted Diana or any of the wolves here.

Bee and I skidded to a halt as we ran across the threshold to the main dining hall.

The Duchess was sitting in a chair, with two women on the ground in front of her, shaking and clinging to each other, a young boy at her side whose face was nearly black with soot. The scene was surreal.

Diana, Will, and Dominic were standing in a semi-circle around them, and I wasn't sure if they were protecting her or keeping her hostage as they'd done to Will and Dominic.

Evangeline was covered in dirt, her face coated with it, her clothing ripped and torn, hair tangled with twigs, and yet she sat with her back ramrod straight, a teacup in her hand without so much as a tremble to her muscles.

"Edmund," she said softly, "set the remainder of the harvest girls *free*." She curled her lip on the last word. "Of course, it was a lie. As soon as he released them, he let his closest allies know that they would be fair game, and a hunt ensued. There was nothing I could do but try and save as many as I could. My young friend here helped me." She reached over and gently touched the shoulder of...

"Timmy!" I burst out, running across the room.

He swiveled around to me, eyes wide. "Miss Sienna!"

I scooped him up into my arms, unable to keep the tears completely at bay. He'd been one of those my presence had killed in my dream. A sweet boy, who loved horses. And he'd die if I stayed. I set him down and fought to gain control of myself. "Well done, Timmy."

A hand gently touched my wrist, and I found myself looking into the Duchess's eyes.

"Sienna. You and Bethany, you saved my Will."

I just stared at her, feeling a strange weight to her words. "You knew he was infected with the bloodworm, didn't you?"

She gave me a slow nod. "I did."

"And that my blood had the potential to save him," I whispered and even so I felt the words circulate the room.

Her smile was soft, sad. "I did. I wish I'd known sooner, you could have saved my brother too."

"I'm glad you are alive, and well," I said, meaning every word of it but also feeling strangely formal. I'd been so excited that she would be here and now it felt like there was a distance between us.

Dominic caught my eye, and I shook my head. I took a step back, but the Duchess did not let me go and it was as if we were alone in the room, without an audience to our back and forth. "I see the fear in you, Sienna. You are strong enough for the war that is coming."

My lips trembled. "You don't know what you're saying. I might be strong enough, but you don't know that everyone else is. You don't know what the storm will bring when it rains down upon us all."

CHAPTER 21

Dominic

The room I'd been given, despite its size and rustic grandeur, felt small as I paced the edges of it. My body felt...amazing. Yesterday, I'd still been tired, and my skin felt too tight for my frame. But today, it was as if I'd never stepped into the sun at all. There wasn't a mark on me, not a single pink patch, no scars to speak of. And all because of Sienna.

My heart gave a strange thump as I thought of her sleeping in my arms, trusting me to keep her safe. More than that, even though, she'd saved me. She'd saved Will. And her healing abilities were nothing our world had ever seen before.

Which put her in great danger. Every faction of magical being would want to wield that power. And if they couldn't have her for themselves? They would make sure no one else did, either.

"Fuck," I growled the word under my breath as I walked. Sienna in danger yet again was not even something I wanted to think about. But each day that passed, she became more of a target.

The Duchess had arrived in the early hours of the morning, barely making it before the sun rose on the werewolf territories. I was glad to see her physically unharmed, but her story of the release and hunt of the women was only more proof that Edmund was on the warpath. All those girls, slaughtered for the hell of it just when they'd thought they had a chance at freedom. It was meant to be horrific for them, and he'd made sure of it. To prove what? That Edmund was not anything like our father?

My hand flicked to the hip where my sword should have rested, then to my low back where I would have carried my iron staff. A weapon in hand would have made me feel better.

I'd not seen my aunt since her arrival hours before, and I was getting anxious on her behalf.

She was ensconced with Diana alone as if she were the leader to be, and not Will.

But why?

My brother sat at the desk, working away on a piece of paper, scribbling and re-writing his words over and over.

"You'll wear a track in the floor soon," he muttered.

"You've gone through half a tree's worth of paper. I think you aren't the one to be worrying at my pacing," I snapped back. "What in the name of the night gods are they discussing? Should we not all be involved?"

Will raised his head. "Much as I love hearing the same question from you ten times over, I still do not have an answer,

Dom. Whatever they are discussing, I imagine we will hear it soon enough."

I snorted and resumed my pacing.

"It's amazing how opposite you are in so many ways, but how alike you are in others. Just yesterday, it was Sienna pacing a rut in the floor, repeating the same question about whether or not you would awaken." My brother stared across at me. "And speaking of Sienna, what exactly is happening to our girl? She's hidden herself away, and won't let anyone in to speak with her."

"Not ours, mine," I growled.

"Well, if she is yours, then that makes her my sister." He said it so casually. "So. What has happened to her? Last night she was different. As if she'd experienced something more than the shock of the kraken and seeing you roasted like a pig on a spit. She was terrified."

Didn't I know it. Her words alone, about a storm struck something deep within my bones. Almost as if she were prophesying something to come. I didn't like that. I wasn't sure I believed in oracles and magic and prophecies, but I was currently immersed in it all and couldn't seem to see a way out, so I changed the subject.

"The Duchess slid me a note, before she was swept off with Diana."

Will shot out of his chair. "And you waited till now to tell me?"

I pulled the single piece of parchment out and handed it to him to read. The words were etched into my mind.

Scarlett had done it. The Vanators had agreed to our terms and were at the ready. But at what price? Right after my escape, she'd been under a microscope but in her missive, she explained that she'd convinced Edmund she appreciated his attentions, and he'd allowed her more freedom than ever.

The results were exemplary. The means were not, and the thought of what she'd had to do to earn his trust made me ill.

I just prayed we would be reunited soon so I could tell her how sorry I was.

"I have been torn in multiple directions. But if all goes well, then we have more than a chance. We will have you on the throne by the end of the week."

He skimmed the paper, his eyes flicking back and forth several times. "More than a chance, brother, this is excellent! But how, why would she..." he looked at me. "You did this? You set this in motion, didn't you?"

I nodded. "Before I...left...Scarlett and I discussed using the Vanators. She brought them into the fold and will set up the access they needed in order to kill Edmund."

He fell back into his chair as if he'd been shot through the heart, his arms and legs akimbo. "And you never thought to mention it before?"

"It wasn't a sure thing, by any means. I assumed that at best, we might hear of an attack, or his death and then be able to sweep in and set you on the throne. That we have a date and a place, that we can actually be there and ensure that it is done? It is...more than I could have hoped for."

A knock on the door turned both our heads.

Lochlin stepped in. "Diana is ready for you two now."

I glared at him, anger surging through me so hot I barely managed to contain it. Lochlin stared back as if nothing at all was wrong.

"You have something to say, fang face?" he asked.

"You put her in danger," I said. "Our friendship is done."

He snorted. "Go piss on a tree, old man. We didn't know about the kraken. I'm loyal to my Queen, and if you'd been in the same boat you'd have paddled the same as I had. As best you could with the toothpick given to you. When you're ready to see sense, then we can talk about just what I've done to keep you and your kin safe, you damn miserable ingrate."

He left, didn't even slam the door, which just left me staring at it. Angry but also...not.

"You didn't really mean that," Will said.

I grunted. "He's an ass. She could have died."

"But she didn't. In fact, she didn't need anyone to save her at all. She did it herself."

Moving swiftly, I headed to the door and Will followed a pace slower.

While he was doing better, the bloodworm had left him weak. I slowed my pace to match his and, in a few minutes, we were let into the hall.

I expected there to be a full clan assembly, but the only people waiting for us were Diana, the Duchess, and shockingly enough, the old king, Lycan. He stood with his back to the wall, behind the two women. As if he were just observing things.

Will stepped forward. "Your Majesties."

Diana dipped her head. "Prince William. You've met King Lycan?"

Lycan grunted and stepped forward. "I am no king now, lass." The two men closed the distance and shook hands. There was no power struggle, neither was trying to see who could shake the longest.

I bowed to both Diana and then to Lycan. "It is good to see you well and hale, Your Majesty."

"I could say the same. Heard you had a dance with the devil in his furnace." He barked a low laugh. "Only you would find a way to survive the un-survivable, Dominic."

I came up out of my bow. "Thank you?"

He grinned, flashing perfect white teeth. Despite the hint of silver at the edges of his black hair and the smattering of wrinkles on his face, he still looked strong and vibrant. But as he moved, I could see the years on him.

"Lycan and I have spoken and we've got some ideas about how—" Diana began but Will lifted his hand and I let him take the lead, as the soon to be King he was.

"Actually, Your Majesty, before the clan representatives get here, we have more information we need to share with you. An inside informant is working with us, and she has secured the Vanators."

The Duchess did not gasp, but I could see her tense. "Is that wise?"

Will held out the paper that I'd given him as if she'd never seen it. "It is the General's most trusted Captain of the Guard. She will aid the Vanators in their preparations and they will assassinate Edmund."

Diana took the paper from the Duchess and looked it over.

If she didn't agree to this, we were sunk.

"Your Majesty, Captain Scarlett has never failed me. She is preparing everything as we speak. We need to get William to the Green Valley, the north side. As such, he will be first on the ground to 'scatter' the Vanators, and take the throne."

Diana's eyes lifted from the paper. "Why would you not take the credit for the death of Edmund? He is the worst of the monsters in this world. Do you think that some would rather him still on the throne?"

I didn't think it. I *knew* it.

"Diana, may I speak plainly?"

She snorted. "As if you have not already? Yes, go ahead. But be quick. the assembly is due to begin and the clans will be arriving any moment."

I took a breath. "There will always be monsters in the shadows. But they are unleashed even more so when the one who leads them allows for evil to reign freely. Can you say that if you would allow chaos and murder here, that you would not have some wolves gladly take up the monstrosities that you accuse us of?" Her lips pursed and I went on before she could counter me. "With Will on the throne, we can continue to grow our people into a less violent version of ourselves. We can weed out those who would harm others. We can make ties with other kingdoms based on trust and mutual respect." I paused. "And even with all that, there will still be monsters. Just, I hope, fewer. And less bold."

Lycan clapped his hand against the table. "Well said, boyo. Well said."

Will shot me a look and a subtle wink. "Boyo."

Diana looked at the paper. "We—myself and every clan member I have spoken with—would prefer Will to Edmund. We recognize that Edmund presents a danger to not only his own people, but ours as well. If he is willing to slide back to the dark ages so easily, it will only be a matter of time before he begins to poach our lands and hunt our people. Ever since the Veil came down, it's as if our world has been slowly unraveling. Lycan tried to reach out to King Stirling. To tell him that we need to come together and figure out how to repair it, but Edmund was the one to respond, and he refused to even entertain thoughts of that nature. Despite the weather changing more and more year after year. Despite creatures dying, and even some of my own going mad...it's only a matter of time until we all devolve into sheer chaos. I believe that, Dominic. And I know that Edmund is impossible to convince. So we will roll the dice with Will and hope for better."

Before I could say anything else, the doors behind us were thrown open and a stream of people slid through. The leaders of the different clans were in front, in their full regalia. Cloaks made of animal skin, wooden masks carved as wolf heads, chest plates of hammered copper and studded with jewels. As technologically advanced as the wolves were, they loved their traditions.

Each of the twelve leaders stepped up to what looked like assigned places.

Diana moved to stand in front of them, Lycan once more sliding into the shadows along with the Duchess.

"My family, we have a decision ahead of us, and I thank you for your swift action in answering my call."

Will and I stepped back as Diana spoke to the pack leaders. Telling them that there was a plan in place, and asking them to support William as he took the throne. Explaining that a small contingent from each tribe would travel with William, to ensure he took the throne.

"So there be no war then?" came a disgruntled question.

Diana smiled at him. "No, Cormen. Maybe a skirmish, but if our plans succeed, there will be no war. That is a blessing."

"Bah, I was looking forward to a good sword swinging."

A few laughs rippled through the group at that.

"I ask you now, will you support not only myself in this decision, but the young prince William as he moves to take the throne of the Vampire Territory?"

"What about the girl? The one who tamed the kraken?"

Mutters flew through the room like starlings in a barn.

Diana held a hand up for silence. "Sienna is indeed an enigma. A powerful woman in her own right who is *our friend and ally.*" Her eyes locked onto one pack leader who shifted his feet uncomfortably. His insignia was a star with a cross etched inside it.

It took all I had to keep my growl to myself. For the time being, I had to behave myself. But if I found out for certain that was the wolf who had taken shots at Sienna? We'd have words.

The pack leader tipped his head in acquiescence. "Understood."

Diana looked around the room. "Sienna will remain with us, safe, as we learn more of her abilities. She is favored by the young prince and the General of the Vampire Army, as well as she remains in my confidence. Is that clear enough?"

Not subtle, but it worked. The last of the muttering stopped.

She clapped her hands together, startling a few of them. "Now for the business at hand. We have a chance to remove Edmund the Vile from power. All in favor of backing Prince William and standing with him until he is on the throne as the rightful heir to the vampire kingdom?"

One by one, every pack leader raised their hands in the air and I let out a breath in relief.

We had their support.

I should have been elated, I should have felt like the world was finally righting itself. But without Sienna at my side, even a victory such as this was empty.

CHAPTER 22

Sienna

I stared at the clock and let out a strangled holler of frustration.

What could they possibly be talking about all this time? And worse, why did they have to do it without me?

"The key, my ass," I muttered, flopping onto my bed and spreading out like I was making angels in the snow. Too bad Bethany had decided I was a liability and didn't want to be my friend anymore. At least I could've complained to her about how wrong everyone was treating me.

First Diana, who had been all, "Sienna won't be present for the assembly. Until we know for sure that no one means her harm, we must protect her at all costs." And then traitorous Dom, who had heartily agreed. So now, while the grownups all made plans and got to find out if the wolves had our backs, I was stuck in my room like a disobedient child.

Well, screw them. They could keep me from the meeting, but they couldn't make me stay in my chambers to stew for the next however long it took. I needed some air.

I rolled off the bed and crossed the room to the door. A jiggle of the knob confirmed it wasn't locked, which meant I was free to go as I pleased. I yanked on my boots and then flung the door open, intent on heading down to the courtyard. My plan was cut short by the burly man with his back to me, standing directly in front of my door at attention.

"Miss?" he rumbled without turning his head to glance my way.

"Who are you?"

"Cedric. Her Majesty appointed me to keep an eye on you while the assembly was in session."

"Keep an eye on...like babysit me, you mean?"

He lifted one shoulder but still didn't turn. "I s'pose you could look at it that way. In either case, Miss, you'll need to remain in your room until the meeting is over for your own safety because—"

I slammed the door shut and bit back a scream of frustration. Before I could even plan my next move, there was a knock at the door. I opened it, already locked and loaded. "I don't need a lecture about—" I broke off, surprised to find the guard who'd been there just a second ago gone, and Dom standing in his place.

"Have you just spent the last forty-five making that poor man's life miserable?"

"In fact, I have not," I replied with a haughty glare. "Although, I probably would have if I'd known he was there."

"You know he's just doing his job."

"How nice for him. I'd have liked to have been doing the same if I'm, you know, going to be integral in saving the world or whatever."

"I know you're pissed at me for agreeing with Diana, but if you thought about it rationally, you'd see why we couldn't risk having you there."

His tone was so patient. So tender. It was hard to stay angry, but somehow, I managed.

"I know you bought and paid for me, but that doesn't mean you own me. I need to feel like I have some control over what's happening in my life. Being left out of these conversations makes me feel incredibly vulnerable."

Especially when everything else was so out of my control, and had been since I'd let the Collectors catch me.

Dom looked down at me and nodded. "I get it. So what if I come in and fill you in on what happened? Will that make you feel better?"

That would depend completely on how the meeting went, but I stepped back to make space for him anyway.

"Fine. Come on in."

He did, barely brushing against me as he passed.

"My Captain of the Guard, Scarlett. She was able to put a plan we'd devised into action. The Vanators...vampire hunters, if you recall, are willing to help us defeat Edmund. Scarlett and the men who remain loyal to me will assist the Vanators in ambushing Edmund and his loyalists. The wolves are in agreement and have pledged soldiers to assist in the cause. We will go together to ensure the deed is done, and immediately following, seat Will on the throne."

Brain going into overdrive, I stared up at him for a long moment before making my way to the window nook and lowering myself to sit. I remembered Dominic's captain from my time at the palace. She was beautiful, strong, and I was pretty sure she and Dominic had bumped uglies in the past. That alone made me want to hate her. But part of me couldn't help but admire a woman who had risen so far above her station, to command a position of power in a male-dominated society. Still, this whole plan seemed like a fool's errand.

"So you're inviting your mortal enemy to come into your territory to kill the King. How can you trust they won't kill you, too? And as many of your kind as they possibly can, because, yanno...vampire hunters. And humans, right?" I shrugged and shot him an incredulous look. "Call me a doubting Thomas, but I'm seeing some flaws in this strategy, General."

He nodded and went on. "Like the wolves, they have a vested interest in making sure that Edmund doesn't remain King. They know what he is. And they know any treaties or truces that have been called with the humans will be tossed aside like they never even existed. It will be anarchy. Without those treaties in place, there is nothing at all stopping our kind and all of the Others from going to the other side and picking off their kind like chickens at a coyote convention. Humans don't need much to turn even more monstrous themselves. A few months of constant fear, hiding in their homes, they'll turn on one another and chaos will ensue. Mark me, it would be the end of your civilization as you know it. As well as the Territories."

I couldn't argue with him. I knew firsthand how awful humans could be.

So that meant we were going back to Vampire Territory. I needed to be there to help them negotiate this tricky situation and, if a battle ensued, I could heal the wounded. But assuming all went well, and Will took the throne, it was all up in the air. I would have to come to a decision. Make a break for it with Bee, assuming she still wanted to, and go back to my own world, or stay here in the Empire of Magic.

The Oracle said I was their salvation, but my dreams told me I was their destruction.

Which was true?

The sad fact was, I likely wouldn't know until it was far too late.

"You look exhausted, and I know you're angry. I can go if you want me to." Dominic was eyeing me as if he wanted to do anything but, and as raw and alone as I felt in that moment, I didn't want him to go anywhere.

"Stay with me."

I didn't need to ask twice.

He bent low and scooped me into his arms, holding me so tenderly that it nearly made me weep. Then, he set me on the bed and climbed in on the other side to pull me close, his big body enveloping mine. He seemed content to stay that way, but I wanted more. I *needed* more. This time, though, the sex was different. Bittersweet, all the more precious with the knowledge that this time might be our last. And when it was over, I felt loved, which was almost as terrifying as warring with Edmund the Awful. Dominic's slow, even breaths told me he'd managed to fall asleep, but in spite of my exhaustion, that feeling kept me wide awake.

As much as a huge part of me wished I could stay with him forever, there was no forever promised to the two of us. Even if we did defeat Edmund. Dominic was a vampire, and I was his food. Diana had already warned me about this and now, more than ever, the thought of growing old and dying while he sat by and watched seemed almost as painful as dying by an arrow, or being struck down by Edmund in battle. But my dream had tipped the scales. As much as I believed the Oracle had indeed seen a vision, I trusted my dreams more than the cryptic words of a stranger. After all, hadn't my dreams foretold meeting Dominic long before I'd ever set eyes on him? I couldn't just disregard this latest nightmare.

If I cared for Dominic, the Vampire General–and Gods help me, I did–if I cared for *any* of them, I needed to get as far away from the Empire as possible.

Because if not, they were all as good as dead.

CHAPTER 23

Dominic

"So you're saying that the Vanators have agreed to assist with the coup and then just... leave the Territories peacefully once the job has been done?"

The Duchess stared at me, doubt written all over her face.

Early that morning, Diana had summoned us all—me, Will, Loch, the Duchess, and Lycan, along with Sienna to her war room. But Sienna was absent yet again, and that was entirely my call. She would rip me a new one for leaving her out again, but that was alright. I could handle it. Right now, I had to worry more about getting this lot on board with the plan. Will had ceded the floor to me, and so far, I was meeting a lot of opposition.

"They have everything to gain and nothing to lose. We're handing them an opportunity to rid the world of the worst of our kind in one fell swoop. I don't think it's a stretch to think that they'd leap at the chance."

The Duchess pressed on. "For all they know, this is a trap. We're inviting them into our territory to ambush and kill them all. I think they'd have to be slightly touched in the head to even consider it."

"We've put assurances into place to protect them. Scarlett gave them a written invitation signed by Will, with the royal seal affixed, guaranteeing their safe exit once the job is done. If we break that agreement, we would be sanctioned by the mainland, and all of our treaties beyond the veil would be null and void. It would be all out war with the humans and they know that's the last thing we need right now. Sure, there is a risk that the coup fails and we all die, but we're taking that risk as well."

"Quick question." Will's brows rose high on his forehead as he held up a finger. "Where, pray tell, did they get such an invitation, brother? I know I was addled from the bloodworm, but I'm pretty sure I'd remember signing such a document."

"You were busy skipping through the lilies with my woman and her maid, so I had to write it and sign it on your behalf. Doesn't matter," I continued, waving him off. "Point is, I had precious little time to come up with a plan, and you weren't around to ask. I did what I thought you'd want me to do to save the crown and protect our people. Was I wrong?"

He shook his head and let out an exasperated sigh. "I guess given your hands were pretty tied at that point, no, but I do fear what could happen if this plan fails."

"It will work. Our biggest obstacle is the weather. It's been so uncertain of late. If it's storming, and travel is affected, our timing may be off. And if the winds are really whipping..."

Lycan grimaced and cut in. "You and your damned noses, almost as good as ours. If they're downwind and they scent the Vanators ahead of time, it's all over. There can be no forewarning if we are to succeed."

"I've been working with my tech guy on some masking capabilities. I'll check with them and see how far we've gotten on that front," Diana said, crossing her arms as she studied the map. "I still feel that Sienna should join us to weigh in here. She's arguably the most powerful of all of us. She's going to need to be on the front lines of this, and should have her say."

Sienna had hardly slept at all for the second night in a row after a soul-wrecking forty-eight hours. I wasn't about to have them wake her. "She needs her rest far more than she needs to be here at this early stage of discussion," I replied smoothly. If the Queen wanted to believe Sienna would be on the front lines of anything dangerous, never mind a battle between Edmund and a group of Vanators, I wasn't about to tell her otherwise. Whatever it took for Diana to commit her men and her might to the cause. But Sienna wouldn't be there. Not while I was alive and breathing. The Queen would just have to get over it. She knew what it was like to have to make hard choices, and she wasn't above a little deception or manipulation to get what she wanted.

"Scarlett has cleared the way for the Vanators to enter the territory here." I set a green marble piece in the northernmost part of Blackthorne Bay, near DuMont's estate. "Now that Anthony is dead, his estate is empty and there are only two guards posted in the general area. The Vanators will leave their ship in the Bay and row to shore when the guards are patrolling the grounds to the east. They'll travel due north," I slid the piece along the map, "close to the mountains along the Demon Territory border and then veer east, to the North Fort. That's where they'll await Scarlett's signal."

I rounded the table and selected a red marble piece and set it in front of Diana's keep.

"We'll travel this route, using the northern border bridge to pass through this sliver of Angel Territory and come out at the Northeast corner of Vampire Territory where we will also lie in wait for Scarlett's signal. When she tells Edmund that there's been a sighting of us just east of the North Fort, they will head straight through the forest to run us down where we will easily flank them here and here. Edmund will die, and we will go back to the palace and explain to our people that we'd been on our way home to work things out but found that Edmund and his men were killed by Vanators. Killings that they are more than happy to take credit for. Will there be some who doubt that story? Definitely. But most will want to believe it because it's the best outcome they can hope for. You'll be king and can go back to leading the way your...our father intended."

I looked at Diana expectantly, who looked to Lycan, who, in a strange turn of events, looked to my aunt.

"Evangeline? Do you believe this is a sound strategy?"

She stared back at the old wolf and nodded slowly, her gaze never leaving his.

"Upon listening to my nephew explain it, it does seem like it can work. But how do we know how many men Edmund will bring? What if we're outmatched, even with the Vanators on our side?"

"We'll need to leave it to Scarlett to manage Edmund." I forced myself to shove my guilt aside for the moment. There was nothing I could've done to help her. "She now has his trust. We also cannot discount Edmund's hubris. He won't bring an army because he doesn't think he'll need one. But most of all, Edmund knows that a good part of his army is loyal to me. Three he handpicked to join the hunting party helped me escape. The more men he brings, the more he risks setting up himself for a coup of his own making."

The Duchess nodded and shrugged. "Nicky is right. All that makes perfect sense to me. I say we go for it. After what I've seen Edmund do since taking the throne, I fear his grip on reality is slipping. It's as if this taste of power has made him even more bloodthirsty and crazed. If we don't stop him soon, I truly believe he will start wars that we can never win and make us a pariah of the Empire and enemy to all."

Lycan dipped his head and gave the Duchess one last, long look before turning to face me.

"Do we have Malach's leave to pass through their territory?"

"I can help there," Diana piped in. "The winged ones owe me a favor, and I'm happy to collect."

We all stared at the map on the table a moment.

"While I do think there are some risks, I have to agree with my aunt," Will said, pursing his lips. "Edmund seems to be spiraling, as the Duchess says, and I don't think we're going to come up with anything better quickly enough to stop him before he does irreparable damage to the crown's reputation. We need to act and we need to act fast."

Lochlin spoke up for the first time. "With my Queen's blessing, I can start to put together a team of volunteers. I'd rather have those passionate about the cause than recruit anyone with doubts about working with the vamps."

Diana nodded. "Send me the list when you have it and I can add to it if need be. Let's work on getting everyone well fed, rested, and armed in the next two days, and then we move out." She eyed me for a long moment, and then turned to the others. "If you can clear the room, I'd like to speak to Dominic alone about a few matters."

The others talked amongst themselves as they stood and filed out of the room. I couldn't help but notice how Lycan trailed behind, waiting for the Duchess so they might exit together.

"What's with the two of them?" I asked the second they'd all gone.

Diana's expression was flat as she lifted one shoulder. "I have no idea what you mean."

I was suddenly sure she did, but I had bigger things to worry about than what was likely idle gossip about the past, so I eyed her expectantly. "You wanted to speak to me alone?"

"I hope I'm not speaking out of turn when I tell you this, but...you realize that Sienna still plans to escape the moment she gets the chance, don't you?"

I gritted my teeth and nodded. "I do. But I also believe by the time we enter Vampire Territory, I'll have changed her mind on that front."

In fact, if it wasn't for her ill-timed and meaningless nightmare, I was pretty sure she'd already have been convinced.

"And at no point did you tell her that, even if we agreed to allow her to go, it can never happen?"

An oil-slick of nausea settled in my belly. "She never asked."

Diana scoffed, a mixture of disbelief and pity clear in her dark green eyes. "Why would you allow her to hold onto hope like that?"

"Sometimes hope is the only thing that keeps us going when we feel we just can't go on anymore."

"Dominic?"

A low voice called my name from the doorway, and I squeezed my eyes closed.

No, I prayed silently to the Gods, not like this.

I opened my eyes and turned to see Sienna standing there, looking like she'd just witnessed a beheading.

"What do you mean, I can never go home?"

CHAPTER 24

Sienna

I was stuck here. Forever.

I stared at Dominic, unable to see anything else in that moment. Fear was the first emotion that registered but it was swiftly drowned by a tidal wave of anger.

"What do you mean, I *can't* leave? Because I doubt very much you mean the keep here," I asked, my voice sounding unnaturally calm even to my own ears. I'd caught the conversation's tail end, but it was enough for me to know I wasn't supposed to know.

Dominic started toward me, "It is complicated Sienna, far more than anyone—"

Diana smacked her hand on her thigh, the crack of flesh on leather cutting him off most effectively. "It most certainly is not."

Reluctantly, I turned my eyes to her. "Tell me."

The pity in Diana's eyes was nearly my undoing. "You planned to come here, didn't you? Somehow found a way to the Territories, to save your friend?"

My throat tightened. "How did you know?"

"Jordan is loyal to you, but he has a family now, the first he has known. He told his mother and asked her what he should do. She of course passed on the information to me."

I struggled to breathe. "That's why he hasn't been in the kitchens? You're keeping him from me?"

"Yes." She dipped her head. "And I will continue to do so. He has the mind of a child and he trusts you, but he is far safer here than anywhere else. And you would strip him of that safety and take him to certain death."

My breaths were coming in shallow gasps as the truth of my situation continued to sink into my bones.

"How do you know for sure?"

"Because it's the truth," Diana went on. "If in fact, you were able to escape and found your way back to the mainland with Jordan and your friend Bethany, you would all be marked."

"Marked?" I managed that one-word question.

"Diana," Dominic growled. "I will tell her."

Diana snorted. "You most certainly will not because you will try to confuse her with your professions of love, and then she will not know the truth of her situation."

I looked at Dominic, still wanting to believe that he wouldn't use my emotions to manipulate me, that he would be brutally honest but...there was nothing in his eyes but fear. Fear and pain.

Forcing myself to look back at Diana I tipped my head at her. "Go on."

"You would be marked as a threat to all in the Empire. You've been here, and you know too much. Within a matter of days, one of our agents on the mainland would hunt you down and kill you all. Your bodies would be disposed of in a way that no one would ever find you." She looked hard at me. "Do you understand, Sienna?"

My heart was beating hard. If I took Jordan or Bethany with me, they would be hunted down along with me. "Why, why would you care if someone got away?"

Diana spread her hands and looked around us. "The Territories are an open secret now, Sienna, but the monsters that reside here, and I include all of the races in that, know that should word get out about how we live, the remainder of the human world would not tolerate it. How easy it would be to whip up a revolt that could risk our treaties with the mainland."

I stared at her. "You defeated us once, soundly."

Dominic stepped into my line of vision. "That was when the entire territories were united. A one-time truce against a common enemy, that I doubt we'd be able to make happen again."

My eyes finally locked on him. "And you knew all this, of course, and let me believe I could get away?"

"You are not the first to think they could leave," he said gently.

I stepped back from them both. "But I've heard of people escaping..."

"Never for long."

"That can't be true."

Diana and Dominic shared a look I didn't like, one that made me feel yet again like a child with the adults speaking over her.

"Look at me!" I snapped the words and they both did. "I do not belong here. I am not a vampire or a werewolf; I'm human! I'm fucking food on a good damn day, and you both know it!"

"No," Dominic said. "That's not true, Sienna. There is a place for you, but it is here. By my side."

I shook my head as I continued to back up through the room, I needed to get away. To escape them both. Even now the dream of the storm and the bodies strewn around me was so real that I knew I still had to try.

"All this time, you let me believe there was a way out. And now you want me to believe that you care for me?"

Dominic's face shuttered. "If when Edmund is disposed of, if you still wish to leave, I will help you. I will find a place for you of safety on the mainland and—"

"No," Diana said softly, but even so the word rippled in the air. "Do not make that promise because I will not stand for it. Sienna is a power in her own right. She belongs here, not on the mainland with the humans. The Oracle said it, she is one of the keys to healing our home. I cannot allow her to just fuck off and wither away with the rest of the humans because the two of you are having a tiff." She tucked her hands behind her back and stared hard at me. "Do you understand? You aren't going anywhere. You, and what you can do, is far too valuable to be wasted, or worse, killed by some random event."

"I'll go to my government then," I threw the words out like a challenge. "I'll go straight to them and—"

"And they will send you right back," she said. "That is if they themselves don't kill you for being a traitor to your own kind."

My jaw dropped, and I stared at her, feeling my eyes widen. "What? No, that's not..."

"There is a treaty in place, that any humans we take within our rights who escape to the mainland are to be returned immediately." She paused. "Of course, those that truly run your country are too excitable and the others that we know who have gone to their leaders for help just...disappeared. Poof."

My back was against the door now, and I fumbled for the handle. Out, I needed out of this room before I heard anything else.

"Starshine..."

I pointed a finger at Dominic—no, the *General*— "Do not ever call me that again. Ever. Whatever you thought was between us is done. Gone. Burnt to a crisp as if you walked out into the sun again."

"Ouch," Diana said softly, but even I heard it.

I didn't care that she was witness to our fight. I didn't care one bit if it embarrassed the General. In that moment, all I cared about was getting away from them both.

I fumbled with the door, yanked it open and strode through. Lochlin was there, his eyebrows in his hairline.

"Lass—"

"Don't you fucking Lass me, you're as bad as those two!" I snapped as I strode past him. Not running, but walking as fast as I could. Getting to the stables was my only thought, my only pretend escape was Havoc. My chest was tight for so many reasons.

For losing Jordan completely. For losing Bethany's friendship.

For losing the man I...had been falling for, and all in one fell swoop. A few simple words and my world, what was left of it, had been torn into pieces and scattered to the storm winds that I knew were coming.

I may have let out a sob as I picked up speed, rushing past people, past doors.

How could he have done this to me? How could he have let me believe that he truly cared...and to think that I was falling for him. Maybe even loved him? Another sob that I caught on the back of my hand.

The world was a blur, my traitorous eyes leaking. Where was I? I'd gotten myself turned around.

A hand on my arm spun me about, and I went with the momentum, my fist clenched. Without even thinking, I snapped it up and into his jaw.

Dominic's head snapped back and a grunt escaped him, but he didn't let me go. "Sienna, stop. Please let me explain."

"There is nothing to explain, General." My words were laced with tears and crying and I hated it, but there you go. My emotions were so heightened after the last few days I don't think I could have stopped the tears had my life depended on it. "I forgot my place. Food. Fucking. That's it."

He grabbed my other arm. "No, that's not true."

"Let me go." I didn't struggle against him, and he reluctantly dropped his hands. Tears streaming, I stared up into the face that was as fascinating as the day I'd seen him at the auction. The one from my dreams. "Do not ever touch me again, General. Ever."

His face tightened as if I'd stabbed him with his own sword. A shudder ran through his body, and he took a step back and bowed from the waist. "As you wish."

My own body felt as though I were tearing it to pieces from the inside out. Lies and deceit, love and hate, terror and safety. Nothing was as I'd thought.

Spinning away from him, I ran now, blindly, through the keep. Taking a corner sharply, I collided hard with someone and bounced off them, sprawling to the ground.

"I'm sorry," I said as I pushed up, dashing away the tears as best I could, but they only fell faster.

"Sienna?"

I blinked at Bee. "I didn't see you. Excuse me." I made as if to brush past her and she touched my arm.

"Are you okay?"

I shook my head. "No. But there is nothing anyone can do for it."

Fully expecting her to go the opposite direction, I was surprised when she fell into step beside me. "Where are you going?"

"To the stables, I need to ride," I said.

"Maybe I could come with you?" she asked timidly. "I'd like some fresh air."

I closed my eyes and then nodded. We hadn't spoken in several days now, and the distance between us was palpable. I hated it. "Of course."

We walked in silence all the way to the main door before she cleared her throat and spoke. "What's wrong? I don't think I've ever seen you so upset before."

"I'm sorry." I shook my head and dove in. "For everything. For putting you in danger, for dragging you to the Hunters, for just not being a great, or even a good friend. I thought...I thought I could get us out of here if I just kept trying and just kept fighting and then I find out...that..." my voice caught and

I gulped down the sob, "That there is no way, Bee. Even if we made it to the mainland, we'd be killed to keep us quiet."

Her gasp was soft, and then she reached over and took my hand. "You don't have to apologize, Sienna. You're passionate and fierce and I love that about you. I...want to be more like you. I thought if I was more like you, Will would want me maybe."

I shook my head hard as I stopped and turned to stare at her. "He would be so lucky to have you as you are, Bee. Neither of those bastards deserve us."

She reached up and brushed away some tears off my cheek. "He hurt you."

Not a question. I nodded, and the tears streamed more. "He knew all along that there was no going back, and he just let me keep on believing in something that wasn't possible."

Of course, it was all compounded by the intimacy we'd shared, the moments of vulnerability and softness where I thought at least there was an understanding there.

"I'm a fool," I whispered.

Bee linked her arm with mine and dragged me now toward the stables. "No, I don't think you're a fool, not at all. How can we possibly understand what we are up against when the rules of the game are hidden from us?"

Her words struck something in me. The rules of the game were hidden. But if I stayed here, never mind my own life, I was condemning everyone I cared about—including Jordan, who I'd come to save.

I was damned if it did, and damned if I didn't.

"You're right, Bee." I squeezed her arm. "The rules are hidden."

What if I made my own rules?

Like a burst of light, a singular memory rushed to the front of my mind. I thought about the man that I'd met on the night I'd lost Jordan, the one who'd said he'd escaped from the Territories. How strange it had been and how the stars had seemed to align for that meeting. I hadn't thought about him, not once since he'd told me his story, but now it came back in a rush and clear as a bell.

Demons, he'd belonged to the demons for a time, and eventually escaped by way of the wolves' territory. He'd said that their soon to be queen possessed a pair of magically imbued items that allowed the wolves to move about undetected when they came to the mainland and he knew, if he took one, he could go home. He'd given me a wicked grin and turned his head, flashing a brilliant ruby stud in one ear. The light had caught it, giving it a preternatural gleam. Then he'd touched me on the side of the head and....

"Until you need this memory, forget it. Some can read minds there. Kismet brought us together. There is always a way."

"Kismet," I said softly, drying my tears on the back of my sleeve.

"What?" Bethany tipped her head sideways, looking at me.

I shook my head and motioned toward the stables. Even at that distance, I could hear Havoc whinnying, demanding to be let out. "Come, let's ride and for a little while, pretend we are free, yes?"

Bethany's smile wobbled. "Yes. For a little while."

As we made the last few steps to the stable and as I tacked up Havoc and another horse for Bethany to ride, I knew that my game was not run yet. Perhaps Diana and Dominic thought me broken, perhaps they thought they'd won.

A smile flitted over my lips as I pulled myself up onto Havoc's back and a new plan, a dangerous plan began to form. Come hell or high water, I would find my way out of the Territories, to save them all.

Even though it would mean leaving what was left of my heart behind. And while I told myself that I meant Jordan and Bee, and all the people I'd met along the way, I knew the truth. I would never forget the General, no matter how far I ran.

CHAPTER 25

Dominic

Ares was agitated as hell, dancing and snorting, plunging forward as if he would take off at a flat-out run. I held him back, but barely.

"You don't beat him around the head for bad behavior? I never would of course, but I assumed your training methods would be like the rest of the vampire tactics I've seen. Blunt and violent," Diana asked, riding beside me on a large gelding who was as placid as Ares was hot.

I chose not to rise to her dig. "It's not his fault. He's picking up on the energy in the group." I patted my horse's neck, and he gave another snort but otherwise didn't acknowledge that he was being an ass.

"Or he's just picking up on your energy, General. I would say that disposing of one brother via enemies you don't trust, putting the younger on the throne via allies you aren't sure you can trust, and having your balls handed to you by the woman you supposedly love—in public no less—would be enough to cause you some irritation."

I shot a look at her. "Your jokes aren't funny."

Her grin was instant, and I saw a flash of something familiar in her wide smile. For that brief second, she reminded me of Will when he was teasing me. "I think they're fucking hilarious."

Ignoring her, I looked around our small contingent. In the end, Sienna had remained at the keep, surprising both me and Diana. She'd sided with me and pointed out that if there was anyone who needed healing it would be best if the healer was not pin cushioned by arrows at the battle.

The thought of a single arrow piercing her flesh was enough to make me turn nauseous and ragey.

Will, on the other hand, was here. At his insistence, and despite the danger. Being the one we were trying to crown, I could only argue with him so much before giving in. He did have a right to be here. That didn't mean I had to like it. We also had Rafe and Jack, who had followed me willingly, brave lads that they were.

We'd crossed through the slice of Malach's lands, watched closely from above. Though we couldn't see the winged ones, we'd given them the numbers and description of our party and they'd ghosted along through the night sky, hidden by the heavy cloud cover.

"If we tried to bring even one more person through, the deal would have been off." Diana explained to Will as soon as we were through and firmly onto our land. "Malach and I have an uneasy understanding."

I looked out over the men who'd followed Diana, who'd come to see Edmund die. A few of the clan leaders, but most of the men were actually the noble second and third sons. Set out to find their glory in battle and begin their own list of war wounds, of losses and wins.

"You seem uneasy, brother. Do you think the plan will fail?" William's voice turned me in his direction.

"The plan is good. With Scarlett on our side, I have no doubt that it will succeed and by morning you will be on the throne."

He waved a hand at me, his nose wrinkling up. "Then what is bothering you?"

Will damn well knew what was bothering me and I shot him a look. I was not going to—yet again—discuss Sienna in front of Diana. Bad enough that the Queen was pushing Sienna further away from me...I shook my head. "Nothing."

A runner slid through the trees and the darkness ahead of us, marked as a messenger. He approached the Queen and bowed. "We found them as the General said they would be. Edmund is there, with a contingent of his men. As far as we can tell there are only the fifteen that we were expecting."

I nodded at the same time as Diana. We'd brought double the men, as many as we felt could travel in secret, but even so things could go wrong. The Vanators were to sweep in and target only Edmund. We would sweep in at the same time and block

Edmund's men from saving him. If it came down to Edmund surviving, I would step in and kill him myself.

I had not told anyone this, because I knew they would argue. But the truth of it was, I was expendable. I wasn't even a spare, I was a General, trained and hardened to die for my king. And my king would always be William, no matter who held the crown. I would be drawn and quartered for treason—even William on the throne would not save me from that fate—but my people would be safe.

Sienna would be safe.

Diana held up her hand and gave a low hoot. As a unit, every single man turned to her, waiting, expectant. Despite our differences, I knew she was a good Queen. She loved her people and she and Will would work well together.

Her fingers flashed rapidly and half the men who'd come in nothing but pants began to shift into their wolf forms. The cracking of bones, the air expelling from their lungs as they went from two to four legs in a matter of seconds.

"Fifteen seconds," William breathed. "I remember when father said that they took five to ten minutes."

Diana raised an eyebrow. "That is the difference between a king and a queen. I made them eat their vegetables and meditate and practice daily instead of focusing only on weapons training."

I grimaced. Lochlin could shift in the blink of an eye, but he was different. Part fae.

I'd noted that Lochlin was not in the group that would take down Edmund.

I tried not to feel badly about the fact that we'd not have one last battle, side by side. It was not to be.

Once more Diana's fingers flashed, and we began to circle to the left. The wrong way. I reached out and grabbed her by the forearm.

She leaned across her saddle, and I urged Ares to close the distance between us. "This is to be sure of our safety. I told you I won't put my men in undue danger. From the left side of the valley, we can just as easily ride in. But your contact is not expecting it."

My jaw ticked. "He could recognize her as the traitor. She could die because we are moments slower." Of course, Diana probably knew that she would do this, and had not told me so I would not pass it on to Scarlett. Gods be damned.

"But my people will not," Diana said. "And that is as important as taking Edmund out."

Gods the woman was...fuck, I could not deny that she was protecting those who trusted in her, but it was at the expense of those who trusted in me. Of Scarlett and the others who would help us overthrow Edmund.

Will looked at me, his question silent. He would follow me in this moment because I was the one with the experience in battle.

I shook my head. We couldn't go against the Queen. Not at this juncture.

Instead, I followed the Queen and her men, riding to the very edge of the forest that curled around the green valley. A steady mist curled up from the grass, leaving the valley in a deep fog.

Putting a hand to Ares' neck, I tapped him three times with my fingers, and he went absolutely still, only his ears swiveling. The last thing we needed was a horse snort to give our position away.

I motioned for the others who were mounted to do the same. It was—as Sienna had said—a Jedi mind trick to train the horses to remain silent right before battle. She'd seen me show Diana and then when we'd made eye contact, she'd turned and stormed off.

Diana lifted a hand and clenched her fist. The tension mounted as we waited.

The unmistakable sounds of horses galloping broke the silence first. Then the cries and whoops of...well it didn't sound like men prepped for battle. That was good. But then had Edmund just brought some of the nobles out?

The night mist shifted, and the clouds broke, allowing a sliver of light from the half-moon to shine down. Edmund was there in the center of the men he'd brought to the Green Valley, Scarlett off to one side of him.

She was looking to where we should have been.

"William," Edmund called out in a sing-song voice that cut through my heart. "Dear William, you didn't think your little plan would stay secret, did you?"

He waved and a group of people were dragged out from behind the main group.

Humans. Vanators.

"You thought I wouldn't know?"

Gods above and below, someone had betrayed us. Was it Frank? Why had he spared me in the first place if he was going to do *this*?

My question was answered swiftly as Edmund reached back and pulled something from his saddle bag. A head.

Frank's head.

Edmund tossed it in the direction of where our ambush was supposed to come from. I had no time to grieve my father's brave friend and confidant as my brother spoke again.

"I owe it all to my beloved, my future queen." He held his hand out to her. Drew her forward and my vision narrowed to a tunnel.

Scarlett smiled up at him adoringly.

Betrayer.

The word rocked me and all I could do was stare and do my best not to push Ares out there, to take the battle to them. I'd trusted her with my life. Being dragged off and leaving her behind had been agonizing. And all the while...

Will reached across and put a hand on my arm.

He breathed words to me. "We cannot let them kill the Vanators. Or my word is nothing."

I looked at Diana. "Will you ride out with us? A distraction. Then your men can get the humans out."

Her eyes glittered as she let out a howl that sent my blood tingling down my spine. The wolves she'd brought spread out, disappearing into the forest around us.

"He knew where you'd be, which means there are traps waiting for you," Diana said.

"He brought nobles," I said as I bumped Ares lightly in the sides so that we stepped out of the darkness of the trees. "They came to witness his triumph. They can't fight worth shit. Which means there will be others in the woods."

Will looked across at our older brother. "Can we take him?"

Even as he asked the question, chaos erupted in the spot we *should* have been. The howls and snarls of wolves. The clash of weapons.

Laughing, Edmund pulled a sword and sliced the head off the Vanator closest to him.

A trap.

"No, we save as many as we can. Drive the humans out, Edmund will come at me."

Insanity to think about saving humans that were out to kill our kind, but I knew why. Part of it was as Will said. Breaking the agreement would mean another battle, but this time with those on the mainland. But the other part? Was because Sienna would want me to. And maybe that's why Will wanted us to, as well. Because of Bethany.

Because our women were human, and they would think less of us if we didn't.

Edmund didn't turn our way until the three of us were almost on top of him.

Scarlett was the one to warn him, driving her horse between me and her betrothed. "Dominic."

She growled my name, and there wasn't an ounce of shame on her face. No, she stared me down and fucking smiled at me.

"You betrayed me. You were my most trusted friend!" I roared the words at her.

"Fuck you, Dominic. Or rather. Not." She sneered at me, her face twisted into a visage I didn't recognize. How could I have not seen her duplicity?

My hesitation nearly lost me my head. I ducked, and Ares kicked out at Edmund's horse as he circled me.

"You really thought you had me?" Edmund demanded. "Was it your plan? What am I asking, of course it was. William is too fucking weak to think of having assassins do the work."

The nobles ranged around us as the Vanators made a run for it straight into the woods.

"I'm happy to take your head first." Edmund smiled without mirth. "How that will weaken poor little Will, without his protector. Honestly, I'm shocked he's still alive. It won't be long now. Bloodworms. Nasty business."

He was trying to distract me. Circling around and around, while Scarlett did the same. She struck out at me and I batted her attempt away.

I had to keep them both on their toes, and their eyes locked on me.

"Enjoying my leftovers, *brother*?" I flashed my teeth at Edmund, knowing full well that he didn't share. At all.

Scarlett let out a hiss. "Lies. He'd say anything to save himself at this point."

I laughed. I couldn't help it. "Night gods, that is not something I would admit to if it weren't true. To fuck a betrayer? You were rather good at sucking me off though. That little twist of your mouth at the end, right when I came was really quite good."

A move she'd told me she'd perfected and I had no doubt she'd have shared with Edmund.

I was right.

Edmund's face tightened and he turned not to me, but toward Scarlett. The distraction was all I needed. Ares leapt as though I'd spurred him, only from me leaning forward in the saddle.

We crashed against Edmund's horse, but yet again he was saved by Scarlett.

With a scream she drove her staff straight at my head like a spear. I had to veer away from Edmund in order to save my own head which set me and Ares off, galloping away from the skirmish.

No one followed. A look over my shoulder was all it took to see that the Vanators and Will were well out of range, the wolves carrying many of those who could not move swiftly enough.

Diana caught up to me. "The plan was not to go deep."

I shrugged as we galloped side by side through the trees, weaving our way towards her men. "Were any hurt?"

"One. Dominic, I don't think he's going to make it."

Her stricken expression gave me pause. She was a seasoned warrior, acquainted with loss.

"Will?" I demanded, yanking at the reins and turning to search the faces in the distance. Not possible. I'd just seen him. He was upright on his horse...

"No, thank the gods. It's the servant. The simple one from the Killian clan. He wasn't even supposed to be here, but apparently he wanted to make his new family proud and–"

Fuck. I closed my eyes.

"Gods damn it!"

CHAPTER 26

Sienna

*H*ooves pounded the soft ground beneath me as Havoc tore across the open stretch ahead, headed straight for the harbor. But it wasn't a ship we were rushing toward. It was the water itself, and the creature lying in wait just below the surface. Hot tears streamed down my face as I tugged the horse to a halt right as the water met the shore. What the hell was wrong with me? I should be happy. Escape was moments away. Freedom from this fucked up place where treachery and danger lurked around every corner. But all I felt was loss.

Jordan. Bee.

The betrayer whom I refused to name.

A tentacle snaked from the depths, beckoning me closer.

If I wanted to ensure those I cared for had a chance at surviving, I had to leave. There was no other way.

But it was killing me.

I dismounted and paused to give Havoc a pat and a murmur of reassurance. Then, I walked into the water. The icy waves lapped *at my ankles as the kraken moved closer, wrapping a tentacle gently around my waist.*

"Sienna?"

Bee's voice called to me in the distance, even as the kraken pulled me deeper into the water.

"Sienna!"

I jerked upright and swallowed a gasp. Bee stood over me bathed in moonlight, her face marred with worry.

"Are you alright?"

I nodded dumbly but didn't reply. My heart was pounding out of my chest. A feat, to be sure, considering the grisly old muscle felt shattered beyond repair.

"You're crying," Bee murmured, wiping at my cheeks gently with the sleeve of her nightdress.

"*You're* crying," I shot back as I swung my legs over the side of the mattress and pushed myself upright. This was all going to be hard enough without having to explain it to Bee. What would be the point? It wouldn't change anything. My path was clear and there was nothing to do now but get on it. "It was just a stupid dream. I'm going down to the kitchen to make some warm milk. Go back to sleep. I'm fine."

Her eyes narrowed some like she didn't believe me, but bless her soft heart, she didn't press.

"Okay, but if you want to talk, don't hesitate to wake me."

The woman was a saint. Neither of us had slept more than a handful of hours in the two days that had passed since Diana and her little army had left for the Vampire Territory. It was only in the wee hours of the morning that we'd finally succumbed to exhaustion, and I'd woken her up whimpering like a child.

"You need your rest, my friend. Besides, if you're dead on your feet, who's going to do my hair for me in the morning?" I added with a wink.

She grinned and rolled her eyes, but let me get away with it as she returned to her bed a few yards from mine.

"Fine, but go get your milk and come right back. You have a habit of getting into trouble when I'm not around to babysit."

I flipped her the double bird and backed out of the room before turning and scurrying down the hall.

Strange how she knew me so well already. Strange and irritating. Apparently sharing trauma and enduring a version of hell on earth together had bonded us more quickly than if we were, say, co-workers at the local Quick-E-Mart.

Who knew?

I skidded to a stop at the end of the corridor and then paused.

Warm milk was for babies and lunatics. I'd accidentally fallen into a fitful sleep while biding my time until all the servants were in bed so I could go on a little treasure hunt, and that's what I was going to do.

If I were a super secret, special ruby earring that didn't want to be found, where would I be?

I glanced down the adjacent hallway toward Diana's study and then at the wide, sweeping staircase.

She had people in and out of her study all the time. Surely she wouldn't hide something so precious in a place with a lot of foot traffic. Her bedroom, on the other hand? I'd never seen anyone precede or follow her there. Not even her maid. And I was also pretty sure the ice-queen wasn't sneaking a secret lover in. If she was, I'd have surely seen him frozen on the limb of a tree outside her window.

"Meow," I muttered in a rare moment of self-awareness. Who was I to judge this woman? She had a lot of weight on those strong shoulders. If she needed to put up walls to keep her soft bits safe, more power to her.

I wish I'd done the same. Maybe mine wouldn't feel like chopped meat right now.

"Bedroom it is."

I made a beeline for the staircase and padded up the steps on silent feet. Other than the sound of the once again whipping winds outside, the keep was silent. The servants were tucked away in their quarters on the opposite wing, which meant I could roam freely, so long as Bee didn't get too curious.

Which meant I was likely on borrowed time.

I sidled down the long hallway and then stopped when I reached the first of two doors. It was massive and ornately carved, far more ostentatious than any of the rest in the keep and fit for a queen. Breath suspended, I gave it a jiggle and groaned.

Of course it was locked. Why wouldn't it be? For a second, I hesitated. It would be one thing to walk into an unsecured room and play lost and stupid if I got caught. Literally breaking and entering was another ball of wax.

A snort-laugh bubbled out of me.

What were they gonna do, kill me?

At this point, it wasn't looking like the worst option.

I tugged the butterfly pin from my hair and set to work. It took longer than it should have due to shaky hands and limited visibility via moonlight, but eventually, the lock gave way with a resounding snick.

Excellent.

I slipped the pin in my pants pocket and turned the knob. I wasn't sure what I was expecting, but the space that awaited me blew any of those expectations out of the water. Rather than heavy furniture hewn of iron and steel and tapestries of long ago battles adorning the walls, I found myself in the midst of a zen garden. Moss green, textured wallpaper gave off the sense of being in a peaceful forest. Oversized chairs in soft fabrics of dusty rose were placed strategically around a mystical mermaid fountain that dribbled water into a pond filled with pebbles and technicolor koi fish. Centered against the back wall sat a massive, circular mattress, low to the floor. Fat, downy pillows wrapped in rose and green cases were piled at the head of the bed, and hanging just above it? An ethereal picture of the full moon that almost glowed with life and promise.

This wasn't a bedroom. This was Diana's sanctuary. And suddenly I became very aware of the fact that I was an intruder.

I blew out a breath and shook off the sense of unrest. Get in, find the gem, and get out. I wasn't doing this for me. I was doing this for all of us.

I walked the room like a grid, pouring over every nook and cranny. Luckily, because it was a place of peace, there wasn't a lot of clutter despite the room's size. For all the books and knick knacks she had in her study, this space was an exercise in minimalism. Twenty or so minutes later I finally yanked my hand from under the two-ton mattress with a grunt.

I'd traced my fingers over every piece of furniture, scanned every wall, fondled every lamp, and shook out each pillow but come up empty. There was only one place left to search, and the thought filled me with dread and hopelessness.

I turned to face the koi pond and let out a groan. Finding a gem mixed in with what had to be a hundred million teeny tiny stones lining the bottom of the fountain would be impossible. Maybe if I could turn on some lights, get a shovel, and dump them onto the floor in batches, I'd have had a chance. But if I wanted to come and go without Diana knowing I'd been there for at least a little while—long enough to get back home—then I needed to be careful.

Sorrow rolled through me as the life I'd been so willing to lose just minutes before suddenly seemed precious.

My being here meant certain death for those around me, so I needed to go home. And going home would be the death of me.

The thought of all the things I'd meant to do but never did came rushing in, nearly laying me low as I stared at the fountain that had all but sealed my fate.

At least Jordan would be safe and happy. At least Will would take the throne.

At least I'd tasted love—or what I'd believed was love—for a moment.

I was still fully in the midst of my pity party of one when something caught my eye, giving me pause.

The mermaid...she was holding something in one hand. A clamshell.

Blood whooshed in my ears as I made my way closer, squinting in the dim light. Impossible. There was no way—

I climbed onto the wall of the fountain and reached for the shell. The second I touched it, a hidden hinge gave way, and it opened.

"Gods damn it, you gorgeous, fishy bitch, you!"

Staring up at me sat a tiny stone so glorious, I could barely look at it. Despite its crimson color, it wasn't a ruby at all. It was like some magical amalgamation of many stones, giving off the fire of a ruby, but the ice of a diamond. The soul of an emerald, but the heart of sapphire. Unlike the one my swashbuckling friend had been sporting, this gem was unset. Just the stone itself, in all its glory. Dry-mouthed and still shaking, I reached for it, but stopped short as I noticed a strange shimmer in the air around it, almost like a pulse of energy.

Of course Diana hadn't left the stone completely unprotected. She was far too smart for that. The thing was booby-trapped. Had to be. Now, to figure out how to bypass said trap...

A shout in the distance stopped me cold.

"Sienna?"

Son of a—

"Be right there!" I called back to Bee. I tried not to let the weight of disappointment crush me. At least I knew where the gem was now. I just had to figure out how to get it.

With a cursory glance around the room to ensure I'd left everything as I'd found it, I rushed headlong out the door, locking it behind me.

By the time Bee found me, I was leaning against the staircase like I didn't have a care in the world.

"Hey," I said, pinning a smile to my face.

"Hey yourself," she grumbled as she trudged up the final step to join me. "What are you doing up here?"

I shrugged. "I had some milk and then decided to take a tour. This place is huge. Did you know there is a room solely used to showcase artwork created by the various clans?"

I had no idea if that was true, but it could be, and that was all that mattered.

"Hmm, I guess that's a nice touch," Bee acknowledged reluctantly. "But I'm pretty sure the Queen would rather we stick to our quarters and the main rooms of the house."

"Spoilsport," I said, skirting around her and heading back down the stairs. "Maybe you want to tell her I stole a handful of cookies while I was in the kitchens, too?"

"Depends. Did you save me one?" she asked, following my lead as we made our way toward our bedroom.

"I did not, but because I'm such a good friend, I can go get you one. Meet me in the room, be there in a sec."

I was halfway down the hall when a strange feeling rolled over me.

"Bee! Don't open the door!" I cried as I wheeled around and raced toward her.

But it was too late. She'd already pushed it open when she turned to face me. "What? Why n—"

The thwack of an arrow burying itself into the wall of the corridor sent an icy rage pouring through me. I didn't think. I just acted, shoving past a stunned Bee and barreling into the room. A man stood there, wild-eyed, bow in hand. "I don't care what she or the Oracle has to say about it. If yer with the bloodsuckers, you're an enemy to me and mine." He tossed the bow aside and flexed, his muscles bulging and writhing. Then, he began to change, right before my eyes. His face stretching, jaw cracking as he shifted into his wolf form.

I didn't wait for him to finish. I reached into my pocket, gripped Hannah's butterfly pin tightly, and leapt at him with a howl of fury. He lifted one clawed hand to block me, but I wouldn't be stopped. With another guttural cry, I swung with all my might, driving the long, wickedly sharp pin directly into his furry ear.

The sound that escaped him was a cry of shock, and he stiffened for a second before crumpling to the floor. For a long moment, I just stood there, unable to move.

"Did he hurt you, Sienna?"

Bee's voice seemed a million miles away as it registered exactly how close we'd both come to dying. Yet again.

"Sienna, please tell us. Are you harmed in any way?"

This time, it was Diana speaking. The surprise of it brought me back into my body and I turned to face her.

"I don't even know how to kill a werewolf," I murmured, my voice still breathy with shock.

"Well, you've managed it quite well. Gold directly into the brain or heart will do it," Diana said, sparing the half-man, half-wolf one last sorrowful glance. "I thought we'd come to an understanding, but I believe the after-Veil madness had taken him. I'm so sorry you had to do that, Sienna."

I didn't fully understand her words, but I nodded anyway.

"And Edmund? Is he defeated then?" Is Dominic alright? But I left the question that truly haunted me unspoken.

"It...did not go as planned. Sienna, I need you to come down to the great room. There's been a grievous injury, and we need your healing powers."

Her words spurred me into action like no other, and I let out a strangled cry as I dashed down the corridor.

"Dominic?" I called, looking around frantically as I entered the great hall. It didn't take long to spot him standing at the opposite entrance, the limp form of a man in his arms. Relief flowed through me as I crossed the room. Dominic the betrayer was alive, and I knew I could handle whatever else came next.

But when I got close enough to see the look on his face, and the man in his arms, I realized just how wrong I was.

"Jordan! Nooo!"

CHAPTER 27

Dominic

The keening wail that came from Sienna's throat cut through me like a blade.

"I'm so sorry," I said softly, wishing I could spare her this pain.

She bit down hard on her trembling lip and shook her head.

"Nope. Don't say that. Set him down on the couch. I can fix him."

She tugged at my forearm, pulling me across the room as William and I exchanged a glance.

There was no fixing this. He wasn't dead yet, but he was as good as. Maybe, with Sienna's powers, he'd have stood a chance right when it happened. But the arrow that had pierced his heart had struck true, and there was so much blood now. More than I'd ever have imagined could've fit in such a small body. If we removed the arrow, he would be dead in an instant. Leaving it there was only prolonging the inevitable.

"Sienna..."

"Put him down!" she shouted, wringing her hands as I lowered him to the sofa. The boy's lids flickered as she laid her hands over the broken arrow jutting from his wound, chanting and pleading under her breath.

Bee and Diana held back, giving her space, but I could tell by their expressions they knew it as well as I did. It was too late.

"Come on Jordan, please wake up. Don't leave me like this," she pleaded, rocking forward and back as she squeezed his hand. For one, breathless moment, his eyes opened, and I thought I was witnessing a miracle, but then he let out one last broken sigh. "Goodbye, Ceecee."

His head lolled to the side, and I clenched my fists, anger at the injustice of it all burning a hole in my belly like pure acid.

Sienna stood and turned to face me, her golden eyes flashing flames instead of tears.

"Who authorized this?" she demanded, studying each of our faces in turn, searching for the answer. She stalked toward Diana, stopping only when their noses nearly touched. "Did you recruit him to join this mission? Because if you did—"

"I'm going to stop you before you say something you can't take back, Sienna," Diana cut in gently. "I'm still the Queen here and a threat against me is a threat against my people and this territory, no matter the reason for it." She laid a hand on Sienna's shoulder as she continued on, "He wasn't recruited, and in fact, we didn't even know he'd volunteered. He basically snuck into the lineup in full gear. With everything going on, no one caught on to his presence until it was too late."

"After he was hit, I picked him up from the ground and held him on my horse in front of me," Will chimed in. "He was awake and speaking. He told me he had no regrets. That his clan alpha believed Edmund would be the downfall of the Empires. He wanted to honor his new family and make them proud by fighting for the cause. He died a hero."

Sienna's laugh was hollow. "Ah yes. A dead hero. That and two dollars will buy you a can of pop where I'm from." She turned her gaze to me and cocked her head. "And you? The great General Dominic Blackthorne had no idea that a frail, human male had joined your forces?"

The affection that had been in her eyes only days before, grudging though it might have been, was gone. In its place was a sneering disgust that made my chest feel like Jordan's looked.

"I won't argue. I have no excuse." And because of what it had done to Sienna, it would haunt me.

I could see her throat work as she struggled not to cry.

"And the final person to blame for this, other than me, of course...Who fired the weapon? Was it Edmund himself?"

I doubted it. Edmund liked to kill up close so he could see the light leave his victim's eyes. But who else could've made such a clean shot at that distance?

I made my way over to the boy and reached for the broken shaft of the arrow. Sienna hurried to my side.

"No! Leave him alone."

"Do you want to know who killed him?"

She nodded, a fierce light entering her eyes as she stepped back. "I do."

I tugged the projectile free in one, swift motion and held it close. Rage pulsed through me as I found what I was looking for. A tiny snake in the shape of an "s" etched into the arrowhead. The insignia of the person who had played me like no other. Who I'd trusted above all except my own brother.

"It was Scarlett. She will pay for it with her life."

"She will. And it will be by my hand." Sienna's snarl was more like that of an animal than that of a woman.

A footman entered the great hall, with the stable boy from my territory looking aggrieved.

"Sirs, Your Majesty, Miss Sienna's horse has escaped! Kicked its way out of the stall and is running around like she's out of her head. She'll listen to her. Can you come help, Miss?"

Sienna sent one last longing look toward Jordan and then rushed to follow Timmy and the footman. I strode after her, refusing to let her out of my sight as Diana pulled up beside me as she shouted directives over her shoulder. "Bethany, William, please wake the Duchess and Lycan. Let them know what's happened. Once we've dealt with whatever is happening down at the stables, I will go speak to the Killian clan to break the news about Jordan."

We made it to the stables just a few minutes later, and it was easy to see what had Timmy in an uproar. The mare was galloping in circles, tossing her head wildly, only stopping to buck and kick before taking off again. Only the whites of her eyes were visible, almost as if she were possessed.

"It's alright, girl. Shh, it's okay," Sienna called, but her voice was barely audible over the wind, and in her panicked state, Havoc wasn't hearing it.

"Maybe you need to get a little closer so she can sense your presence?" Diana suggested, her face a mask of concern.

"Or maybe not," I said flatly. I could easily neutralize the horse if it posed an imminent threat to Sienna, but if she was up close and personal with it, I might not have time to intervene. "Wait until she's out of energy and then approach. She can't carry on like this forever."

Sienna didn't acknowledge either one of us as she moved slowly toward the bucking mare.

"It's me, sweet girl. It's Sienna. Come now, we're alright. We're safe," she crooned, now only a few feet away.

I crouched, at the ready to pounce if need be, but I needn't have bothered. The second she touched the animal, it went dead still.

Sienna's head snapped back and she stared into the night sky through unseeing eyes. For a few terrifying seconds, she jerked and twitched before crumpling to the ground in a heap.

I was at her side an instant later, holding her in my arms. She was alert, clear-eyed, and terrified.

"They're coming," she whispered, her whole body shaking like a leaf.

"Who, Sienna?" I asked gently, stroking her hair as I tried to calm her. "Who's coming?"

"The Hunters, and they're going to kill us all."

CHAPTER 28

Sienna

An hour after we'd secured poor Havoc and I'd calmed her down, we were all seated in the war room. Me, Dominic, Will, Bee, Diana, Lycan, and the Duchess, the latter two who Bee had apparently found in Lycan's quarters together. Jordan's body had been delivered to his family where it would be prepared and buried in the Killian clan plot after a warrior's feast two days from now.

Assuming any of us were still alive to celebrate him.

"Did you get a sense of when the Hunters will come?" Lycan asked, the concern etched on his wizened face.

"Tomorrow."

When I'd first touched Havoc, it had been so vague. I could feel the tension of the birds, and then the deer in the Vampire Territory Forest. An unrest that slowly morphed to abject terror. It wasn't until I was staring down into Edmund's icy blue eyes that I understood their fears.

"My Hunters, tonight you will eat and drink your fill to ensure your strength. In the morning, you will be fit with armor and then released so that you may fulfill your destiny and protect the crown from infidels. Our enemies lie in wait across the bridge. Once you cross, destroy everything in your path. Give no quarter, and show them all the might of the Blackthorne monarchy."

Despite Edmund the Awful's directives, I was in the mind of the Hunters and could sense their irritation. They would finally be set free after far too long in captivity.

"Edmund has instructed them to come straight here and raze everything in their path. They're not in a cooperative mood, though. They're daydreaming of frolicking in the skies, flying over the harbor and letting their wings skim across the water."

"That doesn't sound so bad, then," Bee replied, ever the optimist.

"Yeah, no. It's gonna be really fucking bad," I corrected flatly. "Once they've enjoyed their freedom some, they'll do his bidding and come for us all. They're looking forward to that as well..."

Fantasies of bloodletting and gnashing soft, scrumptious flesh with razor-sharp teeth would follow me to my nightmares.

Bee's face fell as she shot a glance toward Will. "Oh."

"So the question is, what do we do about it?" Dominic said, raking a restless hand through his inky hair.

Diana let out a sigh and looked at each of us in turn, pausing when her gaze landed on Lycan.

"The truth of the matter is that there is no 'us'." She gestured around the table. "There is *us*." She wagged a finger between herself and Lycan. "And there is you lot," she continued, waving a hand toward the rest of the table.

"Diana..." Lycan began, shaking his head, but she cut him off with a sad smile.

"With all due respect, old man, if ever there was a time for me to lead on my own, it is now. Especially when your thinking might be...impaired by matters of the heart." She turned to Will and straightened, the smile slipping from her face. "I'm faced with two choices. I wave the proverbial white flag to Edmund, and ship you all back to him tied up with a bow along with an apology, or I go to war for a cause that is not my own or that of my people."

"I know I'm just the maid, but I'm voting for option number two," Bee said, wetting her lips nervously.

I knew I should feel some sort of way about Diana's words, but it was almost like my brain was protecting me from the truth of my existence right now. My lover had betrayed me, I'd lost my best friend, and in order to avenge him, I was stuck in this horror movie for the duration, all for the privilege of fighting one of the strongest vampires in the world so I could get to his demon-spawn traitor of a girlfriend.

And all I felt was numb.

The Duchess spoke then, pulling me from my reverie. "You speak of your people, child. But what of me? What of your brothers? I know it's been a long time...are we nothing to you now?"

Diana's cheeks went pale and it was like the air had been sucked out of the room.

"She's right, Diana," Lycan murmured. "Evangeline risked everything to protect you. You would forsake her now?"

"What the hell is everyone talking about right now?" Will demanded, rising to his feet, wide-eyed.

But it was Dominic who answered, a knowing gleam in his eye, a twisted smile on his lips. "Diana is—was?—one of us, wasn't she? Our sister. Godsdammit, that makes so much sense. There was something about her that reminded me so much of father. But how. Why?"

It was Diana's turn to stand. "I hadn't planned to get into this right now as we have enough on our plates, but now that the matter is out of my hands," she muttered, shooting the Duchess a frown, "we might as well get it all out in the open. Long ago, before either of you were born and Edmund was a child, my mother found out she was expecting me. It was a shock because babies between humans and vampires were so rare, even before the Veil fell. As a human, the pregnancy was a troubled one, and she nearly lost me a number of times. Rather than have it out in the open and show the potential weakness of his line should I not survive, our father asked that it be kept secret from everyone but a select few. Evangeline being one of them. When I was born, I did not cry. My heart and lungs were far too weak, and I had none of the strength or healing abilities of your kind. It was decided by our father that it was best for me to remain hidden from the public until I grew stronger or perished. Enter young, maniacal Edmund."

She folded her hands behind her back and began to pace.

"While I would never be considered heir to the throne, and enjoyed precious little of our father's time, the little bastard didn't like sharing. When I was three years old, he dragged me to the harbor and tried to drown me. He would have succeeded if it weren't for the Duchess. She had sensed his jealousy, knew of his cruelty, and always ensured that, if I was alone with him, a servant was nearby. When Edmund left me in the water for dead, I was rescued by her."

"And she sent you here. To Lycan," I marveled, drawn into the macabre tale in spite of myself.

Diana inclined her head and shot me a tight smile. "She did."

"How did you not know? Can't you sense one another, even if she is half human?" Bee asked Will with a frown.

Will's gaze never left Diana. "We can. We do. Care to explain...sister?"

"They changed her..." Dominic nodded slowly as if he was just accepting this truth bomb as he said it. "Lycan made her a wolf. Humans can be changed, and I imagine it'd have been easy enough, especially if her vampire genes were weak."

Diana's crack of laughter was so harsh, several at the table flinched.

"Easy?" she hissed. "It was the most excruciating pain I've ever endured. Far more painful than if I'd been fully human. A full day and night of endless agony as the moon and the sun warred for my fealty. But I wouldn't change it, because it made me who I am today." She stopped beside the Duchess and bent low. "The Werewolf Queen. Daughter to Lycan and mother moon. I appreciate what you did for me, Evangeline. You protected me from the apathy of my father, my psychotic brother, and a lifetime of living in a place that cares not about the suffering of others." She straightened, facing the room at large again. "But make no mistake. The only 'us' here is me and the man who raised me, and my only responsibility is to him and the clans we are the stewards of."

Lycan opened his mouth to speak, but the Duchess held up a staying hand as she studied my face intently.

"Sienna has something to tell us. Sienna?"

This brave, beautiful, incredibly astute woman always did have a bead on me...

I took a breath as all eyes turned toward me. This was it.

"A few nights ago, I had a dream that if I stayed here, a storm would come, and everyone would die because of me. Maybe the Hunters were that storm. But now Jordan is dead, our plan for Edmund failed, and I get the sense that everything has changed. I thought my staying would doom you all, but I've finally realized that we need to fight this war together. You and your kind included. According to the Oracle, I am the key to your success. You need me alive and in your service, which I won't be if you hand my friends over to Edmund."

Diana's eyes narrowed as she circled the room, deep in thought. Minutes ticked by before she finally spoke again.

"Fine. I will join you in fighting this war against tyranny, but once we are victorious, I require a favor." She turned to Will. "Once you regain the throne, you must agree to help me form a party to travel to the mainland and find something that has been stolen. Something I need if the Veil is to be restored and the future of the Empires secured. Will you grant me this boon?"

The young prince didn't hesitate.

"I will."

Diana nodded with a satisfied smile that told me this had been her endgame all along.

"Then to war we go."

ALSO BY SHANNON MAYER

The Forty Proof Series
MIDLIFE BOUNTY HUNTER
MIDLIFE FAIRY HUNTER
MIDLIFE DEMON HUNTER
MIDLIFE GHOST HUNTER
MIDLIFE ZOMBIE HUNTER
MIDLIFE WITCH HUNTER
MIDLIFE MAGIC HUNTER
MIDLIFE SOUL HUNTER

The Alpha Territories
TAKEN BY FATE
HUNTED BY FATE
CLAIMED BY FATE

HUNTED BY FATE

The Golden Wolf
GOLDEN
GLITTER

The Honey and Ice Series (with Kelly St. Clare)
A COURT OF HONEY AND ASH
A THRONE OF FEATHERS AND BONE
A CROWN OF PETALS AND ICE

World of Honey and Ice (with Kelly St. Clare)
THORN KISSED & SILVER CHAINS

FOR A COMPLETE BOOK LIST VISIT
www.shannonmayer.com

Hunted by Fate

CHAPTER 9.5

Will & Bethany

NEW YORK TIMES BESTSELLING AUTHOR

SHANNON
MAYER

SCAN TO GET YOURS

Hunted by Fate

THE LOST CHAPTER

Evangeline & Lycan

NEW YORK TIMES BESTSELLING AUTHOR

SHANNON MAYER

SCAN TO GET YOURS

Alpha Territories Merch

Visit my Merch Shop to get all your Alpha Territories Merch!
I've got tote bags, a blanket, stickers, and more.

Plus, you can grab a gorgeous special edition of
Taken By Fate with custom edges, a color art print, foiled case
and more
(There will be matching editions of Hunted By Fate and
Claimed by Fate in the future.)

Don't miss the heart-pounding conclusion to
Sienna & Dominic's story! Order it now.

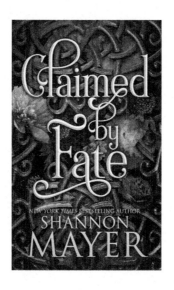

Printed in Great Britain
by Amazon